THE IVORY GRIN

The roller blind was down over the window. Light slanted through the cracks in the blind, supporting a St. Vitus's dance of dust motes. There was a wall switch beside the door, and I jogged it with my elbow. The yellow walls sprang up around me and the ceiling pressed down from overhead, ringed with concentric shadows. The light radiated from a wall bracket directly over Lucy. Its paper-shaded bulb shone down into her face, which was grey as a clay death-mask in a pool of black blood. Her cut throat gaped like the mouth of an unspeakable grief.

I leaned on the door and wished myself on the other side of it, away from Lucy. But death had tied me to her faster than any ceremony.

"Ross Macdonald is one of the best living writers of the whipcord thriller."   *Books and Bookmen*

". . . head and shoulders above his contemporaries."
New York Times

ROSS MACDONALD

The Ivory Grin

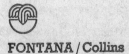

FONTANA / Collins

First published by Wm. Collins 1952
First issued in Fontana Books 1965
Second Impression October 1970
Third Impression October 1971
Fourth Impression July 1973
Fifth Impression March 1974

Copyright 1972 by Alfred A. Knopf, Inc.

Printed in Great Britain
Collins Clear-Type Press London and Glasgow

TO ALL HANDS

CHAPTER I

I found her waiting at the door of my office. She was a stocky woman of less than medium height, wearing a blue slack suit over a blue turtleneck sweater, and a blue mink stole that failed to soften her outlines. Her face was squarish and deeply tanned, its boyish quality confirmed by dark hair cut short at the nape. She wasn't the type you'd expect to be up and about at eight-thirty in the morning, unless she'd been up all night.

As I unlocked the door she stood back and looked up at me with the air of an early bird surveying an outsize worm. I said: "Good morning."

"Mr. Archer?"

Without waiting for an answer, she offered me a stubby brown hand. Her grip, armed with rings, was as hard as a man's. Releasing her hand, she placed it behind my elbow, ushered me into my own office, and closed the door behind her.

"I'm very glad to see you, Mr. Archer."

She had begun to irritate me already. "Why?"

"Why what?"

"Why are you glad to see me?"

"Because. Let's sit down and be comfortable so we can talk." Without charm, her petite wilfulness was disquieting.

"About anything in particular?"

She seated herself in an armchair by the door and looked around the waiting-room. It was neither large nor expensively furnished, and she seemed to be registering those circumstances. Her only comment was to click her ringed fists together in front of her. There were three rings on each hand. They had good-sized diamonds in them, which looked real.

"I have a job for you," she said to the sagging green imitation-leather davenport against the opposite wall. Her manner had changed from girlish vivacity to boyish earnestness. "It's not what you'd consider a big job, but I'm willing to pay well. Fifty a day?"

5

" And expenses. Who sent you to me?"

" But nobody. Do sit down. I've known your name for ages, simply ages."

" You have the advantage of me."

Her gaze returned to me, tireder and older after its little slumming excursion around my antechamber. There were olive drab thumbprints under her eyes. Maybe she had been up all night, after all. In any case she looked fifty, in spite of the girlishness and the boyishness. Americans never grew old: they died; and her eyes had guilty knowledge of it.

" Call me Una," she said.

" Do you live in Los Angeles?"

" Not exactly. Where I live doesn't matter. I'll tell you what does, if you want me to be blunt."

" I couldn't bear it if you weren't."

Her hard dry glance went over me almost tangibly and rested on my mouth. " You look all right. But you sound kind of Hollywood to me."

I was in no mood to swap compliments. The ragged edge on her voice, and her alternation of fair and bad manners bothered me. It was like talking to several persons at once, none of them quite complete.

" Protective coloration." I caught her glance and held it. " I meet a lot of different types."

She didn't flush. All that happened was that her face looked a little congested for a moment. It passed, and the incomplete boy in her came to the point:

" I mean, do you make a habit of cutting your clients' throats? I've had some pretty discouraging experiences."

" With detectives?"

" With people. Detectives are people."

" You're full of compliments this morning, Mrs.——"

" I said just call me Una. I'm not proud. Can I trust you to do what I want you to do and stop? Take your money and go about your business?"

" Money?"

" Here." She produced a crumbled bill from a blue leather pouch and tossed it to me as if it were an old piece of Kleenex and I were a wastebasket. I caught it. It was a hundred-dollar bill, but I didn't put it away.

" A retainer always helps to establish a bond of loyalty,"

I said. " I'll still cut your throat, of course, but I'll give you sodium pentothal first."

She addressed the ceiling darkly: " Why does everybody in these parts work so hard for laughs? You haven't answered my question."

" I'll do what you want me to do so long as it's not illegal and makes some kind of sense."

" I'm not suggesting anything illegal," she said sharply. " And I promise you it makes sense."

" All the better." I tucked the bill into the bill compartment of my wallet, where it looked rather lonely, and opened the door to the inner office.

There were three chairs in it, and no room for a fourth. After I had opened the Venetian blinds, I took the swivel chair behind the desk. The armchair I pointed out for her faced me across the desk. Instead, she sat down in a straight chair against the partition, away from the window and the light.

Crossing her trousered legs, she pushed a cigarette into a short gold holder and lit it with a squat gold lighter.

" About this job I mentioned. I want you to locate a certain person, a coloured girl who used to work for me. She left my house two weeks ago, on the first of September to be exact. It was good riddance of bad rubbish as far as I was concerned, only she took along a few little knick-knacks of mine. A pair of ruby earrings, a gold necklace."

" Insured?"

" No. Actually they're not very valuable. Their value is sentimental—you know? They mean a lot to me, sentimentally." She tried to look sentimental and failed.

" It sounds like a matter for the police."

" I don't think so." Her face closed up solid like brown wood. " You make your living tracing people, don't you? Are you trying to talk yourself out of a living?"

I took the hundred-dollar bill out of my wallet and dropped it on the desk in front of me. " Apparently."

" Don't be so touchy." She forced her grim little mouth into a smile. " The truth is, Mr. Archer, I'm a fool about people. Anybody that ever worked for me, even if they took advantage of me—well, I feel responsible for them. I had a very genuine affection for Lucy, and I guess I still have. I don't wish to make any trouble for her, nothing like that. I wouldn't dream of sicking the police on Lucy. All I really want is a chance to talk to her, and get my things back. And I was so hoping that you would be able to help me?"

She lowered her short bristling lashes over her hard black eyes. Maybe she could hear the music of distant violins. All I could hear was the pushing and hooting of traffic on the Boulevard one story down.

"I think you said she was a Negro."

"I have no race prejudice——"

"I don't mean that. Black girls are unfindable in this city. I've tried."

"Lucy isn't in Los Angeles. I know where she is."

"Why don't you simply go and talk to her?"

"I intend to. First I'd like to get some idea of her movements. I want to know who she sees, before I talk to her, and after."

"That's a pretty elaborate way to go about recovering some jewellery. What's the purpose?"

"It's none of your business." She tried to say it gaily and girlishly, but the hostility showed through.

"I believe you're right." I pushed the bill across the desk towards her, and stood up. "In fact, it sounds like a wild-goose chase. Why don't you try the classified ads in the *Times*? There are plenty of investigators who live on a steady diet of wild goose."

"By God, I think the man's honest." She spoke to one side as if her alter ego was standing there. "All right, Mr. Archer, you have me, I guess."

The image didn't excite me, and I registered a suitable apathy.

"I mean I'm in a hurry. I haven't got time to shop around. I'll even admit that I'm in a spot of trouble."

"Which has nothing to do with petty theft or costume jewellery. You could have thought of a better story. But please don't try."

"I'm not. This is straight. When Lucy was working in my house she naturally got to know my family affairs. Well, there was bad feeling when she left, not on my side, on hers. There are one or two things that could embarrass me if she decided to spread them. So I want to know who she's seeing. From that I can draw my own conclusions."

"If I knew a little more about these embarrassing facts——"

"I'm not going to tell you, that's definite. My whole idea in coming to you is to keep them from getting out. Now what could be franker than that?"

I still didn't like her story, but the second version was an improvement over the first. I sat down again. "What sort of work did she do for you?"

She hesitated briefly. "General housework. She's a maid. Her full name is Lucy Champion."

"And where did she work for you?"

"In my house, naturally. There's no reason for you to know where it is."

I swallowed my irritation. "Where is she now, or is that another secret?"

"I know I seem unreasonable and suspicious," she said. "Believe me, I've been burned. I take it you'll do this job for me?"

"I might as well."

"She's in Bella City, up the Valley. You'll have to hurry to make it before noon. It's a good two hours from here."

"I know where it is."

"Good. A friend of mine saw her there yesterday, in a restaurant on Main Street near the corner of Hidalgo. My friend talked to the waiter and found out that Lucy eats her lunch there every day between twelve and one. It's a combination café and liquor store called Tom's. You can't miss it."

"A picture of Lucy would help."

"I'm sorry." She spread her hands in an automatic gesture that placed her ancestry on the north shore of the Mediterranean. "The best I can do is a description. She's a handsome girl, and so light she could pass for South American or Californian Spanish. She has nice big brown eyes, and not too much of a mouth, like some of them. A nice little figure, too, if she wasn't so skinny."

"How old?"

"Not old. Younger than me—than I." I noticed the self-correction, as well as the self-flattery in the comparison. "In her early twenties. I'd say."

" Hair?"

" Black, in a straight bob. She keeps it straight with oil."

" Height?"

" A couple of inches taller than I. I'm five foot two."

" Distinguishing characteristics?"

" Her legs are her best feature, as she well knows." Una couldn't pay another woman an unmixed compliment. " Her nose is sort of turned up—cute, if her nostrils didn't sort of stare at you."

" What was she wearing when your friend saw her?"

" A black-and-white checkered sharkskin suit. That's how I know it was her. I gave her the suit a couple of months ago. She altered it for herself."

" So you won't want the suit back."

That seemed to strike a nerve. She removed the butt that had gone out in her holder and crushed it violently in the ashtray beside her chair. " I've taken quite a bit from you, mister."

" We're about even now," I said. " I've been keeping score. I just wouldn't want you to think that you were buying very much for a hundred bucks. I have to watch that around here. You're suspicious. I'm touchy."

" You talk as if you were bitten by a bear. Do you have an unhappy home life, by any chance?"

" I was just going to ask you about yours."

" Don't start worrying about my home life. That's one thing —I don't want you talking to Lucy." She had a quick change of mood, or affected one. " Oh hell, it's my life and I live it. We're wasting time. Are you willing to do what I say, no more no less?"

" No more anyway. She mightn't turn up at the restaurant to-day. If she does, I tail her, keep a record of where she goes, who she sees. And report to you?"

" Yes. This afternoon if possible. I'll be registered at the Mission Hotel in Bella City. Ask for Mrs. Larkin." She glanced at the square gold watch on her right wrist. " You better get going. If she leaves town let me know immediately, and stay with her."

She moved deliberately and quickly to the outer door. Her walk was the shortest distance between things she wanted. The back of her neck was heavy under the cropped hair, swollen with muscle as if she had often used it for butting and rooting. Turning at the door to lift a flashing hand in good-bye, she hitched the mink stole higher. I wondered if she used it to conceal that telltale grossness.

I went back to my desk and dialled the switchboard of my answering service. Standing by the window, I could see the sidewalk below through the slats of the Venetian blind. It swarmed with a bright young crowd of guys and girls buzzing and fluttering in pursuit of happiness and the dollar.

Una emerged among them, dark and foreshortened by the height from which I was watching her. She turned uphill, her head thrust forward on her heavy neck, like an irresistible force searching for an immovable object. The switchboard answered in a youthful female gurgle on the fifth ring. I told it I was going out of town for the weekend.

CHAPTER 2

From the top of the grade I could see the mountains on the other side of the valley, leaning like granite slabs against the blue tile sky. Below me the road meandered among brown September hills spattered with the ink-blot shadows of oaks. Between these hills and the further mountains the valley floor was covered with orchards like vivid green chenille, brown corduroy ploughed fields, the thrifty patchwork of truck gardens. Bella City stood among them, a sprawling dusty town miniatured and tidied by clear space. I drove down into it.

The packing houses of the growers' associations stood like airship hangars on the edge of the green fields. Parched nurseries and suburban ranchos offered tomato plants and eggs and lima beans for sale. There was a roadside traffic of filling stations, drive-ins, motels slumping dejectedly under optimistic names. In the road the big trucks went by in both directions, trailing oil smoke and a long loud raspberry for Bella City.

The highway was a rough social equator bisecting the community into lighter and darker hemispheres. Above it in the northern hemisphere lived the whites who owned and operated the banks and churches, clothing and grocery and liquor stores. In the smaller section below it, cramped and broken up by ice plants, warehouses, laundries, lived the darker ones, the Mexicans and Negroes who did most of the manual work in Bella City and its hinterland. I remembered that Hildago Street ran parallel to the highway and two blocks below it.

It was fairly hot and very dry. The dryness ached in my sinuses. Main Street was loud and shiny with noon traffic moving bumper to bumper. I turned left on East Hidalgo Street and found a parking space in the first block. House-wives black, brown, and sallow were hugging parcels and pushing shopping carts on the sidewalk. Above them a ramshackle house, with paired front windows like eyes demented by earthquake memories, advertised Rooms for Transients on one side, Palm Reading on the other. A couple of Mexican children, boy and girl, strolled by hand in hand in a timeless noon on their way to an early marriage.

Two privates appeared from nowhere, pale in their uni-forms like young ghosts trapped by reality. I got out and followed them across Main and into a magazine shop near the corner. The unlit neon sign of Tom's Café was almost directly across the street. Beer on Tap. Steam Beer. Try Our Spaghetti Special.

The soldiers were inspecting a rack of comic books with the air of connoisseurs. They selected half a dozen each, paid for them and left.

" Milk sops." the clerk said. He was a grey-headed man with smeared spectacles. " They draft them in didees these days. Cradle to grave in one jump. When I was in the AEF."

I grunted, stood by the window looking out. Tom's Café had a varied clientele. Business suits and overalls, sport shirts and T-shirts and sweaters went in and came out. The women wore gingham dresses, sunsuits with halters, slacks and shirts, light topcoats over faded flowered silk. There were whites among them, but Negro and Mexican heads were in the majority. I didn't see a black-and-white shark-skin suit.

" When I was in the AEF," the clerk said softly and wist-fully from behind the counter.

I picked up a magazine and pretended to read it, watching the changing crowd on the other side of the street. The light danced in standing waves on the car tops.

The clerk said in a changed tone: " You're not supposed to read them until you pay for them."

I tossed him a quarter, and he was mollified: " You know how it is. Business is business."

" Sure." I said it gruffly to ward off the AEF.

Through the dusty window, the people resembled extras in a street scene in very early colour. The faces of the buildings were depthless and so ugly that I couldn't imagine their insides. Tom's Café was flanked on one side by a pawnshop displaying violins and shotguns in its window, on the other side by a movie house plastered with lurid advertisements for *La Liga de Muchachos*. The crowd hurried faster, it seemed, and then the scene focused on the double swinging doors of Tom's Café. A light-skinned Negro girl with short black hair and a black-and-white checked suit came out, paused on the edge of the sidewalk and turned south.

" You forgot your book," the clerk called after me.

I was halfway across the street when she reached the corner of Hidalgo and Main. She turned left, walking quickly with short steps. The sun gleamed on her oiled hair. She passed within three feet of my convertible. I slid behind the wheel and started the engine.

Lucy carried herself with an air. Her hips swayed pearlike from the narrow stem of her waist, and her stockingless tan legs worked pleasantly below the checked skirt. I let her cover the rest of the block, then followed her by fits and starts from parking place to parking place. In the second block I stopped in front of a frame Buddhist church. In the third, a pool hall where black and Mexican and Asian boys handled cues over green tables. In the fourth, a red-brick school in a yellow desert of playground. Lucy kept on walking due east.

The road degenerated from broken asphalt to dirt, and the sidewalk ended. She picked her way carefully among the children who ran and squatted and rolled in the dust, past houses with smashed windows patched with cardboard and scarred peeling doors or no doors at all. In the photographic light the wretchedness of the houses had a stern kind of clarity or beauty, like old men's faces in the sun. Their roofs sagged and their walls leaned with a human resignation, and they had voices: quarrelling and gossiping and singing. The children in the dust played fighting games.

Lucy left Hidalgo Street at the twelfth intersection and headed north along the green board-fence of a baseball park. A block short of the highway she went east again into a different kind of street. It had a paved road and sidewalks, small green lawns in front of small well-kept houses, white frame and stucco. I parked at the corner, half hidden by the clipped eugenia hedge that surrounded the corner lot. The name of the street was stencilled on the curb. Mason Street.

About the middle of the block, a faded green Ford coupé stood in a driveway under a pepper tree in front of a white bungalow. A Negro boy in yellow swimming trunks was hosing it down. He was very large and strong-looking. At a distance of half a block I could see the muscles shimmering in his wet black arms. The girl crossed the street towards him, walking more slowly and gracefully than she had been.

When he noticed her he smiled and flicked the spray from the hose in her direction. She dodged and ran towards him, forgetting her dignity. He laughed and shot the water straight up into the tree like a jet of visible laughter that reached me as sound a half second later. Kicking off her shoes, she scampered around the car one step ahead of his miniature rain. He dropped the hose and raced around after her.

She reappeared on my side and snatched up the nozzle. When he came around the car she turned the white stream full in his face. He came on dripping and laughing, and wrenched the nozzle out of her hands. Their laughter joined.

Face to face on the green grass, they held each other by the arms. Their laughter ended suddenly. The pepper tree shaded them in green silence. The water from the hose bubbled springlike in the grass.

A door slammed. I heard its delayed percussion like the sound of a distant axe-blow. The lovers sprang apart. A stout black woman had come out on the porch of the white bungalow. She stood with her hands clasped at her thick aproned waist and looked at them without speaking. At least her lips didn't move perceptibly.

The boy picked up a chamois and began to polish the car

top like somebody wiping out the sins of the world. The girl stooped for her shoes with an air of earnest concentration, as if she'd been searching high and low for them. She passed the boy without turning her head and disappeared around the side of the bungalow. The stout black woman went back into the house, closing the screen door soundlessly behind her.

CHAPTER 3

I circled three quarters of the block, left my car short of the intersection, and entered Mason Street from the other end, on foot. Under the pepper tree the Negro boy was still wiping down the Ford. He glanced at me as I crossed the road, but paid me no further attention.

His house was the fifth on the north side of the street. I opened the white picket-gate of the third house, a stucco cottage wearing a television aerial like a big metal feather in its cap. I knocked on its screen door and took a black notebook and a pencil out of my inside breast pocket,.

The inner door was opened a few inches, the thin yellow face of a middle-aged Negro inserted in the aperture. "What do you want?" When they shut, his lips turned inward over his teeth.

I opened the notebook and held the pencil poised over it. "My firm is making a national survey."

"There's nothing we need." The ingrown mouth closed, and the door closed after it.

The door of the next house was standing open. I could see directly into a living-room crowded with old Grand Rapids furniture. When I knocked on the door, it rattled against the wall.

The boy under the pepper tree looked up from the fender he was polishing. "Just walk right in. She'll be glad to see you. Aunty's glad to see anybody." He added: "Mister," as a deliberate afterthought and turned his wedgeshaped back on me.

The voice of the house spoke up from somewhere in the rear. It was old and faded but it had a carrying quality, like a chant: "Is that you, Holly? No, it wouldn't be Holly yet. Anyway, come in, whoever you are. You must be one of my friends, and they visit me in my room now, now that I can't get out. So come on in."

The voice went on without a break, the words linked to each other by a pleasant deep-South slurring. I followed it like a thread across the living-room, down a short hallway, through the kitchen to a room that opened from it. "I used to have my visitors in the sitting-room, that wasn't so long ago. Just lately the doctor told me, you stay in bed now, honey, don't try to cook any more, let Holly do for you. So here I lie."

The room was small and bare, lit and ventilated by a single window, which was open. The source of the voice was a bed beside the window. Propped with pillows against the maple headboard, a Negro woman smiled from a sunken grey face, with great eyes like dark lanterns. Between the smiling blue lips the thread of talk unwound:

"It's a blessing for me, he said, that my joints are frozen solid with the arthritis, because if I tried to run around like I used to, my heart would give out sure. I told him he was a Job's comforter, what good is keeping my heart going like a watch that won't tell time if I can't get up and cook. He said I was one of the stiff-necked generations and I laughed right out in his face, I couldn't help it. That young doctor's a good friend of mine, I don't care what he says. Are you a doctor, son?"

The great eyes shone on me, and the blue lips smiled. I hated to lie when the human element cut across my work. I lied: "We're making a survey of radio users in southern California. I see you have a radio."

There was a small imitation-ivory table radio between her bed and the wall.

"I certainly have." She sounded disappointed. Her grey upper lip, faintly moustached, puckered in many vertical wrinkles.

"Is it working?"

"It certainly is working." The question revived her spirits by giving her a subject for conversation. "I wouldn't give house-room to a radio that wasn't working. I listen to it morning, noon and night, just shut it off the minute before you knocked on the door. I'll turn it on again when you go away. But don't hurry. Come in and sit down. I like to make new friends."

I sat in the room's only chair, a rocker near the foot of the bed. From there I could see the side of the white bungalow next door, with an open kitchen window towards the rear.

"What's your name now, son?"

"Lew Archer."

"Lew Archer." She repeated it slowly, as if it were a short, eloquent poem. "Now that's a pretty name, a very pretty name. My name is Jones, after my last husband. Everybody calls me Aunty. I have three married daughters and four sons in Philadelphia and Chicago. Twelve grandchildren, six great-grandchildren, more on the way. See my pictures?" Above the radio, the wall was studded with thumbtacked snapshots. "It must be relieving to you to get off your feet for a little. This survey job, does it pay much, son?"

"Not much."

"You wear nice clothes, though, that's a comfort to you."

"This job is only temporary. I wanted to ask you, do your neighbours have radios? I couldn't get an answer out of the man next door."

"That Toby man? He's a surly one. They have radio *and* television. Her sigh expressed envy and resignation. "He owns himself a half block of income property down on Hidalgo Street."

I made a meaningless entry in my notebook. "What about the other side?"

"Not Annie Norris. I was as churchy as Annie Norris when I had the free use of my limbs but I was never as stiff-necked as Annie. Never could see the harm in a little radio music. Annie claims that it's a contraption of the devil, and I told her she's not moving with the times. She wouldn't even let that boy of hers go to the moving pictures, and I told her worse things could happen to a boy than a little innocent entertainment. Worse things could and worse things did." She fell silent. One of her gnarled hands struggled up from where it rested on the sheet that covered her knees. "Speak of the devil. Hear that?"

With a surge and lunge of her entire body, she turned her face away, towards the window. Behind the walls of the house next door, two female voices were arguing.

" She's carrying on with her boarder again. Listen."

One voice was a heavy contralto, easily identified with the stout black woman. I caught fragments of what she said: " You listen . . . out of my house . . . making eyes at my son . . . get out . . . my son."

The other voice was soprano, shrill with fear and anger. " I didn't It's a lie. You rented me the room for a month——"

The heavy voice broke like a wave: " Get out. Pack up and get. You can have your money back for the rest of the time. You'll be needing it to buy liquor, Miss Champion."

The screen door slammed again, and the boy's voice spoke inside: " What's going on in here? Mama, you leave Lucy alone."

" You stay out of this. It's none of your affair. Miss Champion is leaving."

" You can't throw her out like this." The boy's tones were high and hurt. " She's paid up to the end of the month."

" She's leaving, irregardless. Alex, you go to your room. What would your father think, he heard you talking to your mother the way you've been talking?"

" You do what your mother tells you," the girl said. " I wouldn't stay here anyway, after the insinuations."

" Insinuations!" The older woman gave the word a savage satiric twist. " These are facts I'm talking, Miss Champion, and they're not the only facts. I wouldn't soil my tongue with the other thing while Alex was listening——"

" What other thing?"

" You know what other thing. I didn't rent my good clean room for any such use as you put it to last evening. You entertained a man in your room last night and don't try to lie your way out of it."

If Lucy made any answer, it was too low to be heard. Mrs. Norris appeared suddenly at the kitchen window. I had no time to move back out of her line of sight, but she didn't raise her eyes. Her face was stony. She slammed the window down, and jerked the blind down after it.

Gasping and smiling, the old woman rolled back onto her

pillows: "Well! It looks as if Annie's lost her boarder. I could have told her she was borrowing trouble, renting a room to the young Lucy creature with a grown boy in the house." She added with the candour of the very old, who have nothing but life to lose: "Shucks, if she really goes, there won't be no more arguments to listen to."

I got up and touched her thin flannelette shoulder. " It was nice to meet you, Aunty."

"Same to you, son. I hope you get yourself a better job than that walking job you got. I know what it does to the feet. I cooked all my life in big houses. You take good care of your feet. . . ." The voice trailed me out like a cobweb spun endlessly into space.

I went back to my car and drove it forward a few yards into a position from which I could watch the Norris house. My job was a walking job and a driving job, but mainly a sitting and waiting job. It was hot under the top of my car, but I needed it for cover. I took off my coat and sat and waited. The seconds piled up slowly into minutes like rows of hot bright pennies.

At two by my dashboard clock, which was working, a yellow cab entered Mason Street from the other end. It slowed and honked in front of the Norris house, turned in the driveway behind the Ford coupé, and backed into the curb. Lucy Champion came down the driveway with a suit-box under her arm and a hat on her head. Behind her Alex Norris, fully clothed now, carried a pair of matched grey suitcases. The driver put them in the trunk and Lucy got into the back seat with a reluctant awkwardness. Alex Norris watched the cab out of sight. From the porch, his mother watched him.

I drove past them with my head averted, and followed the cab to Hidalgo Street, along Hidalgo Street, then south on Main. The railway station lay in that direction, and I half expected Lucy to take a train. Her cab turned into the circular drive by the station, deposited her and her luggage on the platform. Lucy went into the station. I parked behind it and headed for the back door of the waiting-room. At the same moment, Lucy came out. Her face was heavily powdered, and her hair tucked up under her hat. Without a glance at me, she walked to the taxi rank on the other side of the building and climbed into a black-and-white cab. While its driver was picking up her luggage from the platform, I turned my car.

The black-and-white cab went north on Main to the highway, then west along the highway for two blocks. It slowed and turned sharp left under a canvas sign stretched between two poles: MOUNTVIEW MOTEL AND TRAILER COURT. I drove by it, U-turned at the next intersection, and came back in time to see the black-and-white cab pull out with its back seat empty.

I parked short of the canvas sign and slid to the other side of the seat. The Mountview Motel and Trailer Court stood in the social badlands between the highway and the railroad tracks. It had a view of the mountains in the sense that every building in Bella City had. Through a wire-net fence to which vines clung halfheartedly, I could see twenty or thirty house trailers lying like beached whales in the dusty court. Around and under them, children and dogs were playing. The near side of the court was half enclosed by an L-shaped building made of concrete blocks, pierced with twelve windows and twelve doors. The first door was marked Office. Lucy's suitcases stood on its low concrete stoop.

Lucy came out, followed by a fat man in a T-shirt. He picked up her suitcases and escorted her to the seventh door, in the corner of the ell. Even at a distance, she looked rigid with strain. The fat man unlocked the door and they went inside.

I drove into the court and parked in front of the office. It was a dismal cubicle, divided by an unpainted wooden counter. A frayed canvas settee stood by the door. On the other side of the counter there was a rolltop desk stuffed with papers, an unmade studio bed, an electric coffee-maker full of grounds, over all a sour coffee smell. A dirty printed card scotch-taped to the top of the counter announced: We Reserve the Right to Choose Our Clientele.

CHAPTER 4

The fat man came back to the office, his belly rising and falling under the T-shirt. His forearms were marked with blue tattooings like the printing on sides of beef. One on the right arm said: I Love You Ethel. His small eyes said: I love nobody.

"Any vacancies?"

"You kidding? Vacancies is what we got plenty of." He looked around his office as if he suspected something the matter but couldn't exactly place it. "You want a room?"

"Number six if it's empty."

"It ain't."

"How about number eight?"

"You can have eight." He rummaged in the desk for a registration blank, which he pushed across the counter. "You on the road?"

"Uh-huh." I signed my name illegibly, omitting my license number and home address. "Hot to-day."

"You ain't seen nothing." His defensive tone was accentuated by an asthmatic wheeze. "It's barely a hundred. You should of been here around the first of the month. It was darn near a hundred and ten. That's what keeps the tourists away in droves. The room is two and a half single."

I gave him the money and asked to use the phone.

"Long distance?" he wheezed suspiciously.

"A local call. Private, if you don't mind."

He produced a telephone from under the counter and ambled out, slamming the screen door behind him. I dialled the number of the Mission Hotel. Una's voice answered immediately when the switchboard called her room:

"Who is it?"

"Archer speaking from the Mountview Motel. Lucy Champion checked in here a few minutes ago. She was evicted by her landlady, a coloured woman named Norris on Mason Street."

"Where is this motel?"

21

"On the highway two blocks west of Main. She's in room seven."

"All right, fine," on a rising note. "Keep a close watch on her. I'm going to pay her a visit. I want to know where she goes after I talk to her."

She hung up. I moved into room eight by placing my overnight bag in the middle of the worn rag rug and hanging my jacket on the one wire hanger in the cardboard wardrobe. The bed was covered with a sleazy green spread that failed to conceal the economic depression in its middle. I didn't trust the bed. I sat on a straight chair that I placed beside the front window and lit a cigarette.

The window gave me a view of Lucy's door and window across the inner corner of the ell. The door was closed, the green roller-blind drawn down over the window. The smoke from my cigarette rose straight up through the stagnant air to the yellow plaster ceiling. A woman groaned behind the wallboard partition in the next room, number nine.

A man's voice said: "Anything the matter?"

"Don't talk."

"I thought something was the matter."

"Shut up. There's nothing the matter."

"I thought I hurt you."

"Shut up. Shut up. Shut up."

My cigarette tasted like burning grass. I butted it in the lid of a coffee can which had been left in the room as an ashtray and thought of the people who had lain alone or in pairs on the iron bed and looked at the yellow ceiling. Traces of their dirt remained in the corners, their odours clung to the walls. They had come from all over the country to look at the yellow ceiling, stir in the iron bed, finger the walls and leave their indelible marks.

I moved across the floor to the partition between my room and Lucy's. She was sobbing. After a while she said something to herself that sounded like: "I won't." And after another while: "I don't know what to do."

People were always sobbing to themselves and saying that they didn't know what to do. Still, it was hard to listen to. I went back to my chair by the window and watched the door, trying to imagine I didn't know what was going on behind it.

Una appeared in front of it suddenly like a figure in a dream. A marijuana dream. She had on leopard-spotted slacks and a yellow silk shirt. Leaning towards the door like an eager fighter, she struck it two backhanded blows with her right fist.

Lucy opened the door. Her curled brown hands came up to her mouth and hooked on her lower lip. Una pushed in like a small garish battering-ram, and Lucy fell back out of my line of vision. I heard her staggering heels strike the floor. I moved to the partition.

" Sit down," Una said briskly. " No, you sit on the bed. I'll take the chair. Well, Lucy. What have you been doing with yourself?"

" I don't want to talk to you." Lucy's voice might have been soft and pleasant if fear hadn't been playing tricks with it.

" You don't have to get excited."

" I'm not getting excited. What I do is my own business. It's no business of yours."

" I wonder about that. Just what does your business cover?"

" I've been looking for a job, a *decent* job. When I save a little money, I'm going back home. It's not your business, but I'm telling you anyway."

" That's a good thing, Lucy. Because you're not going back to Detroit, now or ever."

" You can't stop me!"

There was an interval of silence. " No, I can't stop you. I will tell you this. When you step off that train, there'll be a reception waiting for you. I phone Detroit long distance every afternoon."

Another, longer pause.

" So you see, Lucy, Detroit is out for you. You know what I think you should do, Lucy? I think you made a mistake leaving us. I think you should come back with us."

Lucy sighed very deeply. " No, I can't."

" Yes. You come back. It'll be safer for you and safer for us, safer for everybody." The bright clatter of Una's tone took on an illusive softness: " I'll tell you what the situation is, dearie. We can't just have you running around loose the way you have been. You'll get into trouble, or you'll have

a teensy bit too much to drink in the wrong company, and
then you'll blab. I know you people, you see. Blabber-
mouths every one of you."

"Not me," the girl protested. "I'd never blab, I promise
you faithfully. Please leave me go on the way I been, minding my own business, *please*."

"I've got my duty to my brother. I'd like to leave you
alone, Lucy. If you'd co-operate."

"I always co-operated before, before it happened."

"Sure you did. Tell me where she is, Lucy. Then I'll leave
you alone, or you can come back to us on double the salary.
We trust you. It's her we don't trust, you know that. Is she
here in town?"

"I don't know," Lucy said.

"You know she's here in town. Now tell me where she is.
I'll give you a thousand dollars cash on the barrelhead if
you'll tell me. Come on now, Lucy. Tell me."

"I don't know," Lucy said.

"A thousand dollars cash on the barrelhead," Una repeated.
"I have it right here."

"I won't take your money," Lucy said. "I don't know
where she is."

"Is she in Bella City?"

"I don't know, mum. She brought me here and left. How
do I know where she went? She never told me nothing."

"That's funny, I thought you were her regular little con-
fidante." Harshly, with a sudden change of pace: "Was he
hurt bad?"

"Yes. I mean, I don't know."

"Where is he? In Bella City?"

"I don't know, mum." Lucy's voice had sunk to a stolid
monotone.

"Is he dead?"

"I don't know who you talking about, mum."

"Rotten little liar!" Una said.

I heard a blow. A chair scraped. Someone hiccuped once,
loudly.

"You leave me be, Miss Una." The pressure of the situation had thrown Lucy back into sullen nonresistance, and
slurred her speech. "I don't have to take nothing from you.
I'll call the *pol*lice."

"I'm sorry, honey. I didn't mean to hit you. You know my bad temper, Lucy." Una's voice was husky with false solicitude. "Did I hurt you?"

"You didn't hurt me. You couldn't hurt me. Just stay away from me. Go away and leave me be."

"Why should I?"

"Because you won't get nothing out of me."

"How much are you holding out for, honey?"

"And don't you call me honey. I'm no honey of yours."

"Five thousand dollars?"

"I wouldn't touch your money."

"You're getting pretty uppity for a nigger gal that couldn't get a job until I gave her one."

"Don't you call me that. And you know what you can do with your job. I wouldn't go back to it if I was starving to death."

"Maybe you will," Una said cheerfully. "I hope you do starve to death."

Her footsteps marched to the door, and the door slammed. In the hollow silence that ensued in the room, a series of slow dragging movements ended in the creak of bedsprings and another yawning sigh. I went back to my window. The sky blazed blue in my eyes. At the entrance Una was climbing into a taxi. It went away.

Two cigarettes later, Lucy came out and locked her door with a brass-tagged key. She wavered on the concrete stoop for a moment, gathering herself like an inexperienced diver for a plunge into cruel space. Thick powder clung like icing sugar to her face, imperfectly masking its darkness and its despair. Though she was wearing the same clothes, her body looked softer and more feminine.

She left the court and turned right along the shoulder of the highway. I followed her on foot. Her steps were quick and uncertain, and I was half afraid she might fall in front of a cab. Gradually her stride took on the rhythm of some purpose. At the first traffic-lights, she crossed the highway.

I went ahead of her and ducked into the first store I came to, which happened to be an open-front fruit-and-vegetable market. Bent over a bin of oranges with my back to the street, I heard her heels on the pavement and felt her shadow brush me, like a cold feather.

CHAPTER 5

The street was one block west of Main and parallel to it. Its pitted asphalt was lined with Main Street's leavings: radio and shoe repair shops, re-upholsterers, insect exterminators, flytrap lunchrooms. A few old houses survived among them as flats and boarding-houses.

Lucy paused in front of a house in the third block and looked up and down the street. A hundred yards behind her, I was waiting at a bus stop on the corner. In a sudden flurry of movement, she ran across the shallow yard of the house and up the verandah steps. I walked on.

The house she had entered leaned with an absent and archaic air between a mattress-cleaning plant and a one-chair barbershop. Three-storied and weirdly gabled, it had been built before the invention of California architecture. Wavy brown watermarks streaked its grey frame sides. The lower panes of the ground-floor windows, painted white, faced the sun like a blind man's frosted glasses. Beside the double front-door there was a name on a board, printed in large black letters: SAMUEL BENNING, M.D. A card above the bell-push said, in English and Spanish, Ring and Enter. I did.

The air in the hallway was a thin hospital-soup compounded of cooking odours, antiseptic, dimness. A face swam at me through it. It was a big man's face, too sharp and aggressive. I shifted my feet instinctively, then saw that it was my own face reflected in murky glass, framed in the tarnished curlicues of a wall mirror.

A door let light in at the end of the hall. A dark-haired woman came through it. She wore the grey striped uniform of a nurse's aide, and she was handsome in a plump and violent way. Her black eyes looked at me as if they knew it. " You wish to see the doctor, sir?"

" If he's in."

" Just go into the waiting-room, sir. He will take care of you presently. The door on your left."

The waiting-room was unoccupied. Large and many-windowed, it had evidently been the front parlour of the house. Its present quality was a struggling lack of respectability, from the shredding carpet to the high discoloured ceiling. Against the walls there were some wicker chairs that someone had recently brightened up with chintz. And the walls and floor were clean. In spite of this, it was a room in which the crime of poverty had left clues.

I sat down in one of the chairs with my back to the light and picked up a magazine from a rickety table. The magazine was two years old, but it served to mask my face. Across the room from me, in the inner wall, there was a closed door. After a while a tall black-haired woman wearing an ill-fitting white uniform opened the door. I heard a voice that sounded like Lucy's say something unintelligible and emotional, several rooms away. The woman who had opened the door closed it sharply behind her and came towards me:

"Do you wish to see the doctor?"

Her eyes were the colour of baked blue enamel. Her beauty cancelled the room.

I was wondering how the room had happened to deserve her when she interrupted me: "Did you wish to see the doctor?"

"Yes."

"He's busy now."

"Busy for how long? I'm in a hurry."

"I couldn't say how long."

"I'll wait for a while."

"Very well, sir."

She stood with perfect calm under the pressure of my stare, as if it were her natural element. Her beauty wasn't the kind that depended on movement or feeling. It was plastic and external like a statue's; even the blue eyes were flat and depthless. Her whole face looked as if it had been frozen with novocaine.

"Are you one of Dr. Benning's patients?"

"Not yet."

"Can I have your name, please?"

"Larkin," I said at random. "Horace Larkin."

The frozen face remained frozen. She went to the desk and wrote something on a card. Her tight, lumpy uniform made me restless. Everything about her bothered me.

A bald man in a doctor's smock jerked the inner door open. I raised the magazine in front of me and examined him over its edge. Large-eared and almost hairless, his head seemed naked, as if it had been plucked. His long face was dimly lit by pale worried eyes. Deep lines of sorrow dragged down from the wings of his large vulnerable nose.

" Come here," he said to the receptionist. " You talk to her, for heaven's sake. I can't make head or tail of it." His voice was high-pitched and rapid, furious with anger or anxiety.

The woman surveyed him coldly, glanced at me, and said nothing.

" Come on," he said placatingly, raising a bony red hand towards her. " I can't handle her."

She shrugged her shoulders and passed him in the doorway. His stringy body cringed away from hers, as if she radiated scorching heat. I left the house.

Lucy came out ten minutes later. I was sitting in the barber shop beside Dr. Benning's house. There were two men ahead of me, one in the chair having his neck shaved, the other reading a newspaper by the window. The newspaper-reader was an unstylish stout in a tan camel's-hair jacket. There were purple veins in his cheeks and nose. When Lucy passed the window heading south, he got up hurriedly, put on a soiled panama, and left the shop.

I waited, and followed him out.

" But you are next, sir," the barber cried after me. I looked back from the other side of the street, and he was still at the window, making siren gestures with a razor.

The man with the veined nose and the panama hat was halfway to the next corner, almost abreast of Lucy. She led us back to the railway station. When she reached it, a passenger train was pulling out towards the north. She stood stock-still on the platform until its smoke was a dissolving haze on the foothills. The man in the camel's-hair coat was watching her, slouched like a barely animate lump of boredom behind a pile of express crates under the baggage-room arch.

Lucy turned on her heel and entered the station. A narrow window under the arch gave me a partial view of the waiting-room. I moved to another window, ignoring the man behind the express crates but trying to place him in my memory.

Lucy was at the ticket window with green money in her hand.

The man edged towards me, his stout body wriggling along the wall as if the shade-latticed air offered solid resistance to its movement. He laid two soft white fingers on my arm:

"Lew Archer, *n'est-ce pas*?" The French was deliberate clowning, accompanied by a smirk.

"Must be two other people." I shook the fingers loose.

"You wouldn't brush me, boysie. I remember you but vividly. You testified for the prosecution in the Saddler trial, and you did a nice job too. I combed the jury panel for the defence. Max Heiss?"

He took off his panama hat, and a shock of red-brown hair pushed out over his forehead. Under it, clever dirty eyes shone liquidly like dollops of brown sherry. His little smile had a shamefaced charm, acknowledging that he had taken a running jump at manhood and still, at forty or forty-five, had never quite got his hands on it.—If it existed, the smile went on to wonder.

"Heiss?" he said coaxingly. "Maxfield Heiss?"

I remembered him and the Saddler trial. I also remembered that he had lost his licence for tampering with prospective jurors in another murder trial.

"I know you, Max. So what if I do?"

"So we toddle across the street and I'll buy you a drink and we can talk over old times and such." His words were soft and insinuating, breaking gently like bubbles between his pink lips. His breath was strong enough to lean on.

I glanced at Lucy. She was in a telephone booth at the other end of the waiting-room. Her lips were close to the mouthpiece and moving.

"Thanks, not this time. I have a train to catch."

"You're kidding me again. There isn't another train in either direction for over two hours. Which means you don't have to be anxious the girl will get away, *n'est-ce pas*? She can't possibly use that ticket she just bought for over two hours." His face lit up with a practical joker's delight, as if he had just palmed off an explosive cigar on me.

I felt as if he had. "Somebody's kidding. I'm not in the mood for it."

"Now don't be like that. You don't have to take offence."

"Beat it, Max."

"How can we do business if you won't even bat the breeze?"

"Go away. You're standing in my light. "

He waltzed in a small circle and presented his smirk to me again: "*Avee atquee valee* boysie, that means good-bye and hello. I'm on public property and you can't push me off. And you got no monopoly on this case. If the true facts were known, I bet you don't even know what case you're on. I got a priority on you there."

I couldn't help being interested, and he knew it. His fingers returned like a troupe of trained slugs to my arm:

"Lucy is my meat. I won her in a raffle by dint of sheer personal derring-do. Signed her up for a seven-year contract and just when I'm thinking of converting the deal into cash, lo and behold I stumble into you. In my alcoholic way."

"That was quite a speech, Max. How much truth is there in it?"

"Nothing-but-the-truth-so-help-me-God." He raised his palm in mock solemnity. "Not the whole truth, naturally. I don't know the whole truth and neither do you. We need an exchange of views."

Lucy came out of the telephone booth. Whenever she left an enclosed space her body huddled protectively into itself. She sat down on a bench and crossed her legs, leaning forward as if she had stomach cramps.

Heiss nudged me softly. His moist eyes shone. He might have been confiding the name of his beloved. "I do know there's a great deal of money in it."

"How much?"

"Five grand. I'd be willing to go fifty-fifty with you."

"Why?"

"Simple panic, chum." Unlike most natural liars, he could use the truth effectively. "Hit me and I black out. Shoot me and I bleed. Frighten me and I lose my controls. I'm not the courageous type. I need a partner who is, one that won't tear me off."

"Or a fall guy?"

"Perish the thought. This is strictly legal, believe me. You don't often pick up twenty-five hundred legally."

"Go on."

" In a minute. *Exchange* of views is what I said. You haven't told me a thing. What tale did the lady tell you, for example?"

" Lady?"

" Woman, dame, whatever she is. The one with the boyish bob and the diamonds. Didn't she hire you?"

" You know everything, Max. How can I tell you something you don't know?"

" You can try. What was her story to you?"

" Something about missing jewels. It wasn't very convincing even at the time."

" Better than the guff she handed me. Do you know what she gave me? That the girl was her late husband's servant, and when he died he left a legacy to her, and she was the executrix of the estate. And oh mercy me I owe it to my poor dead husband to find Lucy and pay off." With a nasty wit, he mimicked Una's accents of false sentiment. " She must have thought she was dealing with an imbecile or something."

" When was this?"

" A week ago. I spent a good solid week picking that black girl up." He shot a vicious glance through the window at Lucy's impervious back. " So I found her, and what happened? I phoned up the good executrix and asked her for further instructions, and she fired me."

" What's she trying to cover up, Max?"

" Are we in business?"

" That depends."

" The hell. I offer you a half interest in a big deal, and you say that depends. *That depends*. I bare my bosom to you, and all you do is play clam. It isn't ethical."

" Is the five grand ethical?"

" I promised you it was. I've been burned, I lost my licence once——"

" No blackmail involved?"

" Absolutely not. If you want the honest truth, the things so legal I'm afraid of it."

" All right, here's what I think. It isn't Lucy she wants at all. Lucy's a decoy duck for somebody else."

" You catch on rapidly. Do you know who the somebody else is, though?"

"I haven't identified her, no."

"Uh-uh. Not *her*." He smiled with superior knowledge. "*Him*. I've got his name and description and everything else. And that black babe is going to lead us to him, watch."

Heiss was emotionally carried away. His sherry-brown eyes slopped round in their sockets, and his hands congratulated each other. To me, his story sounded too good to be true. It was.

Lucy straightened suddenly and jumped up from the bench, heading for the back door of the waiting-room. I left Heiss standing. When I turned the rear corner of the station, Lucy was climbing into a green Ford coupé. Alex Norris was at the wheel. The Ford was rolling before the door slammed.

There was one taxi at the stand beside the station. Its driver was sprawled asleep in the front seat, his peaked cap over the upper part of his face, his mouth wide and snoring. Out of the tail of my eye, I saw the Ford turn north towards the highway.

I shook the driver awake. He was little and grey-haired, but he wanted to fight. "Take it easy, for Christ's sake. What goes on?"

I showed him money. "Follow that Ford coupé."

"All right, take it easy."

Max Heiss tried to get in beside me. I shut the door in his face, and the taxi pulled away. We were in the street in time to see the Ford turn left at the highway intersection, towards Los Angeles. At the intersection a red light stopped us. It was a long time before it turned green again. We drove fast out of town, passing everything on the highway. No green Ford.

Five miles beyond the city limits, I told the driver to turn around.

"Sorry," he said. "I couldn't run that light with all the traffic going through. You have trouble with those people?"

"No trouble."

When I got back to the station, Max Heiss had gone. That suited me just as well. I ordered breakfast, always a safe meal, in the station lunchroom, and discovered when I started to eat it that I was hungry.

It was shortly after five o'clock when I finished my bacon and eggs. I walked back to the Mountview Motel.

CHAPTER 6

Lucy's key, with the numbered brass tag dangling from it, was in her door. I obeyed my impulse to knock. There was no answer. I looked around the court, which was sunk in the somnolence and heat of late afternoon. On its far side trailer children were chirping like crickets. knocked again, listened to answering silence, turned the knob and stepped inside. Lucy was lying almost at my feet. I closed the door and looked at my watch. Five seventeen.

The roller blind was down over the window. Light slanted through the cracks in the blind, supporting a St. Vitus's dance of dust motes. There was a wall switch beside the door, and I jogged it with my elbow. The yellow walls sprang up around me and the ceiling pressed down from overhead, ringed with concentric shadows. The light radiated from a wall bracket directly over Lucy. Its paper-shaded bulb shone down into her face, which was grey as a clay death-mask in a pool of black blood. Her cut throat gaped like the mouth of an unspeakable grief.

I leaned on the door and wished myself on the other side of it, away from Lucy. But death had tied me to her faster than any ceremony.

One of her arms was outflung. Beside the spread upturned hand something metal glinted. I stooped to look at it. It was a hand-made knife with a curved six-inch blade and a black wooden handle ornamented with carved leaves. The blade was stained.

I stepped across Lucy towards the bed. It was identical with the bed in my room, its green rayon cover wrinkled where she had lain on it. At its foot her suitcases stood unopened. I opened one of them, using a clean handkerchief to mask my fingerprints. It was neatly packed with nurses' uniforms, crisped and starched from the laundry. Like the private compartment of a divided life, the contents of the other suitcase were a jumbled mess. It had been packed in a hurry with a tangle of stockings, wadded dresses, soiled blouses and underwear, an *Ebony* and a sheaf of romance

33   B

magazines, an Ellington album wrapped in red silk pyjamas.
I found an envelope tucked among the powders and creams
in a side pocket.

It was addressed to Miss Lucy Champion, c/o Norris, 14
Mason, Bella City; and postmarked Detroit, Mich., Sept. 9.
The letter inside lacked date or return address:

DEAR LUCY

*Am very sorry you lost your job we all thot you got yourself
fixed up for Life but you never know what is going to come,
sure we want you back honey can you raze the fair am afraid
we cant. You father is out of work agin and am the soul
sport of the family again, hard to make ends meat. Can
always give you a bed to sleep in honey something to eat,
come home things will be better. Brother is still in school
doing real good writing this for me (hi sis). Hope you can
raze fair stay off the roads.*

MOTHER

P.S.—*How are you sis am fine, you know who.*

I put the letter back where I had found it, and closed
the suitcase. Its catch clicked loudly, like a final tick of time.

Lucy's purse lay in a nest of dust in the corner behind her
bed. It contained lipstick and a handkerchief stained with it,
a few ten- and five- and one-dollar bills and some change, a
one-way ticket to Detroit, a social security card, and a newspaper clipping. The clipping was printed in old-fashioned type
under a single-column head:

MOTHER OFFERS REWARD FOR MISSING MAN

Arroyo Beach, Sept. 8 (Special to the BELLA CITY PRESS.)
Mrs. Charles A. Singleton, socialite resident of this resort
town, to-day posted a reward of $5,000 for information
concerning the whereabouts of her son. The son, Charles
A. Singleton, Jr., disappeared from the public rooms
of a local hotel one week ago, on the evening of September 1st. His friends and relatives have not heard from
him since that date.

Singleton, a Harvard graduate and wartime Air Force
Lieutenant, is of medium height and athletic build, with
curly brown hair, hazel eyes and a ruddy complexion.
When last seen he was wearing a grey worsted suit,
white shirt, dark red tie, and black shoes, without hat

or topcoat. The missing man, son of the late Major Charles A. Singleton, is heir to the Singleton agricultural enterprises. His maternal grandfather was Colonel Isaac Carlyle, who married Maria Valdes, daughter of the founder of the great Valdes land-grant estates.

Local police are inclined to reject suggestions of foul play, though Mrs. Singleton herself expresses fears for her son's safety. County Sheriff Oscar Lanson states: "Kidnapping seems out of the question. There has been no ransom note, for one thing. As for foul play, the evidence indicates that Mr. Singleton left Arroyo Beach under his own power, for his own reasons. It is to be remembered that he is a young, unattached man, with a background of travel. We are, however, doing everything we can to locate him, and will welcome any information from the public."

Anyone having information as to Singleton's whereabouts was urged to contact Capt. Kennedy of the Arroyo Beach sheriff's office.

I read the report twice, fixing the names, times, places, in my head, then replaced the clipping in the purse and the purse in the corner. In a way I knew less than before, as something written in a foreign language extends the range of your ignorance. I looked at my watch, Five twenty-four. Seven minutes since I had found Lucy.

In order to reach the door I had to step over her again. I looked down into the grey face before I switched off the light. Alienated and deeply sunk beyond time already, the face told me nothing. Then it was swallowed by shadows.

In the court, the yellow sunlight looked thin and faded, as if it had been late afternoon for an insupportable time. An old car turned in from the highway and rolled across the gravel to the trailers, leaving a feeble flurry of dust on the stagnant air. I waited for the dust to settle before I started across the court to the office. Before I reached it I saw that Alex Norris was watching me from the gate.

Moving with awkward speed in a pressed blue suit too small for him, he ran at me. I went to meet him and crouched for the onset. He was heavy and strong, and he knew how to use his weight. His shoulder took my midriff and laid me on the gravel on my back. I got up. He didn't know how to use his fists. I stepped inside a wild swing and bent him with a body-blow. It brought his head forward for an uppercut. Instead, to save my knuckles and his face, I locked his right arm and used it as a lever to turn him away.

" Let me go," he said. " Fair fight. I'll show you."

" You showed me. I'm too old to fight. Me and Joe."

" He could beat your brains out," the boy cried defiantly.

" Turn me loose, I'll do it myself. What were you doing in Lucy's room?"

" Something's happened to her."

Bowed and immobilised by my hold, he had to crane his neck sideways to look at me. His black forehead was sprinkled with droplets of sweat, and his eyes were large and bright with expectations of disaster. " You're a liar. Let me go."

" Will you stand and talk to me, like a sensible man?"

" No." But the word lacked force. The brightness of his eyes was glazing, would turn to tears in a minute. He was a boy in a man's frame. I released him.

He straightened slowly, rubbing his cramped arm. Beyond him, on the other side of the court, a ragged line of spectators was moving slowly towards the lure of violence.

" Come into the office, Alex."

He stiffened. " Who's going to make me?"

" Nobody's going to make you. Come on, anyway."

" I don't have to."

" How old are you, Alex?"

" Nineteen, going on twenty."

" Ever been in trouble?"

" I never have. Ask my mother."

" Lucy your girl friend?"

" She's not my girl friend. We're going to get married." He added, with pathetic irrelevance: " I can support a wife."

" Sure you can."

His bright gaze was painful on my face. " Is something the matter? Why did you go in there?"

I groped back for the impulse that had made me knock on Lucy's door and go in. " To talk to her. To warn her to leave town."

" We are leaving, to-night. That's what I'm waiting for.

She came to get her things." As if it were being turned by a long-handled wrench against his will, his head turned on his shoulders to look at the closed door of number seven. "Why doesn't she come out? Is she sick?"

I said: "She's not coming out."

The gallery of onlookers from the trailers was straggling across the court, uttering small sounds of menace and excitement. I pulled the office door open and held it for Alex. He went in past me, moving nothing but his legs.

The man who loved Ethel and nobody else was sitting on the studio bed with his back to the door, a half-empty Coke bottle in his fist. He rose and padded to the counter, casting a backward glance at the studio bed. From the cover of a magazine spread open on its pillow, a bare-bosomed woman screamed soundlessly for assistance.

Disregarding her pleas, the pink-haired man said: "What can I do for you?" Then his slow nerves reacted to the black boy: "What does he want?"

"The telephone," I said.

"Local call?"

"The police. Do you know the number?"

He knew it. "Trouble?"

"In number seven. Go and take a look. I wouldn't go in, though. Don't let the others, either."

He leaned on the counter, his belly oozing over its edge like cottage cheese in a bag. "What happened?"

"Look for yourself. Give me the telephone first."

He handed me the telephone, hustled to the door and out. Alex tried to follow him. I kept my right hand on the boy's arm and dialled with my left. When he heard what I had to say to the desk sergeant he fell forward across the counter, catching his weight on his forearms. The upper half of his body was shaken by an inaudible sobbing. The desk sergeant said that he would send a car right out.

I shifted my hand to the boy's back. He shied away from it as if I were trying to stab him.

"What were you doing out there, Alex?"

"Minding my own business."

"Waiting for Lucy?"

"If you know you don't have to ask me."

"How long were you waiting?"

"Nearly half an hour. I drove around the block a couple of times and came back."

I looked at my watch: five thirty-one. "She went in about five o'clock?"

"It was just about five."

"Did she go in alone?"

"Yes. Alone."

"Did anybody else go in afterwards?"

"Not that I saw."

"Did anybody come out?"

"You did. I saw you come out."

"Besides me. Before me."

"I didn't see. I drove around the block."

"Did you go in?"

"No, sir. I didn't go in."

"Why not?"

"She said she'd only be five minutes. Her bags, they were still packed."

"You could have gone in."

"I didn't want to. She didn't want me to."

"Lucy was passing, wasn't she?"

"What if she was? There is no law against passing in this state."

"You're well informed," I said. "Going to school?"

"I just started junior college. But I'm quitting."

"To get married?"

"I'll never get married. I'll never marry anybody now. I'll run away and lose myself." With his head dejected below his shoulders, he was speaking to the scarred top of the counter.

"You're going to have to stick around and answer a lot of questions. Pull yourself together."

I shook him roughly by the shoulder. He wouldn't turn or move until the siren whooped on the highway. Then his head came up like an animal's at bay.

CHAPTER 7

A black patrol-car ground to a stop on the gravel outside the office. A plainclothesman got out, mounted the stoop, and filled the doorway. In spite of his grey fedora and baggy grey clothes, he looked as if he had always been a policeman—had teethed on handcuffs, studied his lessons in the criminal code, pounded out his career on broken pavements, in nocturnal alleys. Scarred and seamed by fifty years of sun and other weather, his face was a relief map of life in the valley.

"I'm Brake, lieutenant of detectives. You the one that phoned?"

I said I was. "She's in room seven, at the end of the court."

"Dead?"

"Very."

Alex let out a choked noise. Brake took a step towards him and looked him over closely. "What are you doing here?"

"Waiting for Lucy."

"She the one that's dead?"

"Yes, sir."

"You're going to have a long wait. Did you cut her?"

Alex looked at the detective as if he were a tree too thick to climb. "No, sir."

"You're Annie Norris's boy, aren't you?"

"Yes, sir."

"How's your mother going to like this?" Before Alex could answer, Brake turned to me: "Did he cut her?"

"I doubt it. He stayed around after it happened. They were on their way to get married, he says."

"He says."

"I didn't cut her," Alex said. "I wouldn't hurt a hair of Lucy's head." He was leaning slackly against the counter on his elbows, as if he no longer had a use for his body.

The fat key-clerk came in, letting the door close softly on his heel. He moved sideways along the wall and around the end of the counter to his world of paper bosoms, dirty sheets,

39

silent screams for assistance. The sight of death had reminded him of the buried guilts in the graveyard of his mind, and he jumped when Brake said to his back:

" Are you the key-clerk?"

" Yes, sir."

" I want a key to number seven, all the keys in fact."

" They're both out, Mr. Brake." He came forward placatingly, offering his quivering body as a sacrifice. " I give her one when she rented the room, and then when she came back she asked me for the duplicate. She said she lost the other. I said she'd have to pay——"

I cut in: " The key's in the door, lieutenant."

" Why didn't you say so?"

Brake stepped outside and summoned his driver to keep an eye on Alex. A second police-car drew up behind the first. The ring of spectators broke and re-formed around it. A uniformed sergeant pushed through them to join Brake. He had a folded tripod and camera under one arm and a finger-print kit in the other hand. " Where's the stiff, lieutenant?"

" Over yonder. Call the deputy coroner?"

" He's on his way."

" She'll spoil before we get to her, at this rate. Now take it easy, folks. Gangway."

The crowd made way for them and surged in their wake. Inside the office, Alex and his guard sat in glum intimacy on the settee. The guard was a large young cop in a blue traffic officer's uniform. Beside his thick-chested frame Alex looked smaller and thinner. His gaze was turned inward. He seemed to be seeing himself for the first time as he was: a black boy tangled in white law, so vulnerable he hardly dared move a muscle.

Behind the counter, the key-clerk was comforting himself with the remnant of his Coke. I sat on the studio bed beside him:

" I'd like to get that straight about the keys."

" Questions!" He belched pathetically. Brown liquid trickled from the corner of his mouth into a red rash on his chin. " You prob'ly won't believe me, I look like a healthy constitution, only I got delicate nerves. I'm still on partial disability from the Army, and that's the proof of it. I can't take all this cross-questioning and stuff. The way the lieutenant looked at me, you'd think I done her in." He pouted like a bloated dilapidated imbecile little boy.

"When did you see her last?"

"Must of been around five o'clock. I didn't look at the time."

"She needed another key?"

"That's correct. I asked her what happened to the one I give her when she checked in. She said she must of lost it. I said that would be fifty cents extra and she paid me the money right then. She said she was checking out. Little did I know she had a rendezvoose with murder."

"Did she seem disturbed?"

"I don't know. I didn't specially notice. I was the one that should of been disturbed. Why'd she want to come here to get herself chopped? They'd do it for her down on Hidalgo any day of the week."

"It certainly was tough on you," I said, "and inconsiderate of her."

"You're bloody right." Self-pity gurgled in his throat like a hæmorrhage beyond the reach of irony or cautery. "How did I know she was passing herself for white? That she was going to bleed all over my floor? I got to clean it up."

On the other side of the counter Alex sat with his guard. All I could see of him was the top of his head, but I could hear him breathing.

"After the girl went into her room," I said, "did anybody else go in?"

"Not that I saw. I don't pay no attention half the time. They go and come." The phrase pleased him, and he repeated it: "Go and come."

"You didn't see anybody?"

"Naw. I was sitting down in here passing the time. They come and go." A flash of anger galvanised him feebly: "I *wisht* I seen him. Just lemme get my hands on the guy that done it and mussed that floor——"

"You think it was a man?"

"Who said so?"

"You said ' guy.' "

"Only a manner of speaking. Anyway, why would a woman cut a woman?" Leaning towards me, he said in a loud stage whisper: "You want my honest opinion, I think that young buck done it. They're always cutting their wenches, you know that."

There was a scuffle of feet. Alex Norris came over the counter head first and lighted on all fours in front of us. Scrambling to his feet, he landed a back-handed blow on the side of the clerk's head. The clerk screamed gently and swooned across my legs.

Alex dived for the open window. Unable to get to my feet, I yelled: "Stop it, Alex! Come back!"

He kicked out the screen and hoisted one leg over the sill. The coat of his blue suit was split down the back.

His guard strode round the end of the counter, lifting the right side of his uniform blouse. His black police-holster snapped open and a revolver popped up in his hand like a lethal jack-in-the-box. Its safety clicked off. Alex was still in the window struggling to force his other leg through the narrow opening. He was a sitting duck, and the range was almost point-blank.

I rolled the key-clerk off my knees to the floor and stepped across the line of fire. The trigger-happy guard cursed me and said. "Get out of the way."

Alex was out of the window. I went out after him. He was pounding across a field of tall dry grass towards the fence that ran along the highway. It was a seven-foot wire fence. He ran up to it and vaulted over in a single fluid motion. His Ford coupé was parked on the shoulder of the highway.

I got over the fence and fell on the other side. A gun went off behind me. Alex was in his car, kicking the starter. A bullet struck the hood of the Ford with the plop of a heavy raindrop, leaving a hole. As if stung, the Ford jumped forward, its rear wheels churning the gravel. I ran for it and got one arm hooked through the open right window.

Alex didn't turn his head over the wheel, but he braked suddenly, swerved, and accelerated. I lost my precarious grip on the door. When I hit the ground, I rolled. The coloured world spun into grey monochrome and blacked out for a second. The young traffic-cop with the gun hauled me to my feet. The Ford was out of sight.

" Listen, you." He cursed me unimaginatively a few times. " I could of pinked him, if you hadn't been in the way. What you trying to pull?" The revolver in his right hand seemed to be threatening me. His left hand was automatically brushing gravel off the back of my jacket.

"You wanted him alive. If you shot him you'd be in the soup. He wasn't under arrest."

His face went white under the tan, as if I had turned a valve on its blood supply. Almost furtively, he put the revolver away.

Brake came out through the gate of the court, running swiftly and cumbrously like a bear on its hind legs. He had grasped the situation before he reached us:

"You're wasting time, Trencher. Take after him. Use the other car. I'll get on the radio. What's his number?"

"I didn't get it lieutenant."

"You're doing great work, Trencher." Brake waved him away.

I gave him the licence number. Moving with alert impatience, Brake went back to the patrol-car and shut himself in to radio his headquarters. I waited for him beside it:

"What's the story, lieuetnant?"

"General alarm. Roadblocks." He started for Lucy's room.

The crowd of trailer people, men and women and children, blocked his path. One of the men spoke up: "The boy get away from you, captain?"

"We'll get him back. Incidentally, I want all you people to stay home to-night. We'll talk to you later."

"Is it murder?" The question fell into a hush, which was broken by a sparrowlike twittering from women and children.

"I'll guarantee this:" Brake said, "she didn't cut herself shaving. Now break it up. You people go back to your houses."

The crowd drew back muttering. Advised by his glance to come along, I followed Brake to the door of number seven. Inside, the identification officer was taking measurements and photographs. Lucy lay under his ministrations with the bored expression of a hostess whose guests' antics were getting out of hand.

"Come in," Brake said. "Shut the door."

One of the suitcases was open on the bed, and he returned to his examination of it. I stayed by the door, watching his large practised hands go through the white uniforms.

"Trained nurse, apparently." He added very casually: "How did you happen to find her?"

"I knocked on the door and she didn't answer. The door wasn't locked. I looked in."

"Why do that?"

"I'm in the room next door."

His narrow grey gaze came up to my face. "You know her?"

"Never met her."

"Hear any noise? See anybody?"

"No." I made a quick decision. "I'm a private detective from Los Angeles. I've been trailing her since noon."

"Well." The grey eyes clouded. "That makes it interesting. Why were you doing that?"

The identification man, who was dusting the second suitcase for fingerprints, turned his head to give me a sharp-faced look.

"I was hired to."

Brake straightened up and faced me. "I didn't think you were doing it for fun. Let's see your identification."

I showed him my photostat.

"Who hired you?"

"I don't have to answer that."

"You weren't hired to kill her, by any chance?"

"You'll have to do better than that, if you want any co-operation from me."

"Who said I wanted any co-operation from you? Who hired you?"

"You get tough very quickly, lieutenant. I could have blown when I found her, instead of sticking around to give you the benefit of my experience."

"Can the spiel." He didn't needle easily. "Who hired you? And for God's sake don't give me the one about you got your client's interests to protect. I got a whole city to protect."

We faced each other across the drying moat of blood. He was a rough small-city cop, neither suave nor persuasive, with an ego encysted in scar-tissue. I was tempted to needle him again, to demonstrate to these country cousins how a boy from the big city could be hard in a polished way. But my heart wasn't in the work. I felt less loyalty to my client than to the dead girl on the floor, and I compromised:

"A woman who gave her name as Una Larkin came to my office this morning. She hired me to tail this girl, and told me where to pick her up at lunchtime. Tom's Café on Main Street. I picked her up there and followed her home to Alex Norris's house, where she was a roomer——"

"Save the details for your statement," Brake said. "What was that about the client's name? You think it was a phony?"

"Yes. Am I going to make a statement?"

"We'll go downtown soon's we finish up here. Right now I want to know what she hired you for."

"She said Lucy worked for her, and left a couple of weeks ago with some of her jewellery—ruby earrings and a gold necklace."

Brake glanced at the identification man, who wagged his head negatively. He said to me: "You'll have to take it up with the County Administrator. Or is that story phony, too?"

"I think so."

"The woman live in town here?"

"I doubt it. She was very cagey about who she was and where she came from."

"You giving it straight, or suppressing information?"

"Straight." Una had bought that much with the hundred that was lonely in my wallet.

"It better be. Did you call us as soon as you found her?"

"There was a few minutes' time-lag. On my way across the court to the office, young Norris attacked me."

"Was he going or coming?"

"Neither. He was waiting."

"How do you know?"

"I held him and questioned him a little. He said he'd been waiting for Lucy to get her things since five o'clock. They were going away to be married. He didn't know she was dead until I told him."

"You read minds, huh?" Brake's face slanted, chin out, towards me, cracked and red like Bella Valley earth above the irrigation level. "What else do you do, Mister Experience?"

"When I make a statement, I try to keep the record straight. The physical facts are against Norris. It looks like consciousness of guilt, running out like that——"

"You don't tell me," Brake said heavily, and his assistant

snickered. " I never would have thought of that by myself."

" He ran because he was scared. He thought he was going to be railroaded, and maybe he was right. I've seen it happen to black boys, also to white boys."

" Oh sure, you've been around. You've had a lot of experience. Only I don't want the goddam benefit of your goddam experience. I want the facts."

" You're getting them. Maybe I'm going too fast for your powers of assimilation."

Brake's small eyes crossed slightly. His large face became congested with dark blood. The developing situation was interrupted by someone opening the door behind me, and singing out: " Break it up, boys. I have a date with a lady. Where's the lady?"

It was the deputy coroner, a plump young medical man bubbling with the excessive cheerfulness of those who handled death as a regular chore. He was accompanied by a white-coated ambulance driver and a black-coated undertaker who strove to outdo him in gaiety. Brake lost interest in me and my selection of facts.

Samples of blood were taken from the floor. The stained bolo knife and Lucy's smaller belongings were packed in evidence cases. Its position having been outlined with chalk, the body was lifted onto a stretcher and covered with canvas. The undertaker and the ambulance driver carried it out. Brake sealed the door.

It was twilight, and the courtyard was almost empty. Around a pole in its centre, a group of women stood in the spill of light from a single arc-lamp. They were talking in loud self-righteous tones about murders they had seen or read or heard about or imagined. Their voices sank to an uneasy protesting murmur as Lucy's cortege went by them. Their eyes, bright-dark in faces splashed with white by the lamp on the pole, followed the covered stretcher to the back door of the waiting hearse. The sky was a dingy yellow ceiling.

CHAPTER 8

The Mission Hotel was the most impressive building on Main Street. It was a concrete cube pierced with four rows of windows and surmounted by a broadcasting mast that thrust a winking red light towards the stars. Its flat white façade was stained red by a vertical neon sign over the entrance.

The lobby was deep and gloomy, furnished with dark wrinkled-leather chairs. Those near the half-curtained windows at the front were occupied by old men sitting in stiff impromptu positions, as if a flood had lodged them there years ago and then receded forever. On the wall above their heads an obscure mural depicted U.S. cavalrymen riding strange horses with human knees in pursuit of still stranger Indians.

The desk-clerk was a mouse-coloured little man who was striving against heavy odds to confer distinction on himself and his surroundings. With hair and eyebrow-moustache scrupulously brushed, a cornflower in his buttonhole matching the delicate pin-stripe in his flannels, and at his languid elbow a vase of cornflowers to underline his point, he might have inspired a tone poem by Debussy. He answered my question in tones of careful elegance, implying that he hadn't always manned an outpost in the wilderness:

" I beileve Mrs. Larkin is in her suite. I haven't seen her go out, sir. Whom shall I say is calling?"

" Archer. Don't bother announcing me. What's her room number?"

" One hundred and two, Mr. Archer. I think she's expecting you."

It was opposite the elevator on the second floor. At the end of the corridor a pair of curtained French doors had a red-lit sign above them: FIRE ESCAPE. I knocked on the door of 102. The elevator creaked and thumped behind me like an old heart running down.

A wan voice called through the door: " Who is it, anyway?"

" Archer."

47

" Come in."

The door was locked, and I said so.

" All right, all right, I'm coming." The door swung inward.

Una looked sick. The olive-drab patches under her eyes had darkened and spread. In red Japanese pyjamas she looked less like a woman than a sexless imp who had grown old in hell.

She stood back to let me enter the room and closed the door softly behind me. It was the sitting room of the bridal or gubernatorial suite, if honeymooners or politicians ever came there. The two tall windows that overlooked the street had drapes of dark-red plush. They were lit from outside by a red neon glow that competed with the light of a parchment-shaded floor lamp made of twisted black iron. The tall carved Spanish chairs looked unsat in and unsittable. The only trace of Una's occupancy was a leopard coat hanging over the back of a chair.

" What's the trouble?" I said to her back.

She seemed to be supporting herself on the doorknob. " No trouble. It's this foul heat, and the waiting and the uncertainty." She saw where that was leading her, into candour, and switched off the little-girl whine. " I have a migraine, God bless it. They hit me regularly."

" Too bad." I added, with deliberate tactlessness: " I have a headache myself."

She turned on me with a hypochondriac's fierce competitive smile. " Not migraine, I bet. If you haven't had migraine you don't know what it is. I wish I could have my head amputated. Wouldn't that be stylish, though, a headless torso strutting around?" She was making an effort to master her self-pity and carry it off as a joke. " Men wouldn't know the difference."

Una was flattering herself again. Even in lounging pyjamas, her torso was no more interesting or curvilinear than a brick. I backed into one of the unsittable chairs, and said: " You're a great admirer of men."

" They're an admirable race. Well?" She stood above me, her changed tone indicating that there was no more time for comedy.

" I have a report to make. Why don't you sit down?"

"If you say so." The chair was too big for her, and her feet dangled clear of the floor. "Go ahead."

"Before I do, there are a couple of matters that need straightening out."

"What does that mean?" The pain behind her tongue gave it a vicious twang.

"You lied once to me this morning, about the theft of some jewellery. It's possible that you lied twice."

"Are you calling me a liar?"

"I'm asking you."

"You've been talking to her."

"Not exactly. Is that what I'd find out if I had? That you're a liar?"

"Don't put words into my mouth, I don't like it. I gave you the reason I had for wanting Lucy followed."

"The second time."

"The second time, then."

"You didn't say very much."

"Why should I? I've got a right to some privacy."

"You had this morning. Not any more."

"What is this?" she asked the room in perplexity. Her hands twisted, and their diamonds caught and reflected red light from the window. "I pay a man a hundred dollars to do a job for me, so he wants to know my grandfather's middle name. It was María, curiously enough."

"You're very frank about things that don't count. But you haven't given me your own name yet. I don't even know where you live."

"If it was any of your business, I'd tell you. Who do you think you are?"

"Merely an ex-cop trying to hustle a living. I sell my services on the open market. It doesn't mean I have to sell them to anybody."

"That's tall talk for a peeper. I can buy and sell you twenty times over——"

"Not me. You should have taken my advice and gone to the classifieds. There are bums you can hire for fifteen dollars a day to do anything short of murder. Murder comes higher."

"What about murder? Who said anything about murder?" Her voice had dwindled suddenly to a bodiless whisper that buzzed and wavered like a mosquito's flight.

"I did. I said it was expensive, in more ways than one."

"But why bring it up, what's the point? You haven't been talking to anybody? One of these bums you mentioned?"

She was thinking of Maxfield Heiss. I said I hadn't.

"Not Lucy?"

"No."

"But you have been staying close to her?"

"As close as possible."

"Where is she? Where did she go?"

"I don't know."

"You don't know! I paid you good money to tail her. That was the whole point."

She slid off the chair and faced me with clenched fists. I was ready to catch them if she flung herself on me. Instead, she used them on herself, beating her bony flanks in staccato rhythm. "Has everybody gone crazy?" she yelped at the ceiling.

"Settle down. You sound as if you have. I wouldn't put homicidal mania past you——"

"Homicidal mania!" Her voice rose to the narrow limit of its range, and broke. "What about homicidal mania? You *have* been talking to Lucy."

"No. I overheard you talking to her, though, this afternoon. I didn't like the sound of it. There's violence in my business but I don't like cold-blooded violence, or people who threaten other people with it."

"Oh. That." She looked relieved. "I slapped her face for her, not very hard. She had it coming."

"Tell me more."

"You can go to hell."

"Later, perhaps. Before I kiss you good-bye, I want some information. Who you are, where you came from, why you were after Lucy. Also what were you doing at five o'clock this afternoon. We'll start with that."

"Five o'clock? I was right here, in this room. Is it important?" The question was neither rhetorical nor defiant like most of her other questions. She knew or sensed what was coming.

"Never mind that. Can you prove it?"

"If I have to. I made a telephone call around five." Her hands were moving over and over each other, trying to warm themselves at the cold fire of the diamonds. " I wouldn't want to use that unless I have to. You haven't even told me what it is I need an alibi for."

"Who were you calling?"

"You wouldn't be interested. I said I can prove it if I have to. It was long distance. They keep a record." She retreated to a leather hassock and crouched uneasily on its edge.

"I'm interested in everything about you, Una. A little while ago I made a statement to the police, and I couldn't leave you out."

"You went to the cops?" Her voice was incredulous, as if I had leagued myself with the forces of evil.

"They came to me. I found Lucy with her throat cut shortly after five o'clock."

"Did you say throat cut?"

"I did. She was dead in her motel room. I had to explain what I was doing there. Naturally your name came up—the name you're using."

"Why aren't they here?"

"I didn't tell them you were in town. I thought, before I threw you to them, I'd give you a chance to level. I'm also a little curious about who I'm sticking my neck out for, and why."

"You sap! They might have followed you here."

"Sap is the word." I stood up. "I haven't thought of a word for you, but I will."

"Where are you going?"

"Down to the station to amplify my statement. The longer I wait, the more trouble it's going to make for me."

"No, you can't do that." She scrambled to her feet and ran jerkily to the door, spreading her arms across it like a crucified marionette. "You're working for me. You can't turn me in."

I took the hundred from my wallet and tossed it at her feet. She stooped for it, watching me anxiously to see that I didn't escape:

"No. Please take it back. I'll give you more."

"You haven't got enough. Murder comes very high on my price-list."

"I didn't kill her, you—Mr. Archer. I told you my alibi."

" Telephone alibis are easy to fix."

" I didn't fix it. There's no way I could have fixed it. I was here in this room. Ask the switchboard. I haven't been out of here since early this afternoon."

" And that's why you're taking it so calmly, eh?" I reached for the doorknob.

" What are you going to do?"

Her cold hand closed over mine. The bill fell like a crumpled green leaf to the floor. Braced against the door, breathing with terrier quickness, she didn't notice it.

" I'll see the switchboard girl, if the same one's still on duty."

" It was the desk-clerk who handled the call. I recognised his voice."

" All right, I'll talk to the desk-clerk. Then you and I are going into this thing in detail."

" Not with cops?"

" It's up to you. We'll see how your story checks."

" No. Stay here. You can't do this to me." The words were punctuated by gasping breaths.

I turned the knob and pulled on it. She sat down against the door and began to scream wordlessly. The opening door pushed her sideways. Legs straddled, mouth wide open, she looked up at me in the reddish murderous light and I looked down at her. She was making a steady unbearable sound like the screech of tearing metal. I closed the heavy door, cutting off the sound.

The desk-clerk beamed with pleasure at the sight of me. I was the fortunate traveller whose lady-friend in the expensive suite wore genuine leopardskin and probable diamonds.

" I'm looking after things for Mrs. Larkin," I said. " May I see her room account?"

" Certainly, sir." Plucking a large card from a filing drawer beside him, he leaned confidentially across the polished counter top. " I do hope Mrs. Larkin isn't checking out. She tips quite beautifully. It's good for general morale among the help." His voice sank to a bashful murmur: " She isn't a Hollywood personality, by any chance?"

" I'm surprised she told you."

" Oh, she didn't *tell* me. I deduced it. I recognise real class. Of course I did have a clue."

His polished oval fingernail pointed to the top of the card. Una had given the Hollywood-Roosevelt Hotel as her home address. Below it, only three items were listed on the account: twelve dollars for the suite, which had been paid in advance; a telephone charge of $3.35; and $2.25 for room service.

" She's been here less than one full day," I said in a penny-pinching way. " Three thirty-five seems like a lot of money for phone calls."

His small moustache rose towards his nostrils as if it was about to be inhaled. " Oh no, it's perfectly legitimate. It was all one call, long distance and person-to-person. I took care of it myself."

" Isn't that unusual?"

" I wish it were. The daytime operator goes off at five, and the night operator was a little late. I was at the switchboard myself when Mrs. Larkin called down."

" At five?"

" Maybe one or two minutes after. I'd just sat down in front of the board that minute. Switchboards have always fascinated me."

" You're sure it was Mrs. Larkin?"

" Oh, absolutely. Her voice is quite unique. Is she an actress of some kind, a character actress?"

" You're quite acute," I said. " She is also a character in her own right. It's hard to believe she'd spend that much money on a single phone call."

" Just ask her!" He was cut to the quick, which was very near the surface. " Go and ask her."

" Mrs. Larkin doesn't like to be bothered with these trivial details. She employs me to protect her from them, in fact. Now, if it was a call to Detroit, I could understand it."

" Ypsilanti," he said eagerly. " It was to the Tecumseh Tavern in Ypsilanti. That's right outside Detroit, isn't it?"

I assumed a thoughtful expression. " Let's see now, who does Mrs. Larkin know in Ypsilanti?"

" His name was Garbold. She asked for a man called Garbold, person-to-person." But his eagerness was beginning to fade at the edges. He looked down at his vase of corn-flowers as if he suspected that noxious insects might be concealed among them

" Of course. Garbold. Why didn't you say so? There's no

trouble there. Mrs. Larkin will take care of it." I scrawled my initials at the bottom of the card and left him quickly.

Una had been quicker. I knocked once on her door and got no answer. What I got was the feeling you get when you go to a great deal of trouble to hit yourself a sharp blow at the base of the skull with a rubber hammer.

The door wasn't locked. The leopard coat was gone from the back of the chair. Bedroom and bathroom were as clean as a whistle. I left as Una had, by the fire escape.

In the alley behind the hotel, a woman in a shawl and a dragging black skirt was hunched over an open garbage-can. She looked up at me from an infinite network of wrinkles.

" Did a lady come down here? In a spotted coat?"

The ancient woman removed something from her mouth's eroded crater. I saw it was a red steak-bone she had been gnawing. " *Si,*" she said.

" Which way did she go?"

She raised the bone without speaking, and pointed up the alley. I dropped the change from my pocket into her mummified hand.

" *Muchas gracias, señor.*" Her black Indian gaze came from the other side of history, like light from a star a thousand years away.

The alley led to the hotel garage. Mrs. Larkin had taken her car out within the last five minutes. It was a new Plymouth station-wagon. No, they didn't keep a track of licence numbers. Probably she'd left a forwarding address at the desk. Try there.

CHAPTER 9

I climbed the oil-stained concrete ramp to the sidewalk and stood at its edge, undecided what to do. I had no client, no good leads, not much money. Regret for Una's hundred-dollar bill was gnawing at me already, like a small hungry stomach ulcer. The crowd went by like a kaleidoscope continually stirred, in which I only just failed to discern a pattern.

It was an early Saturday-night crowd. Farmhands in jeans and plaid shirts, soldiers in uniforms, boys in high-school windbreakers, roved singly and in pairs and packs among women of all ages and all shades. Hard-faced women in hats towed men in business suits. Ranchers hobbling in high-heeled boots leaned on their sun-faded wives. Under the winking yellow lights at the intersection, long shiny cars competed for space and time with pickup trucks, hot-rods, migrant jalopies. My car was still in the court of the Mountview Motel. I stepped out into the crowd and let it push me south, towards the highway.

Above the highway corner there was a cigar store with a pay-telephone sign. Under the sign a quartet of Mexican boys were watching the world go by. They leaned in a row, one-legged like storks, their lifted heels supported by the window-sill of the shop, displaying mismatched fluorescent socks under rolled jeans. Keep Your Feet on the Sidewalk Please was lettered on the wall beside them in vain.

I detached myself from the crowd and went in through the shop to the telephone booth at the rear. Three taxi-drivers were shooting craps on the back counter. I looked up Dr. Samuel Benning's number in the local directory, and dialled it. At the other end of the line the phone rang twenty times. My nickel jangled in the coin return with the fanfare of a silver-dollar jackpot.

Before I reached the front door a young woman passed the window, walking south by herself. The four boys sprang into a burlesque routine. The one at the end pushed the one beside him, who almost caromed with the woman. He recovered his balance and rumpled the ducktail haircut of the third, who punched the fourth in the stomach. They staggered around in front of the entrance, breathless with simulated laughter.

I pushed out through them. The woman looked back in disdain. Though she had changed her striped grey uniform for a white batiste blouse and a white skirt, I recognised her face. She was the plump dark-eyed woman who had directed me into Dr. Benning's waiting-room. The back of my neck began to itch where the bitch goddess coincidence had bitten me before.

The woman walked on, switching her red-ribboned horse-tail of black hair above the soft round rotation of her hips. I followed her, with compunction. She reminded me of Lucy for some reason, though she was wide and low-slung where Lucy had been lean and high-stepping. She walked, with a similar air of knowing where she was going, into the section in which I had first seen Lucy. When she crossed the street and entered Tom's Café, my compunction turned acute.

She paused inside the glass door to get her bearings. Then she set her course for one of the rear booths. A man was sitting in the booth with his back to the door. His panama hat showed above the low plyboard partition. He rose to greet her, buttoning his camel's-hair jacket, and stood above her in an attitude of delight while she inserted her hips between the seat and the table. As a final mark of devotion he removed his hat and smoothed his stubbly shock of brown hair with fat white fingers, before he sat down opposite her. Max Heiss was exerting charm.

I went to the bar, which covered the whole left wall of the café. The booths along the opposite wall were full, and the bar was packed with Saturday-night drinkers: soldiers and shrill dark girls who looked too young to be there, hard-faced middle-aged women with permanented hair, old men renewing their youth for the thousandth time, asphalt-eyed whores working for a living on drunken workingmen, a few fugitives from the upper half of town drowning one self to let another self be born. Behind the bar a hefty Greek in an apron dispensed fuel, aphrodisiac, opiate, with a constant melancholy smile.

I ordered a short rye and took it standing, keeping an eye on Heiss in the bar mirror. He was leaning far over the table towards the dark-eyed woman, and she was registering pleasant shock.

The booth behind him was vacated, and I crossed to it before the table was cleared. The room was surging with noise. A juke box bawled above the babel of tongues at the bar. An electric shuffleboard beside the liquor counter at the front gave out machine-gun bursts of sound at intervals. I propped myself in the corner of the seat with my ear pressed to the plyboard. A yard away, Heiss was saying:

"I been thinking about you all day, dreaming about those great big beautiful eyes. I been dreaming about those great big beautiful etcetera, too, sitting and dreaming about 'em. You know what an etcetera is, Flossie?"

"I can guess." She laughed, like somebody gargling syrup. "You're a great kidder. Incidently, my name isn't Flossie."

"Florie, then, what does it matter? If you were the only girl in the world, which is what you pradically are as far as I'm concerned, what does it matter? You're the girl for me. But I bet you've got plenty of boy friends." I guessed that Max had been drinking all day, and had reached the point where anything he said sounded like poetry set to music.

"I bet I have, not. Anyways, it's no business of yours, Mr. Desmond. I hardly know you." But she knew the game.

"Come on over on this side and get to know me better, kid. Florie. Sweet name for a sweet kid. Did anybody ever tell you you got a mouth like a flower, Florie?"

"You certny got a line, Mr. Desmond."

"Aw, call me Julian. And come on over. I warn you it isn't safe. When I get close up to a great big beautiful etcetera, I want to take a bite out of it, I warn you."

"You hungry or something?" I heard the rustle and creak of the girl's movement into the near seat. "Incidentally, Julian, I'm kind of hungry. I could eat something."

"*I'm* going to eat *you*." Max's voice was muffled. "I guess I better fatten you up first, huh? You want a steak, and something to drink? After that, who knows? *Quien sabe*, isn't that how you say it?"

"I only talk American," she answered him severely. Having established that, she relaxed again: "A steak will be swell, Julian. You're a real fun guy."

Heiss hailed the waitress. She crossed the room, a lank henna-head mincing on tender feet. "What'll it be?"

"A steak for the little lady. I've already dined myself."

"Let's see, you're drinking sherry."

"Very dry sherry," said Desmond-Heiss.

"Sure, very dry." She turned her head to one side and threw the line away: "Maybe you take it in powder form."

"An Alexander for me," the girl said.

"Sure, kiddie, have yourself a time." But there was an undertone in his voice, the no-expense-account blues. "Nothing's too good for Florie."

A woman came in from the street and walked quickly along the row of booths. Her wide-shouldered black coat swung out behind with the energy of her movement and showed the white uniform underneath. She didn't see me but I saw her and straightened up in my seat. She stopped beside Heiss and Florie, her blue eyes glittering in her cold porcelain face.

" Hello, Mrs. Benning. You want to see me?" Florie's voice was small and tinny.

" You didn't finish your work. You can come and finish it now."

" I did do my work, Mrs. Benning. Everything you said."

" Are you contradicting me?"

" No, but it's Saturday night. I got a right to my Saturday nights. When do I get a chance to have some fun?"

" Fun is one thing. What you're doing is peddling my private affairs to a dirty snooper."

" What's that?" Heiss put in brightly. " I beg your pardon, lady?"

" Don't ' lady ' me. Are you coming Florie?" The woman's voice was low, but it hummed like an overloaded electric circuit.

" I hope there ain't no trouble, ma'am," the waitress said briskly behind her.

Mrs. Benning turned to look at her. I didn't catch the look, because the back of her dark head was towards me. The waitress backed away, holding the menu card as if to shield her chest:

Heiss stood up, not quite so tall as she was. " I don't know who you are, lady. I can tell you this, you got no call to molest my girl friend in public." His face was groping for an attitude. Then his liquid gaze met hers and drooled away.

She leaned towards him, talking in a low buzzing monotone: " I know who you are. I saw you watching the house. I heard you talking to Florie on the office extension. I'm warning you: stay away from her, and especially stay away from me."

" Florie has a right to her friends." Heiss had found a manner, that of man-of-the-world, but it went bad immediately. " As for you, Mrs. Benning, if that's what you call yourself, I wouldn't touch you. I wouldn't buy you for cat's-meat——"

She laughed in his face: " You'd never have the chance,

little man. Now crawl back down your hole. If I ever see you again, I'll knock you over with a stick the way I would a gopher. Come on, Florie."

Florie sat head down with her arms on the table, frightened and stubborn. Mrs. Benning took her by the wrist and hauled her to her feet. Florie didn't resist. With dragging feet, she followed Mrs. Benning to the door. There was a taxi waiting at the yellow curb outside. By the time I reached the street it had pulled away and lost itself in the traffic.

I had a bad feeling that history was repeating itself in spades. The bad feeling got worse when Heiss came up behind me and touched my arm. He touched people whenever he could, to reassure himself of his membership in the race.

"Go and take gopher poison," I said.

The veined nose stood out on his pale face. "Yeah, I saw you in there. I thought you run out on me, boysie. I was consoling my bereavement with a nice fresh chunk of Mexican cactus candy."

"Pumping her, you mean."

"You unnerestimate me. I pumped Florie dry long since! They can't resist me, boysie. What is it I got that they can't resist me, I wonder." His mobile mouth was working overtime, talking him back into his own good opinion.

"What's the pitch, Max?"

"No dice, Archer. You got your chance to cut in, this aft. You couldn't be bothered with me. Now I can't be bothered."

"You want to be coaxed."

"Not me. Lay a small pinkie on me and I scream my head off." He cast a smug eye on the crowds streaming past us, as if he was depending on them for protection.

"You don't know me well," I said. "Those aren't my methods."

"I know you as well as I want to," he said. "You gave me the quick old brush this aft."

"Forget it. What's the tieup with this missing man in Arroyo Beach?"

"Come again, boysie." He leaned against the corner post of the storefront. "I should give you something for nothing. Nobody ever gave me something for nothing. I got to roust and hustle for what I get." With a lipstick-stained handkerchief, he wiped his face.

" I'm not trying to take something from you, Max."

" That's jakeroo, then. Good night. Don't think it ain't been charming." He turned away.

I said: " Lucy's dead."

That stopped him. " What did you say?"

" Lucy had her throat cut this afternoon."

" You're stringing me."

" Go to the morgue and take a look for yourself. And if you won't tell me what you know, tell it to the cops."

" Maybe I will at that." His eyes shone like brown agates lit from behind. " Well, *bon soir* again."

He moved away, with one or two furtive back-glances, and joined the northward stream of pedestrians. I wanted to go after him and shake the truth out of him. But I had just said those weren't my methods, and the words stood.

CHAPTER 10

I picked up my car at the Mountview Motel and drove to Dr. Benning's house. There were no lights behind its white painted windows. From the overgrown yard it looked like a house no one had lived in for a long time. Its tall grey front stood flimsily against the dark red sky like a stage set propped by scantlings from behind.

When I rang the door bell, the house resumed its dimensions. Far in its interior, behind walls, the buzzer sounded like a trapped insect. I waited and rang again, and no one answered. There were old-fashioned glass panels, ground in geometric patterns, set in both of the double doors. I pressed my face to one of them and looked in and saw nothing. Except that the glass was cracked in one corner, and gave slightly under pressure.

I slipped on a driving-glove and punched out the cracked corner. It smashed on the floor inside. I waited and looked up and down the street and rang the bell a third time. When nobody answered and nobody passed on the sidewalk I eased my arm through the triangular hole and snapped the Yale lock.

I closed and relocked the door with my gloved hand.

Broken glass crunched under my heel. Feeling along the wall, I found the door of the waiting-room. A little light fell through the windows from the street, lending the room a vague beauty like an old woman with good features, heavily veiled.

I located the filing cabinet behind the desk in the corner. Using my pocket flash and shielding its light with my body, I went through the Active Patient drawer of the file. Camberwell, Carson, Cooley. There was no card for Lucy Champion.

Dousing the light, I moved along the wall to the inner door, which was a few inches ajar. I pushed it open wider, slid through and closed it behind me. I switched on the flash again and probed the walls and furniture with its white finger of light. The room contained a flat-topped oak-veneer desk, a swivel chair and a couple of other chairs, an old three-tiered sectional bookcase not quite full of medical texts and journals. Above the bookcase on the calcimined wall, there was a framed diploma issued in June 1933 by a medical school I had never heard of.

I went through an open door into a room with figured oilcloth walls and a linoleum floor. Brownish stains on the far wall outlined the place where a gas range had once stood. An adjustable examination-table of brown-painted steel padded with black leatherette had taken its place. There were a battered white enamelled instrument cabinet and a steriliser against the wall beside it. On the other side of the room, under the blinded window, a faucet dripped steadily into a sink. I went to the closed door in the wall beyond it, and turned the knob. It was locked.

The second pass-key I tried opened the door. My light flashed on the ivory grin of death.

Six inches above the level of my eyes, a skeleton's shadowed sockets looked down hollowly. I thought in the instant of shock that it was a giant's bones, then saw that the long toe-bones dangled nearly a foot above the floor. The whole thing hung in the closet by wires attached to an overhead crossbar. Its joints had been carefully articulated with wire, and the movement of the door had set it swaying slightly. Its barred shadow wavered on the closet wall behind it.

It looked like a man's bones to me. I had an old brotherly

feeling that I should take him by the unfleshed hand. He was lonely and desolate. I was afraid to touch him.

Somewhere in the house, no louder than a rodent squeak, a door or a floorboard creaked. It caused a croupy tightening in my breathing. I listened and heard the faint wheeze in my throat, and the dripping of the tap. Working with jumping fingers, I relocked the closet door and dropped the key in my pocket.

With the flash unit unlit in my hand, I retraced my steps by blind touch to the door of the consultation room. I had one foot across its metal-strip threshold when the light came on in my face. Dr. Benning's wife stood against the opposite wall with one hand on the light switch. She was so still that she might have been a figure in a frieze, part of the wall itself.

" What goes on in here?"

I squeezed out an answer: " The doctor wasn't here. I came in to wait."

" You a crib-smasher? Junkie? We've got no dope in this office."

" I came to ask a question. I thought the office might answer it for me."

" What question?" The small automatic steady in her hand was gun-metal blue, and her eyes had taken its colour.

" Put the gun away, Mrs. Benning. I can't talk with iron in my face."

" You'll talk." She pulled herself away from the wall and moved towards me. Even in motion her body seemed still and frigid. But I could feel its power, like a land mine under a snowbank. " You're another lousy snooper, aren't you?"

" A fair-to-middling one. What happened to Florie?"

She stopped in the centre of the room, her legs braced apart. The pupils of her gun-coloured eyes were dark and empty like the muzzle of the gun at the centre of her body.

I said: " If that gun went off and hurt me you'd be in a real jam. Put it away, it isn't needed."

She didn't seem to hear me. " I thought I saw you before. You were in the café. What happened to Florie is nobody's business but hers and mine. I paid her off and fired her. I don't approve of my servants stooling to scavengers. Does that take care of the question you had?"

" One of them."

"Fine. Now get out, or I'll have you arrested for burglary." The gun moved very little, but I felt it like a fingernail on my skin.

"I don't think you will."

"You want to stick around and find out?" She glanced at the telephone on the desk.

"I intend to. You're vulnerable, or you'd have called the cops right away. You don't talk like a doctor's wife, incidentally."

"Maybe you want to see my marriage licence." She smiled a little, showing the tip of her tongue between white teeth. "I mean perchance you desire to peruse my connubial document. I can talk different ways, depending on who I'm talking to. To scavengers, I can also talk with a gun."

"I don't like the word scavenger."

"He doesn't like it," she said to nobody in particular.

"What do you think I want from you?"

"Money. Or are you one of the ones that gets paid off in the hay?"

"It's an idea. I'll take a rain check on it. Right now, I'd like to know what Lucy Champion was doing in this office. And if you won't put the gun away, set the safety."

She was still braced and tense, holding on to the gun the way a surfboarder clutches his stick. Muscular tension alone might squeeze the trigger and shoot me.

"The man's afraid." Her mouth was sullen and scornful, but she clicked the safety on with her thumb. "What about Lucy Champion? I don't know any Lucy Champion."

"The young coloured woman who came here this afternoon."

"Oh. Her. The doctor has all kinds of patients."

"Do many of them get themselves killed?"

"That's a funny question. I'm not laughing, though, notice?"

"Neither is Lucy. She had her throat cut this afternoon."

She tried to swallow that without a tremor, but she was shaken. Her braced body was more than ever like a surfboarder's moving fast on troubled water.

"You mean she's dead," she said dully.

"Yes."

Her eyes closed, and she swayed without falling. I took

one long step and lifted the gun from her hand and ejected
the clip. There was no shell in the chamber.

" Did you know her, Mrs. Benning?"

The question brought her out of her standing trance. Her
eyes opened, tile blue again and impermeable. " She was one
of my husband's patients. Naturally he'll be shocked. That
automatic belongs to him, by the way." She had assumed a
mask of respectability and the voice that went with it.

I tossed the gun on the desk and kept the clip. " Is that his
skeleton in the closet, too?"

" I don't know what you're talking about."

" Have it your way. You knew what I was talking about
when I said that Lucy Champion was dead."

Her hand went to her forehead, white under dead-black
hair. " I can't stand death, especially somebody's I know."

" How well did you know her?"

" She was a patient, I said. I've seen her a couple of
times."

" Why isn't there a card for her?"

" A card?"

" In the active file."

" I don't know. Are you going to keep me standing here
all night? I warn you, my husband will be back at any
moment."

" How long have you been married, Mrs. Benning?"

" It's none of your damn business. Now get out of here or
I *will* call the police."

She said it without conviction. Since I had told her Lucy
was dead, there had been no force in her. She looked like a
sleepwalker struggling to come awake.

" Go ahead and call them."

She looked at me with blank loathing. " Augh." It was a
shallow retching sound. " Do your damndest. Do your
dirtiest. Only get out of my sight."

The upper faces of her breasts gleamed through the fabric
of her uniform like cold trembling moons. I walked around
her and let myself out.

CHAPTER 11

The state blacktop unwound like a used typewriter-ribbon under my headlights. It threaded the wilderness of stone that cut off Bella Valley from the ocean, clinging to the walls of precipitous canyons, looping across the shoulders of peaks that towered into darkness. After forty long mountain miles it dropped me down into the lap of the coastal range. A late moon was rising heavily on the sea.

Five minutes north of the junction with U.S. 101 Alternate, the lights of Arroyo Beach began to clutter the roadside. Motels, service stations, real-estate booths, chicken-steak pavilions were outlined in neon on the face of the darkness. I pulled up beside the pumps of a service station; while my car was being gassed I asked the attendant if he had a pay phone. He was a hammered-down elderly man in a uniform of grey coveralls and black leather bow tie, who looked and smelled as if he washed in crankcase oil. He jerked an oil-grained thumb towards the one-room office he had emerged from.

The local telephone directory was a thin pamphlet attached to the wall telephone by a chain. Mrs. Charles Singleton was well represented in it. She lived at 1411 Alameda Topanga, and her telephone number was 1411. A second number was listed for the gatehouse, a third for the chauffeur's apartment, a fourth for the gardener's cottage, a fifth for the butler's pantry.

When the attendant brought me my change, I asked him where Alameda Topanga was.

"Who you looking for, brother?"

"Nobody in particular. I'm sightseeing."

"This is a funny time of the night to be sightseeing." He looked me over. "They got a private patrol, nights, on the Alameda, and you don't look like no member of no garden club."

"I'm interested in real estate. It's a good section, I heard."

"Good ain't the word for it, brother. Since they built the big hotel and the moneybags moved up here from Malibu, that property is worth its weight in gold. I only wisht I had a piece of it. I could of had. Before the war, if the old lady

65   C

would of let me take a little money out of the sock, I could
of had five acres at a steal. I could of been sitting pretty now,
but she says save your money. The place is dead, she says,
the rich set is pulling out for keeps." His laugh was bitter
and compulsive, like an old cough.

"Too bad," I said. "Where is the Alameda?"

He gave me directions, pointing at the dark foothills as if
they rose on the edge of the promised land. I turned towards
them at the next intersection, and drove to the outskirts.
Empty fields strewn with rubbish lay like a no-man's land
between the suburban cottages and the country estates. I
entered an avenue hemmed in on both sides by the grey trunks
and overarched by the branches of eucalyptus trees. It went
by a hedged polo field and across a golf course. Cars were
massed around a lighted clubhouse in the distance, and gusts
of music were blown my way by the wind.

The road ascended hills terraced like the steps of an easy
man-made purgatory. I caught glimpses of glass-and-
aluminium living-machines gleaming like surgical equipment in
the clinical moonlight; Venetian palaces, Côte d'Azur villas,
castles in Spain; Gothic and Greek and Versailles and
Chinese gardens. There was a great deal of vegetable life, but
no people. Perhaps the atmosphere of this higher region was
too rare and expensive for the human breathing system. It
was the earthly paradise where money begot plants upon property. People were irrelevant, unless they happened to have
money or property.

The stone gateposts bearing the number 1411 were backed
up by a Tudor cottage with dark leaded windows. The gates
stood open. A sweeping drive conducted me through a line of
yews like honorary pall bearers to a villa that faced the moon
in white Palladian splendour.

I parked under the columned porte-cochere and rang the
old-fashioned bell at the side entrance. Soft, doubtful footsteps approached the deep-panelled door from the other side.
A key ground in the lock, and a young woman looked out,
soft chestnut hair shadowing her face.

"What is it, sir?" Her voice was soft and doubtful.

"Is it too late to see Mrs. Singleton?"

I handed her my business card. She turned her profile to
the light: soft chin, soft bee-stung mouth, straight and honest

nose. Her eyes were still shadowed, but I saw how young she was.

"Investigator," she said. "Does this mean you're from the agency? It's late for Mrs. Singleton. She isn't terribly well."

"I run my own agency."

"I see. But it is about Charlie—Mr. Singleton?"

"He's still on the missing list, then?"

"Yes. He is."

"I may have a lead for you."

"Really? You think you know where he is?"

"I haven't got that far. It's only to-day I stumbled across—this matter. I don't even know the circumstances of his disappearance. Or if the reward still stands."

"It does," she said with a faint, dubious smile. "If you'll tell me just what it is you stumbled across."

Late or not, I wanted to see Mrs. Singleton. I tossed the girl the heaviest answer I could think of: "A dead body."

Her hand went to her breast like a frightened bird. "Charlie's? Not Charlie's?"

"It was a young coloured woman named Lucy Champion. She had her throat cut. Know her?"

Her answer was slow in coming. I guessed that it was going to be a lie, and that the lie came hard. "No. I don't know her. What possible connection——?" Her voice died.

"She was carrying a newspaper clipping about Singleton's disappearance and the reward. I thought she might have come here about it. The police will probably have the same idea, when they get around to it."

"Was she killed here, in Arroyo Beach?"

"In Bella City." She didn't recognise the name, and I added: "It's an inland town, in the valley, about thirty miles from here as the crow flies."

"Come in." She consulted my card again: "Mr. Archer. I'll ask Mrs. Singleton if she will see you."

She left me standing in the entrance hall and walked along it to a lighted doorway. She was clothed with expensive bad taste in a knitted rust-coloured suit that made her look slightly overblown, at least from the rear. Her movements had an awkward innocence, as if the sudden development of her body had embarrassed her with riches.

I put in several minutes looking at a sequence of Chinese

paintings on the wall. A Chinese gentleman with giant ear-lugs denoting wisdom journeyed on foot through valleys and across rivers and mountains to a snow-line shrine. There were seven paintings, one for each stage of his journey.

The girl appeared in the doorway, her brown hair aureoled by the light behind her. " Mr. Archer. She'll see you."

The room had a lofty white ceiling supported by a Doric cornice. The walls were lined with cases of books uniformly bound in white calf. The cases were interspersed with paintings ; one of them, of a laughing girl in a low-cut bodice, might have been a Watteau or a Fragonard. On a white sofa with a curved back, a heavy grey-haired woman sat.

She had the kind of face, square-jawed and heavy-eyebrowed, that unlucky women sometimes inherit from their fathers. It might have been handsome in a horsey way before age and ego had stiffened the bony framework and thrust it forward under the skin like concealed artillery. The slack body was encased in a black silk dress that would have served for mourning. In the monolithic black lap, the pale yellow hands were conspicuous. They had a constant tremor.

She cleared her throat: " Sit down, Mr. Archer, in this armchair here." And after I had done so: " Now tell me just who you are."

" I'm a licensed private detective. Most of my work is in Los Angeles, and I have my office there. Before the war I was a detective-sergeant on the Long Beach force. I gave the young lady my card."

" Sylvia showed it to me. She told me further that you had some rather shocking information, about a coloured young woman?"

" Her name is Lucy Champion. I found her with her throat cut in a Bella City motel. There was a clipping in her purse from the Bella City paper, concerning your son's disappearance and the reward you offered. It occurred to me as a possibliity that she was killed because she intended to claim the reward. She showed up in Bella City about the same time your son left here, two weeks ago. And I thought she might have approached you."

" Isn't that rather jumping to conclusions, on the very flimsiest grounds?" Mrs. Singleton's voice was low and cultivated. Her hands twitched and plucked at each other like nervous scorpions. "You're surely not implying that we had anything whatever to do with the girl's death? Or with her life."

"I didn't make myself clear."—Though I thought I had. "Assume that your son met with foul play. Assume that Lucy Champion knew what had happened and who was responsible for it. If she was intending to go to you or the authorities with that sort of information, it would explain what was done to her."

Mrs Singleton gave no sign of having heard me. She looked down at her angry hands as if she'd have liked to disown them. "Light me a cigarette, Sylvia."

"Of course." Sylvia rose from her seat at the end of the sofa, took a cigarette from an ivory box, placed one end between the clamped blue lips, applied the flame of a table-lighter to the other.

Mrs. Singleton inhaled deeply, and exhaled from mouth and nostrils. The smoke crawled like fog in the crannies of her head. Even her eyes looked smoky. "You're not implying, I trust, that my son ran off to Bella City with a coloured girl."

"Oh no, Mrs. Singleton!" the girl cried out. "He doesn't mean that." Then she remembered her place, which was to be seen and not heard. She sat down in her corner, looking as if she had given herself a fright.

Mrs. Singleton persisted: "What possible connection could there be between such a person and my son?"

"I'd like to know myself. In fact I'm interested enough to be willing to work on this case on a contingent basis."

"You mean, no doubt, that if you were to qualify for the reward, it would be paid to you. That can be taken for granted."

"Something more definite. Reward money has a way of slipping into policemen's pockets. It has a homing instinct for authority. And I'd like to be sure of my fifty a day and expenses."

"Naturally you would." She exhaled smoke, purring behind it like a cat in a curtain. "What I fail to see is any particular reason why I should underwrite your activities."

"I can't afford to work for fun. It would also be useful to be able to name you as a client."

"That I can understand." Her iron-grey head struck an imperious pose, a little like a late Roman emperor's. Her low voice rose in volume and pitch as if it were preparing to dominate a tea party or repel a barbarian assault. "I do *not* understand why you must interest yourself at all in my affairs. I am employing a detective agency now. They've already cost me more than I can easily afford, and in value received they've given me absolutely nothing. I'm not a wealthy woman." Which probably meant, in her circle, that she could count her millions on the fingers of one hand. She added breathlessly in the ebb of her self-pity: "I'm not unwilling to pay for helpful information, but if a large agency has failed to restore my son to me, as it has, I see no reason to suppose that one man alone might succeed, do you?"

The cigarette in the corner of her mouth was burning short. Sylvia removed it without being asked, and crushed it out in an ashtray.

I said: "Let me kick it around and see what I can do. I intend to find out why Lucy Champion was killed. If and when I do, it may lead to your son. That's my hunch, at least."

"Your hunch," she said contemptuously. "If Charles were being held under duress, for ransom, your visit to me to-night under these circumstances could be interpreted as an overture, from whoever was holding him. Did you know this Negress, the one you claim was murdered?"

"She was murdered. Did you know her?"

Her face radiated a dull white glow of anger. "I warn you not to be insolent, young man. I know how to deal with insolence."

I glanced at Sylvia, who smiled bleakly and almost imperceptibly shook her head:

"You must be very tired, Mrs. Singleton. It's very late."

The older woman paid no attention to her. She leaned towards me, her black silk lap wrinkling stiffly like iron under pressure:

"Only this morning, under circumstances similar to these, a man came here representing himself as a private detective, like you. He claimed that he could find Charles for me, if I would pay him part of the reward in advance. I naturally refused. Then he wasted a full hour of my time, asking me questions. When I tried to ask him a question or two in my turn, he had nothing to say, not a constructive word. What was his name, Sylvia?"

"Heiss."

"Heiss," the older woman repeated vehemently, as if she had invented the name on the spur of the moment. She rolled here eyes towards me. They had been pickled in tears, glassed in grief, but they were still shrewd. "Do you know *him*?"

"I don't think so."

"A most repugnant creature. Eventually he dared to suggest that I sign a contract to pay him five thousand dollars if he should produce my son, alive or dead. He boasted of his connections among the criminal element. I arrived at the conclusion that he was either conspiring to defraud me, or representing a criminal organisation of some sort. I ordered him out of my house."

"And you've cast me in the same role?"

"Oh no," the girl said softly from her corner.

Mrs. Singleton subsided backward, her energy spent. Her head rolled on the curved back of the sofa, exposing a slack throat to an invisible knife. Rising words palpitated feebly in her throat: "I don't know what to think. I'm sick, old, exhausted, bereft. In a world of liars. No one will tell me anything."

Sylvia rose, her soft and anxious look shepherding me to the door. Mrs. Singleton called out with sudden eagerness: "Mr. Archer. Did Charles send you to me? Is that it? Does he need money?" The change in her voice was startling. She sounded like a frightened girl. I turned to look at her face, and saw the same false girlishness touch it with beauty for an instant. The beauty passed like the beam of a searchlight moving across time. It left her mouth curled in a cynical parody of mother-love.

The situation was too complicated for me to understand or try to deal with. I didn't know whether the umbilical cord between Mrs. Singleton and her son had stretched and broken and snapped back in her face and knocked her silly. Or whether she knew he was dead and was talking against despair. Whichever it was, she was ready to believe almost anything and suspicious of nearly everybody. Reality had betrayed her.

"I've never met Charles," I said. "Good night. Good luck."

She didn't answer.

CHAPTER 12

Sylvia went with me to the end of the hall. "I'm sorry, Mr. Archer. The last two weeks have been terribly hard on her. She's been under drugs for days. When things don't fit in with her ideas, she simply doesn't hear them, or she forgets them. It isn't that her mind is affected, exactly. She's suffered so much, she can't bear to talk about the facts, or even think about them."

"What facts?"

She said surprisingly: "Can we sit in your car? I think she really wants me to talk to you."

"You'd have to be a bit psychic to know it."

"I am a bit psychic where Mrs. Singleton is concerned. When you're under a person's thumb, you know."

"You get to know the thumbprint. How long have you worked for her?"

"Only since June. But our families have known each other for a great many years. Charles's father and mine went to Harvard together." She opened the door, leaning across me to reach the knob. "Excuse me, I need some fresh air."

"Is she all right by herself?"

"There are servants on duty. They'll put her to bed." She started towards my car.

"Just a minute, Sylvia. Do you have a picture of Charles? A recent snapshot would be good."

"Why, yes, I do."

"Get it for me, will you?"

"I have one here," she said without embarrassment. She took a red leather wallet from the pocket of her suit and extracted a small snapshot that she handed me: "Is it big enough, clear enough?"

The picture showed a young man in tennis shorts and an open-necked short-sleeved shirt, smiling into the sun. The strength and leanness of his features were emphasised by a short service crew-cut. He was strongly built, with wide sloping shoulders and muscular forearms. But there was an unreal, actorish quality about him. His pose was self-conscious, chest pouting, stomach sucked in, as if he feared the cold eye of the Leica or the hot eye of the sun.

" It's clear enough," I said. " May I keep it?"

" For as long as you need it. It's very like him."

Climbing into my car, she showed a fine round leg. I noticed when I slid behind the wheel that she filled the interior with a clean springlike smell. I offered her a cigarette.

" Thanks, I never smoke."

" How old are you, Sylvia?"

" Twenty-one." She added with apparent irrelevance: " I just received the first quarterly check from Mother's trust fund."

" Good for you."

" About the check, I mean, it's nearly a thousand dollars. I can afford to employ you, if you'll work for me instead of Mrs. Singleton."

" I couldn't promise anything definite. You want him found pretty badly, don't you?"

" Yes." The word had the pressure of her life behind it. " How much money should I give you?"

" Don't bother about it now."

" Why should you trust me?"

" Anybody would. What's more surprising is that you trust me."

" I know something about men," she said. " My father is a good man. You're not like that man Heiss."

" You talked to him?"

" I was in the room. All he wanted was money. It was so —naked. I had to threaten him with the police before he'd leave. It's really a pity. Mrs. Singleton might have opened out to you if he hadn't spoilt things."

" Are there things she could have told me, that she didn't?"

" Charlie's whole life," she said obscurely. " What did this Negro woman look like?"

I gave her a thumbnail description of Lucy Champion.

She interrupted me before I finished: " It's the same one."

She opened the door on her side and began to get out. Everything she did was done gently, almost regretfully, as if an action was a dangerous gamble.

" Do you know her?"

" Yes. I want to show you something." And she was gone.

I lit a cigarette. Before I had smoked a half inch of it, Sylvia came out of the house and climbed in beside me again. " I believe this is hers."

She handed me a soft dark object. I turned on the overhead light to examine it. It was a woman's turban, knitted of black wool and gold thread. Inside, there was a maker's label: Denise.

" Where did you get this?"

" She was here, the day before yesterday."

" To see Mrs. Singleton?"

" I think now that must have been it. She drove up here in a taxicab in the middle of the afternoon. I was cutting flowers in the garden, and I saw her sitting in the back of the cab as if she couldn't make up her mind. Finally she got out, and the cab-driver started away. She stood in the drive and looked at the house for a moment. Then I think she lost her nerve."

" I can understand htat."

" It is imposing, isn't it? I called out to her, to ask her what she wanted, and when she saw me coming towards her she literally ran. I felt like some sort of an ogress. I called to her not to be frightened, but she only ran faster down the drive. Her hat fell off, and she didn't even stop to pick it up. Which is how I happen to have it."

" You didn't follow her?"

" How could I? I had an enormous bunch of 'mums in my arms. The driver saw her running after him, and backed up for her. I had no right to stop her, in any case."

" You'd never seen her before?"

" Never. I thought perhaps she was a sightseer. She was quite smartly dressed, and this is a good hat. The fact that she didn't come back for it made me wonder, though."

" Did you go to the police?"

" Mrs. Singleton disapproved. I thought of asking Denise, but Mrs. Singleton was opposed to that, too."

" You know the woman who made this?"

"I know of her. She has a shop on the ocean boulevard, near the hotel."

"Here in Arroyo Beach?"

"Of course. Isn't it possible, if you questioned her, that she might know something more about Miss Champion?"

"It's very likely. Why didn't you see Denise yourself? You're not that much afraid of Mrs. Singleton."

"No." She was silent for a time. "Perhaps I was afraid of what I might find out. I'm not any more. Charles ran away with a woman, you see." She spoke with reluctance, but she got it out: "I think I was afraid that the Negro girl was—another of his women."

"His mother seems to have shared that idea. Any particular reason for it?"

"I don't know. She knows so much about him, more than she's ever admitted to herself."

"That's a hard saying."

"It's true. These pre-Freudian women know it all, but they never say it, even in their thoughts. Their whole lives are dressing for dinner in the jungle. That's my father's phrase. He teaches philosophy at Brown."

"Who was this woman, the one Charles ran away with?"

"A tall woman with yellow hair, and very beautiful. That's all I know about her. They were seen together in the bar at the hotel, the night he left. The parking lot attendant saw them drive away in his car."

"It doesn't necessarily mean he ran away with her. It sounds more like a pickup."

"No. They had been living together all summer. Charles has a mountain cabin on the Sky Route, and the woman was seen there with him nearly every weekend."

"How do you know?"

"I talked to a friend of Charles's who lives in the same canyon. Horace Wilding, the painter—you may have heard of him. He was very reticent, but he did tell me that he'd seen the woman there with Charlie. Perhaps if you talked to him? Since you're a man?"

I turned up the dash-lights and took out my notebook: "Address?"

"Mr. Wilding's address is 2712 Sky Route. He has no telephone. He said she was beautiful, too."

I turned to look at Sylvia, and saw that she was crying. Sitting quietly with her hands in her lap and tear-tracks bright on her cheeks. "I never cry!" she said fiercely. And then, not fiercely at all: "I wish I were beautiful, like her. I wish I had yellow hair."

She looked beautiful to me, and soft enough to put a finger through. Past the gentle outline of her body, I could see the lights of Arroyo Beach. Between the highway neons and the dotted line of lights hemstitching the shore, the spotlit dome of the great hotel swelled like a captive balloon dragging a cable of light across the sea's surface.

"If you want to be a blonde," I said, "why don't you bleach your hair like all the other girls?"

"It wouldn't do any good. He wouldn't even notice."

"You're in love with Charlie."

"Of course I am." As if every young girl in her senses fell in love with Charlie. I waited for her to go on, and she did: "From the first time I saw him. When he came back to Harvard after the war, he spent a weekend with us in Providence. I fell in love with *him,* not he with me. I was only a child. He was nice to me though." Her voice sank to a confidential murmur. "He read Emily Dickinson with me. He told me he wanted to be a poet, and I thought I *was* Emily, I really did. All through college I let myself imagine that Charles would come for me and marry me. Of course he never did.

"I saw him a few times, once for lunch in Boston, and he was charming to me and that was all. Then he went home, and I never heard from him. Last spring when I graduated, I decided to come west and see him. Mrs. Singleton was looking for a companion, and my father secured the position for me. I thought if I was in the house with Charles he might fall in love with me. Mrs. Singleton rather approved. If Charles had to marry anyone, she preferred someone she could manage."

I looked into her face and saw that she was perfectly sincere. "You're a strange girl, Sylvia. Did you really talk it over with Mrs. Singleton?"

"I didn't have to. She left us together whenever it was possible. I can recognise a fact. Father says that a woman's chief virtue is the ability to see what is under her nose. And when she tells the truth about what she sees, that is her crowning glory."

"I take it back. You're not strange. You're unique."

"I think I am. But Charles didn't. He wasn't even at home very much, so I had no decent chance to make him fall in love with me by propinquity. He spent most of his time in his cabin, or driving around the state. I didn't know about the woman then, but I think she fits in with what he was trying to do. He was trying desperately to break away from his mother and her money and create a life of his own. Mrs. Singleton had all the money, you see, even before her husband died. *He* was the old-fashioned type of rich woman's husband: yachtsman and polo player, and errand boy for his wife. Charles had different ideas from his father. He believed that he and his class were out of touch with reality. That they had to save their individual souls by going down to the bottom of things and starting all over."

"Did he?"

"Save his soul, you mean? He tried. It turned out to be harder than he thought. This summer, for instance, he worked as a tomato-picker in the valley. His mother offered him the managership of a ranch, but he wouldn't take it. Of course he didn't last very long. He had a fight with a foreman and lost his job, if you could call it a job. Mrs. Singleton almost died when he came home with his face all swollen and blue. I almost died, too. But Charles seemed to take a certain satisfaction from it."

"When was this?"

"In July, a few weeks after I came. The middle of July."

"Where did the fight take place?"

"On a ranch near Bakersfield. I don't know exactly."

"After that, did he stay here until the first of September?"

"Off and on. He was often away on trips for two or three days at a time."

"Do you think he's off on another trip this time?"

"He may be. If he is, I don't believe he's coming back this time. Not ever. Not of his own accord."

"Do you think he's dead?" The question was blunt, but Sylvia could take it. Under her air of gentle bewilderment, she had strong reserves.

"I'd know it if he were dead. I don't believe he's dead. I

believe he's made his final break with his mother, and the money from his great-grandfather's land grant."

"Are you sure you want him to come back?"

She hesitated before she spoke: "At least I must know that he's safe and living a kind of life that won't destroy him. For a man who shot down enemy planes during the war, he's such a child, such a dreamer. The wrong woman could break him." She drew in her breath sharply. "I hope I don't sound melodramatic."

"You sound very good to me. But you may be letting your imagination run away with you." I saw that she wasn't listening, and stopped.

Her mind was moving on a remote curve that she was trying to plot in words: "He felt so guilty about the money he'd never worked for, and doubly guilty because he was disappointing his mother. Charles wanted to suffer. He saw his whole life as an expiation. He would choose a woman who would make him suffer."

Against the moonlight her face had a virgin bleakness. The softness of her mouth and chin was broken by angular shadows.

"You know what sort of woman she was, then."

"Not really. All my information is third-hand. A detective interviewed the bartender at the hotel, and told Mrs. Singleton about the woman. She told me."

"Come down there with me," I said. "I'll buy you a drink. I think you could use a drink."

"Oh no. I've never been in a bar."

"You're twenty-one."

"It isn't that. I have to go in now. I always read her to sleep. Good night."

When I leaned across to open the door for her, I could see the tears on her face like spring rain.

CHAPTER 13

A pair of Filipino bell-hops in maroon uniforms gave me an interested look as I went in, and lost interest immediately.

Under a Moorish arch opposite the hotel entrance, an assistant manager stood behind the reservations desk like a tuxedoed saint in a niche. Over an arch in the far corner, a neon sign spelled out *Cantina* in red script. I made my way through the potted-palm formality of the lobby and out to a patio planted with banana trees. Couples loitered in their shade. I crossed to the bar in a hurry.

It was a large L-shaped room decorated with bullfight posters, blue with smoke, pounding with monkeyhouse din. White female shoulders, dinner jackets black, blue, and plaid, swayed and gesticulated three deep at the long bar. The men had the unnaturally healthy, self-assured faces of sportsmen who had never really had to take a chance. Except perhaps on their women. The women's bodies looked more conscious than their heads. Somewhere behind the walls, an orchestra started a samba rhythm. Some of the shoulders and dinner jackets were lured away from the bar.

There were two bartenders working, an agile Latin youth and a thin-haired man who kept a sharp eye on the other. I waited until their business had slacked off, and asked the thin-haired man if he was the regular bartender. He gave me the impervious stare of his trade.

"Sure thing. What are you drinking?"

"Rye. I'd like to ask you a question."

"Go ahead, if you can think of a new one." His hands went on working of their own accord, filling a shot-glass for me and setting it out on the bar.

I paid him. "About Charles Singleton, Junior. You saw him the night he disappeared?"

"Oh no." He glanced up at the ceiling in mock despair. "I tell it to the sheriff. I tell it to the reporters. I tell it to the private dicks." His eyes returned to my level, grey and opaque. "You a reporter?"

I showed him my identification.

"Another private dick," he lamented imperturbably. "Why don't you go back and tell the old lady she's wasting your time and her money? Junior blew with as stylish a blondie as you could hope to see. So why would he want to come back?"

"Why did he go away?"

"You didn't see her. The dame had everything." His

hands illustrated his meaning. "That beast and junior are
down in Mexico City or Havana having themselves a time,
mark my words. Why would he come back?"

"You had a good look at the woman?"

"Sure. She bought a drink from me while she was waiting
for junior. Besides, she was in with him a couple of times
before."

"What was her drink?"

"Tom Collins."

"How was she dressed?"

"Dark suit, nothing flashy. Smart. Not the real class, but
the next thing to it. She was a natural blonde. I could say
this in my sleep." He closed his eyes. "Maybe I am."

"What colour were here eyes?"

"Green or blue, or something in between."

"Turquoise?"

He opened his own eyes. "One question covers a lot of
ground in your book, friend. Maybe we should collaborate
on a poem, only some other day. You like turquoise, I'll
say turquoise. She looked like one of those Polish kids I used
to see in Chicago, but she was a long way off West Madison,
I can tell you that."

"Does anything ever happen that you miss?"

That bought me another thirty seconds of him. "Not
around here it doesn't."

"And junior definitely wanted to go with her?"

"Sure. You think she held a gun on him? They were stuck
on each other. He couldn't peel his eyes off her."

"How did they leave? By car?"

"So I understand. Ask Dewey in the parking lot. Only
you better slip him a little change first. He doesn't enjoy
the sound of his own voice the way I do." Recognising a
good cue-line, he moved out of my range.

I drank up, and went outside. The hotel faced the sea,
across a palm-lined boulevard. The parking lot lay behind a
row of small expensive shops on its landward side. Moving
along the sidewalk, I passed a display of silver and rawhide
pendants, two wax mannequins in peasant skirts, a window
full of jade; and was hit between the eyes by the name
Denise. It was printed in gold leaf on the plate-glass window of
a hat shop. Behind the window a single hat hung on a stand

by itself, like a masterpiece of sculpture in a museum. The shop was dark, and after a second's hesitation, I went on.

Under an arc light at the corner of the parking lot there was a small green-painted shack like a sentry-box. A sign attached to its wall stated: *The sole income of attendants consists of tips.* I stood beside the sign and held a dollar in the light. From somewhere among the sardined ranks of cars, a little man appeared. He was thin and grey. Under his old Navy turtleneck the shoulder-bones projected like pieces of waterworn driftwood. He moved silently in canvas sneakers, leaning forward as if he were being dragged by the tip of his long sharp nose.

" Make and colour? Where's your ticket, mister?"

" My car's parked around the corner. I wanted to ask you about another car. I guess you're Dewey."

"I guess I am." He blinked his faded eyes, innocently contemplating his identity. The top of his uncombed grey head was on a level with my shoulder.

" You know a lot about cars, I bet."

"I bet. People, too. You're a cop, or I miss my guess. I bet you want to ask me about young Charlie Singleton."

" A private cop," I said. " How much do you bet?"

" One buck."

" You win, Dewey." I passed the money to him.

He folded it up small and tucked it in the watch pocket of the dirtiest grey flannels in the world. " It's only fair," he said earnestly. " You take up my valuable time. I was polishing windshields and I pick up plenty money polishing windshields on a Saturday night."

" Let's get it over with, then. You saw the woman he left with?"

" Absotively. She was a pipperoo. I seen her coming and going."

" Say again."

" Coming and going," he repeated. " The blonde lady. She druv up about ten o'clock in a new blue Plymouth stationwagon. I seen her get out in front of the hotel. I was around in front picking up a car. I seen her get out of the stationwagon and go inside the hotel. She was a pipperino." His grey-stubbled jaw hung slack and he closed his eyes to concentrate on the memory.

" What happened to the station-wagon?"

" The other one druv it away."

" Other one?"

" The other one that was driving the station-wagon. The dark-complected one that dropped the blonde lady off. She druv it away."

" Was she a coloured woman?"

" The one that was driving the station wagon? Maybe she was. She was dark-complected. I didn't get a good look at her. I was watching the blonde lady. Then I come back here, and Charlie Singleton druv in after a while. He went inside and come out with the blonde lady and then they druv away."

" In his car?"

" Yessir. 1948 Buick sedan, two-tone green."

" You're very observant, Dewey."

" Shucks, I often seen young Charlie riding around in his car. I know cars. Druv my first car back in 1911 in Minneappolis, Minnesota."

" When they left here, which way did they go?"

" Sorry chum, I can't say. I didn't see. That's what I told the other lady when she asked me, and she got mad and didn't give me no tip."

" What other lady was that?"

His faded eyes surveyed me, blinking slow signals to the faded brain behind them. " I got to get back to those windshields. My time is valuable on a Saturday night."

" I bet you can't remember about the other lady."

" How much you want to bet?"

" A dollar?"

" Double it?"

" Two dollars."

" Taken. She come blowing in a few minutes after they left, driving that blue Plymouth station-wagon."

" The dark-complected one?"

" Naw, this was another one, older. Wearing a leopard-skin coat. I seen her around here before. She asked me about the blonde lady and young Charlie Singleton, which way they went. I said I didn't see. She called me a iggoramus and left. She looked like she was hopping mad."

" Was anybody with her?"

" Naw. I don't remember."

" The woman live around here?"

" I seen her before. I don't know where she lives."

I put two ones in his hand. "Thanks, Dewey. One more thing. When Charlie drove away with the blonde, did he seem to be happy about it?"

" I dunno. He tipped me a buck. Anybody would be happy, going off with that blonde lady." A one-sided grin pulled at his wrinkled mouth. " Me, f'r instance. I ain't had nothing to do with female flesh since I left my old lady in the depression. Twenty years is a long time, chum."

" It certainly is. Good night."

Sniffing lonesomely, Dewey pointed his nose towards the rank of cars and followed it out of sight.

CHAPTER 14

I went back to the hotel and found a public telephone. According to the directory, the Denise Hat Shop was run by a Mrs. Denise Grinker whose residence was at 124 Jacaranda Lane. I called her home number, got an answer, and hung up.

The street twisted like a cowpath between the highway and the shore. Jacaranda and cypress trees darkened the road and obscured the houses along it. I drove slowly, in second gear, turning my flashlight on the house-fronts. It was a middle-class neighbourhood subsiding into bohemian defeat. Weeds were rampant in the yards. Signs in dingy window corners advertised Handmade Pottery, Antiques, Typing: We Specialise in Manuscripts. The numerals 124 were painted in a vertical row, by hand, on the door post of a greying redwood bungalow.

I parked, and walked in under a shaggy eugenia arch. There was a rusty bicycle leaning against the wall on the front porch. The porch light came on when I knocked, and the door opened. A large woman wrapped in a flannel bathrobe appeared in the opening, one hip out. Because her hair was caught up in metal curlers, her face looked naked and very broad. In spite of that, it was a pleasant face. I could feel my frozen smile thaw into something more comfortable.

" Mrs. Grinker? My name is Archer."

" Hello," she said good-humouredly, looking me over with large brown eyes a little the worse for wear. " I didn't leave the darn shop unlocked again, touch wood?"

" I hope not."

" Aren't you a policeman?"

" More or less. It shows when I'm tired."

" Wait a minute." She brought a leather case out of the pocket of the bathrobe and put on tortoise-shell spectacles. " I don't know you, do I?"

" No. I'm investigating a murder that occurred in Bella City this afternoon." I produced the rolled-up turban from my pocket and held it out to her. " This belonged to the victim. Did you make it?"

She peered at it. " It's got my name inside. What if I did?"

" You should be able to identify the customer you sold it to, if it's an original."

She leaned closer under the light, her glance shifting from the hat to me. The dark-rimmed spectacles had gathered her face into a shrewd hard pattern. " Is it a question of identification? You said it belonged to the victim. So who was the victim?"

" Lucy Champion was her name. She was a coloured woman in her early twenties."

" And you want to know if I sold her this turban?"

" I didn't say that exactly. The question is who you sold it to."

" Do I have to answer that? Let me see your badge."

" I'm a private detective," I said, " working with the police."

" Who are you working *for*?"

" My client doesn't want her name used."

" Exactly!" She blew me a whiff of beer. " Professional ethics. That's how it is with me. I can't deny I sold that hat, and I won't deny it was an original. But how can I say who bought it from me? I made it away back last spring some time. I do know one thing for certain, though, it wasn't a coloured girl bought it. There's never been one in my shop, except for a few brownskins from India and Persia and places like that. They're different."

" Born in different places, anyway."

" Okay, we won't argue. I have nothing against coloured people. But they don't buy hats from me. This girl must have found the hat, or stolen it, or had it given to her, or bought it in a rummage sale. So even if I could remember who bought it from me, it wouldn't be fair to drag my client's name into a murder case, would it?" Her voice contained a hint of phoniness, an echo of the daytime palaver in her shop.

"If you worked at it, Mrs. Grinker, I think you could remember."

"Maybe I could and maybe I couldn't." She was troubled, and her voice grew shallower. "What if I did? It would be violating a professional confidence."

"Do milliners take an oath?"

"We have our standards," she said hollowly. "Oh hell, I don't want to lose my customers if I can help it. The ones who can pay my prices are getting as scarce as eligible men."

I tried hard to look like an eligible man. "I can't give you my client's name. I will say that she's connected with the Singleton family."

"The Charles Singletons?" She pronounced the syllables slowly and distinctly, like a quotation from a poem she had always loved.

"Uh-huh."

"How is Mrs. Singleton?"

"Not very well. She's worried about her son——"

"Is this murder connected with him?"

"I'm trying to find that out, Mrs. Grinker. I never will find out unless I get some co-operation."

"I'm sorry. Mrs. Singleton isn't a customer of mine—I'm afraid she buys most of her hats in Paris—but of course I know *of* her. Come in."

The front door opened directly into a redwood-panelled living-room. A gas heater burned low in a red-brick fireplace. The room was warm and shabby and smelled of cats.

She waved a hospitable hand towards a studio couch covered with an afghan. A glass of beer was bubbling its life away on a redwood coffee-table beside the couch. "I was just having a beer for a nightcap. Let me get you one."

"I don't mind if you do."

She went into another room, closing the door behind her. When I sat down on the studio couch, a fluffy grey cat came out from under it and jumped onto my knee. Its purring rose and fell like the sound of a distant plane. Somewhere in the house, I thought I heard a low voice talking. Denise was a long time coming back.

I set the cat on the floor, and moved across the room to the door she had closed. On the other side of it, she was saying, in clipped telephone accents: " He claims to be employed by Mrs. Charles Singleton." A silence, lightly scratched by the sound of the telephone. Then: " I absolutely won't, I promise you. Of course, I understand perfectly. I *did* want to get your view of the matter." Another scratchy silence. Denise intoned a saccharine good-night, and hung up.

I tiptoed back to my seat, with the grey cat weaving between my legs. It paraded back and forth in front of me, rubbing its sides on my trousers and looking up at my face with remote female disdain.

I said: " Scat."

Denise re-entered the room with a foaming glass in each hand. She said to the cat: " Doesn't the nasty mans like kitty-witties?"

The cat paid no attention.

I said: " There's a story about Confucius, Mrs. Grinker. He was a pre-Communist Chinaman."

" I know who Confucius is."

" It seems a stable burned down in a neighbouring village, call it Bella City. Confucius wanted to know if any men were hurt. He didn't ask about the horses."

It hit her. The foam slopped over the rims of the beer-glasses and down across her fingers. She set the glasses on the coffee-table. " You can like cats and people, too," she said doubtfully. " I have a son in college, believe it or not. I even had a husband at one time. Whatever happened to him?"

" I'll look for him when I finish the case I'm on."

" Don't bother. Aren't you going to drink your beer?" She sat on the edge of the couch, wiping her wet fingers with a piece of Kleenex.

" The case I'm on," I said, " involves one dead woman and one missing man. If your cat had been run over by a hit-run driver, and somebody knew his license number, you'd expect to be told it. Who were you telephoning just now?"

" Nobody. It was a wrong number." Her fingers were

twisting the damp Kleenex into a small cup-shaped object, roughly the shape of a woman's hat.

"The telephone didn't ring."

She looked up at me with pain on her large face. "This woman is one of my customers. I can vouch for her." The pain was partly economic and partly moral.

"How did Lucy Champion get the hat? Does your customer explain that?"

"Of course. That's why it's so utterly pointless to bring her name into it. Lucy Champion used to be her maid. She ran away some time ago, without giving notice. She stole the hat from her employer, and other things as well."

"What other things? Jewellery?"

"How did you know that?"

"I got it from the horse's mouth. Maybe horse isn't the right word. Mrs. Larkin is more of the pony type."

Denise didn't react to the name. Her quick unconscious fingers had moulded the Kleenex hat into a miniature replica of the black-and-gold turban. She noticed what her fingers had been making, and tossed it in front of the cat. The cat pounced.

The woman wagged her head from side to side. The metal curlers clicked dully like disconnected thoughts. "All this is very confusing. Oh well, let's drink up." She raised her glass. "Here's to confusion. And universal darkness covers all."

I reached for my beer. The sagging springs of the studio couch threw us together, shoulder to shoulder. "Where did you pick that up?"

"I went to school once, strangely enough. That was before I came down with a bad case of art. What did you say the name was?"

"Archer."

"I know *that*. The woman's name, who told you about the stolen jewellery."

"Mrs. Larkin. It's probably an alias. Her first name is Una."

"Small and dark? Fiftyish? Mannish type?"

"That's Una. Was she your customer?"

Denise frowned into her beer, sipped meditatively, came up with a light foam moustache. "I shouldn't be talking out loud like this. But if she's using an alias, there must be something fishy." Her dubious expression hardened into self-concern: "You wouldn't quote me, to her or anybody else? My business is on the edge of nothing, I have a boy to educate, I can't afford any sort of trouble."

"Neither can Una, or whatever her name is."

"It's Una Durano, *Miss* Una Durano. At least that's what she goes by here. How did *you* happen to know her?"

"I worked for her at one time, briefly." The afternoon seemed very long ago.

"Where does she come from?"

"I wouldn't know. I'm much more interested in where she is now."

"I might as well tell all," Denise said wryly. "She lives on the Peppermill estate, leased it early last spring. I heard she paid a fantastic sum: a thousand dollars a month."

"The diamonds are real, then?"

"Oh yes, the diamonds are real."

"And just where is the Peppermill estate?"

"I'll tell you. But you won't go and see her to-night?" She pressed my arm with strong fingers. "If you do, she'll realise I told tales out of school."

"This is real life, Denise."

"I know it. It's my personal life. The hundred dollars she paid me for that hat took care of the rent that month."

"What month was it?"

"March, I think. It was the first one she bought in my shop. She's been back a couple of times since."

"It must have looked good on her, if anything could."

"Nothing could. She has no feminine quality. Anyway, she didn't buy the turban to wear herself. She paid for it, with a hundred-dollar bill. But it was the other woman with her who tried it on and wore it out of the shop." Her hand was still on my arm, like a bird that had settled on a comfortable roost for the night. She felt my muscles tense. "What's the matter?"

"The other woman. Describe her."

"She was a lovely girl, much younger than Miss Durano. A statuesque blonde, with the most wonderful blue eyes. She looked like a princess in my hat."

"Did she live with Miss Durano?"

"I can't say, though I saw them together several times. The blonde woman only came into my shop that once."

"Did you catch her name?"

"I'm afraid not. Is it important?" Her fingers were sculpturing the muscle patterns in my forearm.

"I don't know what's important and what isn't. You have been helpful, though." I stood up out of her grasp.

"Aren't you going to finish your beer? You can't go out there to-night. It's after midnight."

"I think I'll have a look at the place. Where is it?"

"I wish you wouldn't. Promise me anyway you won't go in and talk to her, not to-night."

"You shouldn't have phoned her," I said. "But I'll make you a better promise. If I find Charlie Singleton, I'll buy the most expensive hat in your store."

"For your wife?"

"I'm not married."

"Oh." She swallowed. "Well. To get to the Peppermill house, you turn left at the ocean boulevard and drive out to the end of town, past the cemetery. It's the first big estate beyond the cemetery. You'll know it by the greenhouses. And it has its own landing field."

She rose heavily and crossed the room to the door. The cat had torn the Kleenex hat into shreds that littered the carpet like dirty snowflakes.

CHAPTER 15

I drove back to the ocean boulevard and turned south. A fresh breeze struck the windwing and was deflected into my face, carrying moisture and sea smells. Behind the whizzing palm trees on the margin of my headlights, the sea itself streamed silver under the moon.

The boulevard curved left away from the beach. It climbed a grade past wind-tormented evergreens huddled arthritically on the hillside. A stone wall sprang up beside the road, amplifying the hum of the tyres and the mutter of the engine. Beyond the wall, stone angels pointed at the sky ; saints spread their arms in iron benediction.

The cemetery wall ended abruptly, and its place was taken by a spear-pointed iron fence. I caught glimpses through it of a great lawn returning to wilderness, beyond it a flat field with a corrugated-iron hangar at one end, a wind-sock blowing from its roof. I slowed down.

A heavy wrought-iron gate hung between obelisk-shaped gate posts, one of which had a large FOR SALE sign bolted to it. I got out and tried the gate. It was chained and padlocked. Through its bars I could see a long straight drive lined with coconut palms, at its end a massive house surrounded with outbuildings. The sloping glass roof of a conservatory glinted at the end of one wing.

The gate was climbable. Iron leaves between the bars provided foot- and hand-holds. I switched off my headlights and went over it. Circling wide on the lawn away from the drive, I struggled through the waist-high grass and weeds. The travelling moon accompanied me to the house.

The building was Spanish Renaissance with a strong Inquisition hangover. Narrow windows barred with ornamental ironwork were set deep in its wide flat concrete face. A lighted window on the second floor formed a tall yellow rectangle striped with vertical bars. I could see part of the ceiling of the room, vague shadows dancing on it. After a while the shadows approached the window, grouping and solidifying into human form. I lay down flat on my back and pulled my jacket together over my shirt-front.

A man's head and shoulders appeared at the bottom of the tall yellow rectangle I made out dark eyes in a moony blur of face under a tangle of hair. The eyes were raised to the sky. I looked straight up into its dark blue well, moon-washed and dripping with stars, and wondering what the man at the window was seeing there, or looking for.

He moved. Two pale hands sprang out from his dark silhouette and gripped the bars framing his face. He swayed from side to side, and I saw the white blaze on one side of his tangled head. His shoulders writhed. He seemed to be trying to wrench the bars out of their concrete sockets. Each time he tried and failed, he said one word in a low growling guttural.

" Hell," he said. " Hell. Hell."

The word fell heavily from his mouth forty or fifty times while his body tugged and heaved, flinging itself violently from side to side. He left the window then, as suddenly as he had appeared in it. I watched his slow shadow retreat across the ceiling and dissolve out of human shape.

Moving closer to the wall, I worked along it to the ground-floor window in which a faint light showed. This opened into a long hallway with a rounded ceiling. The light came from an open door at its far end. Listening closely, I heard some kind of music, a thin jazz scrabbling and tapping on the lid of silence.

I circled the house to the left, past a row of closed garage-doors, a clay tennis-court patchily furred with twitch grass, a sunken garden overgrown with succulents. From its end a *barranca* widened down to a bluff that overhung the sea. Below the bluff, the sea slanted up like a corrugated-metal roof to the horizon.

I turned back to the house. Between it and the sunken garden there was a flagged patio walled with flowerboxes. Its tables and chairs were sand-blown and rusting, old iron relics of dead summers. Light fell among them from a picture window in the wall overhead. The jazz was louder behind the wall, like music at a dance to which I hadn't been invited.

The window was uncurtained but set too high to give me a view of the room. The black-beamed ceiling was visible and the upper part of the far wall. Its oak panels were crowded with paintings of pigeon-breasted women in lace caps and mutton-chop-whiskered men, narrow-shouldered in black Victorian coats. Somebody's ancestors, not Una's. She had been stamped out by a machine.

Standing on my toes, I could see the top of Una's head covered with short black curls like caracul. She was sitting perfectly still beside the window. A young man was sitting opposite her, his profile visible from the neck up. It was a heavy and amorphous profile, whatever strength it had concealed by pads of flesh under the chin, around the mouth and eyes. He had light brown hair bristling in an unkempt crew-cut. The focus of his attention was somewhere between him and Una, below the level of the windowsill. I guessed from the movement of his eye that they were playing cards.

The music behind the wall stopped and started again. It was the same old record, *Sentimental Lady*, being played over and over. Sentimental Una, I said to myself, just as the howling began. Distant and muted by intervening walls, the howling rose and fell like a coyote baying the moon. Or a man. The hair on the back of my neck prickled.

Una said, loudly enough to be heard through the plate-glass window: " For Christ's sake shut him up."

The man with the crew-cut rose into half-length view. He wore the white-drill smock of a nurse or orderly, but he had none of their air of efficiency. " What do I do, bring him down here?" He clenched his hands together in a womanish gesture.

" It looks as if you'll have to."

The howling rose again. The orderly's head turned towards it and then his body followed. He walked away from the window, out of my sight. Una got up and marched in the same direction. Her shoulders were trim in a tailored black pyjama-jacket. She turned the music louder. It poured through the house like a dark intangible surf, and like a drowning person's, the man's cry rose above it. His howling was stilled suddenly. The music went on, washing over the human echo.

Then there were voices in the room, Una's voice weaving jerkily through the music: " Headache . . . get some peace . . . sedation "; and the growling guttural I had heard before, starting below the music and rising above it:

" I can't. It is terrible. Terrible things going on. I got to stop them."

" Old man Stopper himself. You're the one to stop them all right." It was the younger man's mezzo, with a titter running through it.

" Leave him alone!" Una cried savagely. " Let him have his say. You want him to yell all night?"

There was silence again, except for the swirling music. I stepped across a flowerbox into the patio and leaned my weight on one of the rusted tables. It held firm. Using a chair as a step, I got up onto the tabletop. The table teetered on its base, and I had a bad moment before it levelled back. When I straightened up, my head was almost even with the windowsill ten feet away.

On the far side of the room, Una was standing over a radio-phonograph. She turned it low and walked directly towards the window. I ducked instinctively, but she wasn't

looking at me. With an expression in which outrage and
tolerance were combined, she was watching the man who stood
in the centre of the room. The man with the blaze of white
like a lightning scar on the side of his head.

His small body was wrapped in a robe of red brocaded silk
which hung in folds as if he had borrowed it from a larger
man. Even his face seemed to have shrunk inside its skin.
Instead of jowls he had pale loose wattles that flapped with
the movement of his mouth.

"Terrible things." His broken growl was loud in the silence.
"Going on all the time. I caught the dogs at my
mamma. They crucified my daddy. I climbed up out of the
culvert up on the hill and saw the nails in his hands and he
said kill them all. Kill them all. Those were his last streetcar
I went down into the tunnel under the river and the dead boys
lying the ragpickers strutting around with the rods in their
pants." He trailed off into an obscene medley of Anglo-Saxon
and Italian.

The white-smocked orderly was sitting on the arm of a
leather chair. The light from a standing lamp beside him
gave him the unreality of a pink elephant. He called out like
a rooter from the sidelines:

"You tell 'em, Durano. You got a beautiful engram, old
boy."

Una darted towards him, angry face thrust forward:
"*Mister* to you, you lump of dough. Call him *mister*!"

"*Mister* Durano, then. Sorry."

The man who bore the name raised his face to the light.
The black eyes were flat and shiny, deep-sunk, like bits of
coal pressed into soft snow brows. "*Mister* District Attorney,"
he cried earnestly. "He said there was rats in the river, rats
in the Rouge Plant. He said kill them off. Rats in the
drinking-water, swimming in my blood-veins, Mr. Doctor
Attorney. I promised to clean them out."

"Give him the gun, for Christ's sake," Una said. "Get it
over with."

"For Christ's sweet sake," Durano echoed her. "I seen
him on the hill when I come up out of the culvert. Horse-shoe
nails in his hands, and the dogs at my mother. He give me the
gun, said keep it in your pants boy, you get rats in the blood-
streams. I said I would clean them out." His thin hand dove

like a weasel for the pocket of his bathrobe. It came out empty. "They took my gun. How can I clean them out when they took my rod away?" He raised his doubled fists in an agony of rage and beat his forehead with them. "Give me my gun!"

Una went to the record-player, almost running, as if a wind were hurrying her along. She turned it loud and came back to Durano, struggling step by step against the psychic wind that was blowing in the room. The fat orderly hitched up his smock and took a black automatic from under his belt. Durano pounced on him feebly. The orderly offered no resistance. Durano wrenched the automatic from his hands and backed away a few feet.

"Now!" he said with authority. He uttered a string of obscenities as if his mouth was full of them and he was spitting them out to be rid of them. "Now, you two, hands on the heads."

The orderly did as he was told. Una lined up beside him with her hands in the air, rings flashing. Her face was expressionless.

"This is it," Durano said thickly. There were red welts on his forehead where he had struck himself. His slack mouth continued moving but I couldn't hear what he said under the music. He leaned forward, strained white fingers around the gun. It looked as if it were holding him up in the beating ocean of noise.

Una said something in a low voice. The orderly glanced down with a faint fat smile. Durano took a skipping little step and shot him three times point-blank. The orderly lay down on the floor and pillowed his head on an upflung arm, the faint smile still on his face.

Durano shot Una, three times. She doubled over, grimacing histrionically, and collapsed on a divan. Durano looked around the room for other possible victims. Finding none, he dropped the gun in the pocket of his bathrobe. I had noticed when he began to shoot with it that it was a toy cap-pistol.

Una rose from the divan and turned the music down. Durano watched her without surprise. The man in white hoisted himself to his feet and escorted Durano across the room. Durano looked back from the doorway with a dreaming smile. The self-inflicted bruises on his forehead were swelling and turning blue.

Una waved to him, exaggeratedly, like a mother to a child, before the orderly hustled him out. Then she sat down at the card table by the window and began to shuffle the deck. Sentimental Una.

I climbed down from my perch. Away down below on the beach I could hear the waves playing pattycake in the sand, sucking and gurgling rhythmically like idiot children.

I went around to the front of the house. The barred window on the second floor was still lit, and I could see the shadows on the ceiling. I moved in closer to the front door, which was made of carved black oak and about twelve feet high. It was the kind of door that demanded to be knocked on with the butt end of a gun. I stood in a weed-grown flowerbed, leaned my chin on the iron railing of the portico, fingered the butt of the gun in my jacket pocket. And decided to call it a day.

I lacked the evidence and the power to put Una under arrest. Until I had one or the other, it would be better to leave her where I could find her again, safe in the bosom of her family.

CHAPTER 16

The signpost at the mountain crossroads was splintered by the bullets of trigger-happy hunters. Four painted white boards projected from it. One pointed back the way I had come: ARROYO BEACH 7 MIS. One pointed forward: BELLA CITY 34 MIS. The one to the right said: EAGLE LOOKOUT 5 MIS; the one to the left: SKY ROUTE. The fifth direction, unmarked, was straight up to where a hawk wheeled on banked blue curves of air. It was bright early morning.

I got back behind the wheel of my car and turned onto the Sky Route. It was a hairpinning gravel road that traced the contours of the mountainside. On my left the mountain fell away into a canyon in which occasional rooftops were visible. Beyond the canyon's far edge the sea lay smoothed by distance like wine in a teacup, rimmed by the thin white curve of Arroyo Beach.

I passed a few rural mailboxes standing on posts at the

entrances to steep lanes. The mailbox numbered 2712 also
bore the legend HIGHHOLME, H. WILDING, ESQ., in bold red
block-capitals Wilding's lane widened into a clearing near
the bottom of the canyon. A small stone house sat between
white oaks at the back of the clearing.

There were bantam chickens scratching in the yard. An
old hound cocked a grizzled snoot at me and lifted one eye-
brow, refusing to move out of the path of the car. I set the
emergency brake and got out. He growled at me apathetically,
still without moving. A grey gander ran at me hissing and
flapping, veered at the last moment into the trees. Somewhere
in the wooded canyon below, a gang of kids were talking back
and forth in Indian war-whoops.

The man who came out of the stone house could have
passed for an Indian. He was dressed in a pair of dirty
canvas shorts, and the rest of him was burned almost black
by the sun. His straight black hair, greyed in streaks, hung
down over his ears.

"Hello," he said, strumming a silent overture on his wash-
board ribs. "Isn't it a fine clear day? I hope you noticed
the quality of the light. It's rather special. Whistler might
have been able to snare it in paint, not I."

"Mr. Wilding?"

"Of course" He extended a paint-stained hand. "Delighted
to see you. Delighted to see anybody and anything. Did it
ever occur to you that light creates landscape, so that the
world itself is created daily, in a sense? In my sense."

"It never has."

"Well, think about it," he said earnestly. "Light creates
landscape out of old black chaos. We painters recreate it. I
can't step outside in the morning without feeling like God
himself on the second day. Or was it the third? It doesn't
matter really. I've divested myself of time. I live in pure
space."

"My name is Archer," I said, before I drowned in a
mountain torrent of words. "Two weeks ago——"

"I'm sorry, I've been rude. I so seldom see people, I'm a
veritable gramophone when I do. Archer, you say? Were
you born under Sagittarius by any chance, the sign of the
Archer? If you were," he concluded rather lamely, "that
would be fun."

"Sagittarius is my first name, curiously enough. It's more fun than you can imagine."

Wilding uttered a high loud laugh like a mockingbird's imitation of human mirth. A hooting echo of his laughter came back from the children in the woods.

"Who are you anyway?" he said. "Come in and have a cup of tea. I've only just brewed some."

"I'm a detective."

"On the Singleton case?"

"Yes."

"Oh." He didn't renew his invitation to tea. "There's really nothing I can tell you that I haven't told the others."

"I'm working alone. I haven't talked to the others, and I don't know what they know or what they think. My own feeling is that he's dead."

"Charles dead?" Surprise or some other emotion pulled like a drawstring through his cordovan face and left it wrinkled. "That would be a waste. He was only twenty-nine. Why do you feel that he is dead, Mr. Archer?"

"Analogy. A woman was killed yesterday, apparently because she knew what happened to him."

"The blonde woman, was she killed?"

"A coloured woman." I told him about Lucy.

He squatted Indian-fashion, resting one elbow on his folded bare knees, and drew a design in the dust with his forefinger. It was a long-faced mask in the shape of a coffin, which looked a little like his own face. A bantam rooster came and pecked at his hand.

Wilding stood up, and struck himself lightly over the eyes with the hand that had drawn the coffin. "There's your symbol-making faculty at work in its crudest form. I wonder sometimes if my sainted mother didn't deceive my father with a Navajo." He obliterated the dust-drawing with his sandalled feet, talking on without a pause: "The painter makes objects out of events, the poet makes words out of events. What does the man of action do, Mr. Archer? Suffer them?"

"Your friend Singleton did, I think. I take it he was your friend, or is."

"Certainly he was. I've known Charles since he was a schoolboy. I taught at Arroyo Prep School for a while, before my pictures sold. And he's been coming up here in the summers for nearly ten years. You can see his place from here."

He pointed north along the canyon. Near its head, a half mile or more away, a squat structure of brown oiled logs gleamed dully among the live oaks. "I helped him to build it myself, in the summer of 1941. It's only a one-room affair, but Charles always called it his studio. He came back from his freshman year at Harvard with ideas of becoming a poet. His mother's house on the Hill made him feel cramped and stuffy. Both she and her house—I don't know whether you know them—are crusty with tradition, *not* the kind of tradition that a budding poet could use. Charles came up here to escape from it. He called this canyon his private vale of soul-making."

"I'd like to have a look at his cabin."

"I'll go over with you."

Wilding moved impulsively towards my car, and I followed him. I drove up the lane in low gear and turned left on the gravel road cut into the canyon wall. The second mailbox we came to was stencilled with the name Singleton. I turned left again into a lane that slanted down the side of the canyon. About halfway to the bottom, the log house stood on a natural shelf between the canyon's converging walls. When I parked in front of it and got out, I saw that the front door was sealed with official paper.

I turned to Wilding: "You didn't tell me the place was sealed. Does the sheriff suspect violence?"

"He doesn't confide in me," Wilding said wryly. "When I told him about the shot I heard, he didn't seem to take it too seriously."

"The shot?"

"Sorry, I imagined that you knew. I heard a shot from this direction, late that Saturday night. I didn't think twice about it at the time, for the simple reason that I hear a great many shots, in and out of hunting season. When they questioned me the following week, I mentioned it of course. I believe they went over the premises quite thoroughly after that. They didn't find a bullet or anything of the sort."

"They wouldn't, if the slug went into Singleton."

"Mercy upon us," he said. "Do you really suppose that Charles was shot up here in his own cabin?"

"They must think something happened here, or they wouldn't have sealed it up. What else did you hear that Saturday night?"

"Nothing, absolutely nothing. A single shot around eleven o'clock, and that was all. A few cars went by, but there's always late night traffic on the road."

Wilding went to the large window that balanced the door in the front wall of the cabin. Standing on tiptoe, he peered in past the brown monk's-cloth drapes partly drawn across it. I looked over his shoulder into a square beamed room furnished in primitive luxury with polished wood, home-spun fabrics, copper. Everything seemed to be in order and place. Above the copper-vented fireplace opposite the window, a handsome boy in oils looked out of a bleached wooden frame, over our heads, down five miles of sunlit canyon.

"That's Charles," Wilding said in a whisper, as if the boy in the frame might overhear him. "I painted it myself and gave it to him. He looked like a young Shelley when he was twenty. I'm afraid he doesn't any more. Charles lost his ethereal quality during the war, when he took up with that woman. Or it may have been the war itself that did it. I suppose I have a prejudice against women. I'm a confirmed bachelor myself."

"Is she the blonde you mentioned"

"Did I mention her? I didn't mean to.". He turned and laid a brown hand on my shoulder. "Look here, old chap, are you one of the old lady's investigators? If you are, I don't want to say any more. Naturally I told the whole thing to the sheriff."

"Anything you tell me is between us."

His bright black eyes explored my face like foraging beetles. "What is your interest in Charles, just while we're on the subject?"

"Mrs. Singleton's paid compainon hired me."

"Sylvia Treen? She's a lovely child, very much in love with Charles, I think. But I had no idea——"

"She knows about the blonde."

"Yes. I told her. I thought it might be for the best, in the long run. Whatever happened, Charles would never marry Sylvia. He's not the marrying sort. I *didn't* let Sylvia know how long the affair had lasted."

" She said it was just this summer."

" I let her imagine that. Actually it's been going on for seven or eight years. Charles introduced me to her the year he entered the Air Force. Her name was Bess, I don't recall her surname. She was very young and quite exciting, marvellously coloured. Perfect in every way, until she opened her mouth—but I mustn't tattle." He continued to tattle: " Charles always did have a proletarian penchant you know. In spite of that or because of it, it was clearly a case of true love The children were mad about each other. I shouldn't say children. *She* wasn't a child. She was already married, I understand. Which doubtless suited Charles." He added reflectively: " Perhaps he should have married her."

" You think she shot him?"

" I have no reason to think so. Certainly it's possible. Seven years is a long time for a young lady to wait for a young man to make up his mind."

" Was she here the night he disappeared?"

" I have no way of knowing. I did see a light in the cabin. Actually I haven't seen her for weeks. I do have the impression that they came up here together quite often during the summer, practically every Saturday night."

" And before that?"

He leaned against the sealed door and thought for a while, his thin brown arms folded on his chest. " Their visits haven't been continuous, I know that. Bess first appeared in the summer of 1943, and that was when I met her. I wanted to paint her. Charles was excessively possessive, and he never again asked me back when she was here. After that summer, I didn't set eyes on her again until 1945, when Charles left the Air Force. For the next two or three years I saw her at a distance quite often. Then Charles went back to Harvard in the fall of 1948 to study law, and I didn't see them again until this spring. It's possible that she followed him to Cambridge. I've never asked him about her."

" Why?"

" He's jealous, as I said, and secretive about his private affairs. It's partly his mother's doing. Mrs. Singleton's attitude towards the human libido is austere, to say the least."

" So you don't know where she came from, where she went,

what she was doing in Arroyo Beach, who she was married
to?"

"To all of those questions, I have to answer no."

"You can describe her?"

"If I can find the words. She was a young Aphrodite, a
Velasquez Venus with a Nordic head."

"Try me again, Mr. Wilding, in simple language."

"A Nordic Aphrodite rising from the Baltic." He smiled
reminiscently. "She was perfect until she opened her mouth.
Then it was painfully clear that she had learned to speak
English, if English is the word, in shall we say a rather
barbarous milieu."

"I take it she was a blue-eyed blonde, and no lady."

"*Baltic* blue eyes," he insisted. "Hair like pale young corn-
silk. Almost too dramatic to paint seriously, though I dearly
should have loved to do a nude." His eyes were burning a
figure into the air. "Charles wouldn't hear of it."

"Can you draw her from memory?" I said.

"I could if I wished." He kicked at the dirt like a rebellious
boy. "I haven't really bothered with human material for
years. My present concern is pure space, lit by the intelligible
radiance of nature, if you follow me."

"I don't."

"In any case, I never use my art, or allow it to be used."

"Uh-huh. Very high-minded. You've divested yourself of
time. It happens a friend of yours has done it the hard way,
probably. Most people would climb down off their high
horse and do what they can to help."

He gave me a bitter wrinkled look. I thought he was going
to cry. Instead he let out another of his high inhuman
laughs, which echoed like the cry of a lost gull down the
canyon. "I do believe you're right, Mr. Sagittarius. If you'll
take me home, I'll see what I can do."

He came out of his house a half hour later, waving a piece
of drawing paper:

"Here you are, as representational as I can make her. It's
pastel chalk sprayed with fixative, so don't try to fold it."

I took the drawing from his hand. It was a coloured sketch
of a young woman. Her pale blonde braids were coroneted
on her head. Her eyes had the dull gleaming suavity of tile.

Wilding had caught her beauty, but she was older in time than in the picture.

He seemed to sense what I was thinking: "I had to sketch her as I first saw her. That was my image of her. She'll be seven or eight years older."

"She's changed the colour of her hair, too."

"You know her, then."

"Not well. I'll get to know her better."

CHAPTER 17

I climbed the front steps of Dr. Benning's house and rang the doorbell. The hole I had punched in the corner of the pane had been mended with cardboard and scotch tape. Dr. Benning came to the door in shirtsleeves, with suspenders dragging. His uncombed hair was a fringe of withering grass around the pink desert of his scalp. He had the air of a beaten old man, until he spoke. His voice was crisp and impatient:

"What can I do for you? Weren't you in my waiting-room yesterday afternoon?"

"This isn't a professional call, doctor."

"What kind of call is it? I'm just getting up."

"Haven't the police contacted you?"

"They have not. Are you a policeman?"

"A private detective, working with the police." I showed him my photostat. "We're investigating the murder of a coloured girl named Lucy Champion. She visited your office yesterday afternoon."

"You followed her here?"

"I did."

"Do you care to tell me why?" in the harsh morning light his eyes were pale and strained.

"I was hired to."

"And now she's dead?"

"She got away from me. When I found her again, late yesterday afternoon, her throat had been cut."

"It's curious you didn't get in touch with me before. Since she was my patient, and I was apparently one of the last persons to see her alive."

"I tried to last night. Didn't your wife tell you?"

" I haven't had a chance to speak with her this morning. She isn't well. Come in, though, won't you? If you'll just give me a chance to finish dressing, I'll be glad to help you in any way I can."

He ushered me into the waiting-room. I heard his slippered feet diminuendo up the stairs to the second floor. Then minutes later he came down, dressed in a creased blue store suit, and freshly shaved. Leaning on the receptionist's desk in the corner, he lit a cigarette and offered me the package.

" Not before breakfast, thanks."

" I'm foolish to do it myself. I warn my patients about smoking on an empty stomach. But that's the way of us doctors. Preventive medicine is our watchword nowadays, and half of us are still dying prematurely of overwork. Physician, heal thyself." Benning had put on a professional manner along with his clothes.

" Speaking of premature death," I said.

" I shouldn't be chattering." His quick smile held remnants of boyish charm. " It's a bad habit I've fallen into, from trying to establish *rapport* with my patients. Now about this patient, Miss Champion. You say her throat was cut, Mr.—is it Archer?"

" Her throat was cut, and it's Archer."

" Exactly what sort of information do you want from me?"

" Your observations, personal and professional. Was yesterday the first time she came here to your office?"

" I believe it was the third time. I have to apologise for the conditions of my records. I haven't had trained help recently. And then so many of my patients are one-time cash patients. It's in the nature of a general practice among, well, poor people. I don't always keep full records, except in the cash-book. I do recall that she was in twice before: once in the middle of last week I think, and once the week before that."

" Who referred her?"

" Her landlady, Mrs. Norris."

" You know Mrs. Norris?"

" Certainly. She's often done practical nursing for me. Anna Norris is the finest type of Negro woman, in my opinion. Or dark-complected woman, as she would say."

" Her son is suspected of this murder."

" Alex is?" He swung one nervous leg, and his heel rapped

the side of the desk. "Why on earth should he be under suspicion?"

"He was on the scene. When they arrested him, he panicked and ran. If he hasn't been caught, he's probably still going."

"Even so, isn't Alex an unlikely suspect?"

"I think so. Lieutenant Brake doesn't. Alex was intimate with the girl, you know. He was going to marry her."

"Wasn't she much older?"

"How old was she?"

"I'd say in her middle twenties. She was a registered nurse, with several years of experience."

"What was the matter with her?"

A length of ash fell from his untended cigarette. Absently, he ground it into the carpet with the toe of his worn black shoe. "The matter with her?"

"What were you treating her for?"

"It amounted to nothing really," he answered after a pause. "She had an intestinal complaint which I think was caused by a slight colonic spasm. Unfortunately she knew too much about illness, and too little. She magnified her trouble into a malignant disease. Of course she had nothing of the sort, nothing more than a mild psychosomatic ailment. Do you follow me?"

"Partly. Her symptoms were caused by nerves."

"I wouldn't say nerves." Benning was expanding in the glow of his superior knowledge. "The total personality is the cause of psychosomatic ills. In our society a Negro, and especially a highly trained Negro woman like Miss Champion, is often subjected to frustrations that could lead to neurosis. A strong personality will sometimes convert incipient neurosis into physical symptoms. I'm stating it crudely, but that's what Miss Champion did. She felt cramped by her life, so to speak, and her frustration expressed itself in stomach cramp." He paused for breath.

"What was she doing in Bella City?"

"I'd like to know myself. She claimed to be looking for a job, but I don't think she was registered in California. I'd give a good deal for a social history on her."

"She was from Detroit. Her family is poor and pretty ignorant. Does that help?"

"It doesn't tell me much about her psychic life, does it?"

"Why is her psychic life important?"

"I could see that fear of illness wasn't her only phobia. She had a deeper and more general fear which expressed itself in various ways. I tried to explain that to her, to give her some insight, but she wasn't equal to it. She broke down and cried on my shoulder. Then it came out about her other fears."

"What was she afraid of?"

He spread his hands like a lecturer. "It's hard to say. I'm not a psychiatrist, though I do try to keep up with the literature." He looked around his shabby waiting-room, and an obscure impulse made him add: "Which is more than you can say for my colleagues in this desolate town."

"Was her fear real or imaginary?"

"Precisely the question I can't answer, without knowing more about her." His eyes clouded with thought. "Fear is always real subjectively. The true question about fear is whether it's relevant, justified by the situation. In this case it seems to have been. Miss Champion believed that she was being hunted, that she was marked for death."

"Did she give you any details?"

"No. I didn't have time to gain her confidence. She failed to mention these persecution fears at all until her last visit, yesterday. You've been investigating her life and death, Mr. Archer. Was she really being hunted down by someone? Someone who finally caught her?"

"I don't know. I was trailing her myself, and I did a poor job of it and she caught on. If she was full of fear, that might have been enough to set her off." I asked a question I didn't want to ask: "You don't think she could have killed herself out of pure funk?"

Dr. Benning began to pace back and forth along a worn path that cut across the carpet from one door to the other. When he stopped and faced me, he looked ill at ease: "I'll be frank with you. I was concerned about her in that sense, which is why I did my best to allay her fears."

"You thought she had suicidal tendencies?"

"I took it into account as a possibility. That's all I can say. I'm no psychiatrist." He spread his hands palms upward in a gesture of awkward helplessness. "Was the wound consistent with suicide?"

" It was pretty deep to be self-inflicted. Brake or the deput
coroner can answer that question better than I can. An
Brake will want your statement."

" I'm ready now, if you're going to the station."

I said I was. Benning went into the hall and got his ha
With his bald head covered he looked a good deal younge
but neither handsome nor well-heeled enough to be marrie
to the woman he was married to.

He called up the stairs before we left: " I'm going ou
Bess. Do you want anything?"

There was no answer.

CHAPTER 18

The dirty-white brick city hall was distinguished from the sur
rounding store- and office-buildings by a flagless flagpol
standing in its patch of scorched grass. At the rear a concret
ramp sloped down from a paved parking lot to the scuffe
green door of the police department. Benning turned at th
door, smiling a sour private smile.

" The descent into Avernus," he said.

Inside, in a green-walled corridor, a few wire-netted ceiling
bulbs maintained a bilious twilight. Under the brisk odour
of floor oil and metal polish, the smells of fear and germicide
poverty and old sweat, kept up a complicated human murmur
In the furthest, dimmest corner, opposite a door marked
DESK SERGEANT, a monumental shape sat on a wooden bencl
against the wall.

It belonged to a large Negro woman in a black cloth coat
The hair that showed under the side of her black felt hat wa
the colour and texture of steel wool. I recognised her when
she turned to look at us.

Benning spoke first—" Mrs. Norris!"—and went to he
with his hands out.

She took them, raising her heavy, dark face to his. " I'm
glad to see you, doctor." Cross-hatched by shadow, her nose
and mouth and chin looked like black stone rounded by
years of weather. Only her eyes gleamed sorrowfully with life.
" They've arrested Alex. They're accusing him of murder."

" It must be a mistake," he said in a low bedside voice. " I know he's a good boy."

" He is a good boy." She looked questioningly at me.

" This is Mr. Archer, Mrs. Norris. He's working on the case. Mr. Archer has just been telling me that he thinks Alex is innocent"

" Thank you, Mr. Archer, and pleased to make your acquaintance."

" When was he arrested?"

" Early this morning, in the desert. He was trying to get out of the state. The car broke down. He was a young fool to run away in the first place. It's twice as bad for him, now that they've brought him back."

" Did you get him a lawyer?" Benning said.

" Yes, I'm having Mr. Santana. He's up in the Sierra for the weekend, but his housekeeper got in touch with him."

" He's a good man, Santana." Patting her shoulder, he moved towards the desk sergeant's door. " I'll talk to Brake, and see what I can do for Alex."

" I know Alex has a good friend in you, doctor."

Her words were hopeful, but her back and shoulders sloped in resignation. When she saw my intention of sitting down, she gathered her coat and shifted her body to one side, an involuntary sigh escaping from its concertina folds. I sat on a scrambled alphabet of initials carved in the soft wood of the bench.

" Do you know my son, Mr. Archer?"

" I talked to him a little last night."

" And you don't believe he's guilty?"

" No. He seemed very fond of Lucy."

She pursed up her heavy lips suspiciously, and said in a smaller voice: " Why do you say that?"

" He said it himself. Also, it showed in his actions."

That silenced her for a while. Her diffident black hand touched my arm very softly and retreated to her bosom. A thin gold wedding-band was sunk almost out of sight in the flesh of its third finger. " You are on our side, Mr. Archer?"

" The side of justice when I can find it. When I can't find it, I'm for the underdog."

" My son is no underdog," she said with a flash of pride.

" I'm afraid he'll be treated like one. There's a chance

that Alex may be railroaded for this murder. The only sure way to prevent that is to pin it on the murderer. And you may be able to help me do that." I took a deep breath.

"I believe that you are a righteous man, Mr. Archer."

I let her believe it.

"You're welcome to anything I can say or do," she continued. "It is true, what you said before. My boy was crazy for that woman. He wanted to marry her. I did my best to prevent it, every way I could. Alex is only nineteen, much too young to think about getting married. I planned an education for him, I tried to tell him that a dark-complected man is nothing in this country without an education to stand on. And Lucy wasn't the wife for him. She was older than Alex, five or six years older, and she was fast in her habits. I sent her away from my house yesterday, and then she got herself killed. I confess I made a mistake. I rose up in anger against her. She had no safe place to go. If I'd known what was going to come to her, she could have stayed on with us."

"You don't have to blame yourself. I think what happened to her was bound to happen."

"Do you think that?"

"She was carrying something too heavy for her."

"I had that feeling. Yes. She was afraid." Mrs. Norris leaned towards me with heavy confiding charm: "I had the feeling from the beginning that Lucy Champion was bad luck to me and my house. She was from Detroit, and I lived there myself when Alex was an infant. Last night when they came to me and said she was killed, it was like all the things I'd dreaded for myself and Alex, when we were moving from city to city trying to find a living in the depression. Like those things had suddenly come true for us at last, here in this valley. After all those years I worked and planned, keeping my name respectable."

Looking into her eyes, deep black springs tapping the deep black past, I couldn't think of anything to say.

"I mis-stated myself," she said with renewed energy. "It is not my name I care for. It's my son. I believed if we could get out of those big cities in the North and live in a decent place of our own, I could bring him up straight as his father wished for him. Now he has been arrested."

" Where is his father? It would be a good thing if he stood by."

" Yes, it would be a good thing. Alex' father died in the war. Mr. Norris was a chief petty officer in the United States Navy." She blew her nose with the force and effect of an exclamation mark, and dabbed at her eyes.

I waited a while, and said: " When did Lucy Champion come to your house?"

" She drove up in a taxi on a Sunday morning before church. It must have been two weeks ago to-day. I never like to do business on the Sabbath, but then I had no right to turn her away just for my private indulgence. The decent hotels were closed to her in this city, and most of the houses where our people can rent are not fit for dogs to inhabit. She was well spoken and well dressed. She told me she was on a vacation from her work, and she wanted to stay in a private house. I had the side room empty since the spring, and with Alex commencing college I needed the money.

" She seemed a peaceable little soul, though she was nervous and shy. She scarcely ever went out at all except to get herself lunch. She made her own breakfast, and ate her dinner with us. We had a boarding arrangement."

" Did she eat well?"

" Now that you mention it, she didn't. Picked at her food like a bird. I asked her once or twice if my food was not agreeing with her, but she was vague in her answers."

" Did she mention any illness to you?"

" She never did, Mr. Archer. Excuse me, now, she did. There was some trouble with her stomach. Nervous stomach."

" And you sent her to Dr. Benning?"

" I didn't send her. I said if she needed a doctor, he was a good man to go to. Whether she went to him or not, that I can't say."

" She went to him all right. But she never spoke of Dr. Benning to you?"

" Not that I recollect, except for that one time I recommended him."

" Did she mention Mrs. Benning?"

" Mrs. Benning? Dr. Benning has no wife that I know of."

" I met her last night, in his house. At least I met a woman who calls herself Mrs. Benning."

" You must refer to Florida Gutierrez. She works for the doctor. He wouldn't marry her. Dr. Benning wouldn't marry any woman, not after the bad trouble he had with his first wife."

" Was he a widower??"

" Divorced," she said flatly, unable to conceal her disapproval. She added quickly: " Not that I blame the doctor, except for his foolishness marrying a woman so much younger than him—than he. She was a Jezebel to him, a blonde Jezebel mistreating him without shame. It ended as I expected, with her running off and divorcing him. At least that was the story I heard." She pulled herself up sharp. " I ought to wash out my mouth, repeating gossip and scandal on the Lord's Day."

" What was her name, Mrs. Norris?"

" Elizabeth Benning. Doctor called her Bess. I don't know her maiden name. He married her in the war, when he was a medical officer in the United States Navy. That was before we moved here from the North."

" And how long ago did she leave him?"

" Nearly two years, it was. He was better off without her, though I never dared tell him so."

" She seems to have come back."

" Now? In his house?"

I nodded.

Her mouth pursed up tight again. Her whole face closed against me. Distrust of white men lay deep and solid in her like stone strata deposited through generations of time. " You won't repeat that which I have been saying? I have an evil tongue and I've still not learned to curb it."

" I'm trying to get you out of trouble, not deeper in."

She answered slowly, after a time: " I do believe you. And it's true, she returned to him?"

" She's there in the house. Didn't Lucy mention her at all? She went to the doctor three times, and Mrs. Benning has been working as his receptionist."

She answered positively: " Lucy never did."

" The doctor told me you've had nursing experience. Did Lucy show any signs of illness, physical or mental?"

" She seemed a well woman to me, apart from her eating habits. Of course when they drink, often they don't eat."

" She drank?"

" I learned to my sorrow and shame she was a drinker. And now that you ask me about her health, Mr. Archer, there is this thing that has been puzzling me."

She opened the clasp of her black purse and groped for something inside. It turned out to be a clinical thermometer in a black leatherette carrying case, which she handed to me.

" I found this after she left, in the medicine cabinet over the sink in her room. Don't shake it down now. I want you to look at the temperature."

I opened the case and turned the narrow glass stem until I could see the column of mercury. It registered 107°F.

" Are you sure this was Lucy's?"

She pointed to the initials, L.C., inked on the case. " Certainly it belonged to her. She was a nurse."

" She couldn't have had a temperature like that, could she? I thought 107 was fatal."

" It is, for adults. I don't understand it myself. Do you think I should show it to the police?"

" I will, if you like. In the meantime, can you tell me anything more about her habits? You say she was quiet and shy?"

" Very much so, at first, keeping herself *to* herself. Most of her evenings she just plain sat in her room with a little portable gramophone she brought along with her. I thought it was a peculiar way for a young woman to spend her vacation, and I said so. She laughed at that, but not in a humorous way. She became hysterical, and that was when I realised the strain that she was under. I began to feel the strain in the atmosphere when she was in the house. She was *in* the house twenty-three hours out of the twenty-four, it seemed like."

" Did she have any visitors?"

She hesitated. " No, she never had a one. She sat in her room and kept that jazzy music playing on the radio. Then I discovered her drinking. I was cleaning her room one day when she was out to buy her lunch downtown. I opened up a drawer to put fresh paper in the bottom, and it had whisky bottles in it, three or four empty pint bottles." Her voice was hushed with outrage.

" Maybe it helped her nerves."

She looked at me shrewdly: " Alex said just those words to me when I mentioned it to him. He defended her, which set me to thinking about the two of them living together in the same house. That was the end of last week. Then the middle of this week, late Wednesday night it was, I heard her tromping around in her room. I knocked on her door, and she responded in silk pyjamas and there was Alex with her in her room. He said she was teaching him to dance. To all appearances, she was teaching my son the wicked ways of the world, in red silk pyjamas, and I told her that to her face."

Her bosom heaved with remembered anger, like the after-shock of an earthquake:

" I told her she was degenerating my God-fearing house-hold into a dance-hall, she must let my son alone. She said it was Alex's choice and he backed her up, he said he loved her. Then I was harsh with her. The red silk pyjamas over her insolent flesh, they blinded my eyes to charity. My evil anger rose up and I said she must let Alex alone or leave my house in her nightclothes as she was. I said that I was plan-ning better things for my son than she could give him. Alex spoke up then, saying if Lucy Champion went he would go along with her."

Now in a sense, he had. His mother's gaze seemed to be following his image into the shadows where Lucy had preceded him.

" You let her stay, though," I said.

" Yes. My son's wish is powerful with me. Lucy herself went away next morning, but she left her things behind. I don't know where she spent the day. I know she took a bus somewhere because she complained about the service that night when she came back. She was very excited in her manner."

" Thursday night?"

" Yes, it was Thursday night. All day Friday she was quiet and meek, though worried under the surface. I guessed she was planning something, and I was fearful she intended to run away with Alex. That night there was more trouble. I saw there was going to be trouble on top of trouble if she stayed."

" What was the Friday night trouble?"

" I'm ashamed to speak of it."

"It may be important." Casting back over the quarrel I had eavesdropped on, I guessed what Mrs. Norris was holding back: "She had a visitor, didn't she?"

"Perhaps it is best for me to tell you, if it will help Alex." She hesitated. "Yes, Lucy had a visitor Friday night. I heard him go in by her side entrance and I watched for him and saw him when he left. She entertained a man in her room, a white man. I didn't speak of it that night, mistrusting my anger so. I promised myself to sleep and pray on it, but I slept very little. Lucy slept late and then she went out for lunch when I was at the store. When she came back, she tempted my son. She kissed him in full sight of the public street. It was wanton and shameless. I said she had to go, and she went. My boy wanted to leave me and go with her. I had to tell him then about the man in her room."

"You shouldn't have."

"I know it. I confess it. It was rash and scornful of me. And it failed to turn him from her. The same afternoon she telephoned for him and he went to her call. I asked him where he was going. He wouldn't say. He took the car without asking for my permission. I knew then he was lost to me, whatever happened. He never before refused to do my bidding."

She bowed suddenly, sobbing into her hands, a black Rachel lamenting the wrecked hopes of all mothers for their sons, black and white and tan. The desk sergeant appeared in his doorway and watched her in silence for a while before he spoke:

"Is she all right?"

"She's worried about her son."

"She has a right to be," he said indifferently. "You Archer?"

I said I was.

"Lieutenant Brake will see you in his office now, if you're waiting."

I thanked him, and he retreated quickly.

Mrs. Norris's fit of grief had subsided as suddenly as it rose. She said: "I'm truly sorry."

"It's all right. You've got to remember that Alex can still be decent, even if he did disobey you. He's old enough to make decisions."

"I can accept that," she said. "But that he should leave me for a light, common woman, it was cruel and it was wrong. She led him straight into jail."

"You shouldn't have worked on his jealousy," I said.

"Have you lost your faith in him because of that?"

"No, but it gives him a motive. Jealousy is dangerous stuff to fiddle with, especially when you're not sure of your facts."

"There was no doubt what she was, with a white man with her late at night in her room."

"She had only one room."

"That's true."

"Where else could she have a visitor?"

"In my good front parlour," she said. "I gave her free use of the parlour."

"Maybe she wanted privacy."

"Why, I'd like to know." The question implied its own answer.

"There are plenty of reasons for a man to visit a woman. What did this man look like?"

"I saw him only a second, under the street light at the corner. He was an ordinary-looking man, middle size, middle age. At least he seemed slow in his movements. I didn't lay eyes on his face, not to *see* it."

"Did you notice his clothes?"

"I did. He wore a panama straw hat, and a light-coloured jacket. His trousers were darker in colour. He did not appear respectable to me."

"He probably isn't respectable, Mrs. Norris. But I can assure you he visited her for business purposes."

"Do you know him?"

"His name is Max Heiss. He's a private detective."

"Like you?"

"Not exactly." I rose to go.

She laid a detaining hand on my arm: "I said too much, Mr. Archer. You do still believe that Alex is innocent?"

I said: "Of course." But I was bothered by the motive she had provided.

Mrs. Norris sensed my doubt, and thanked me sadly, withdrawing her hand.

CHAPTER 19

Brake's office was a bare cubicle walled with the same green plaster as the corridor. Close up under the ceiling, heating-pipes like sections of iron viscera hung from metal supports. A single small window, high in the wall, flyspecked a square of sky.

Dr. Benning was sitting uncomfortably with his hat on his knees, in a straight chair against the wall. Brake, with his usual air of alert stolidity, was talking into the telephone on his desk:

"I'm busy or haven't you heard. Let the HP handle it. I haven't been a traffic cop for twenty years."

He hung up, and ran a hand like a harrow through his dust-coloured hair. Then he pretended to be noticing my presence in the doorway for the first time: "Oh. It's you. You decided to favour us with a visit. Come in and sit down. The doc here tells me you're taking a pretty active interest in this case."

I sat beside Benning, who smiled deprecatingly and opened his mouth to speak. Before he had a chance to, Brake went on:

"Since that's the situation, let's get a couple of things straight. I'm no one-man team. I like help, from private cops or citizens or anybody. I'm glad you sent the doc in to fill me in on the stiff, for instance."

"What do you think about suicide?"

Brake pawed my question away. "I'll come to that, I got a point to make first. If you're going to be in on this case, talking to my witnesses and messing around in general, I got to know where you stand and where your client stands."

"My original client ran out on me."

"So what's your interest? The doc here tells me you think we're trying to frame the Norris boy."

"I didn't put it so strongly," Benning said. "I also happen to agree with Mr. Archer, that the lad is probably innocent."

"Is that your opinion, Archer?"

"It is. I'd like to talk to Alex——"

115

"Sure you do. Did his mother hire you, by any chance? To cross me up, by any chance?"

"Having delusions of persecution, lieutenant?"

Hostility darkened his face for a slow instant, like a cloud-shadow crossing a hillside. "You admit it's your opinion that Norris ain't guilty. Before we do any talking, I want to know if you're looking for evidence to hang an opinion on, like a bloody lawyer. Or looking for evidence period."

"Evidence period. I was hired last night by a Miss Sylvia Treen. She's Mrs. Charles Singleton's companion."

Benning leaned forward at the sound of the second name: "Isn't she the woman whose son is missing?"

"That's right," Brake said. "We got a routine circular on him last week. Then we find this clipping about him in Champion's things. I been trying to figure how a missing high-lifer like Singleton fits in with a dinge cutting in the valley here. You got any ideas on the subject, doc?"

"I haven't really thought about it." He thought about it. "At first glance it does appear that the connections may be accidental. I know some of my patients carry all sorts of un-connected things around with them, clippings and what not. Women who are emotionally disturbed often identify them-selves with people in the newspapers."

Brake turned to me impatiently: "What about you, Archer? You got any opinions?"

I glanced at Benning's long conscientious face, wondering how much he knew about his wife. It wasn't my job to fill him in on her background.

"None that you couldn't shoot full of holes with a pea-shooter."

"I favour a .45 myself," Brake said. "What about your client? Miss Treen, is that her name?"

"Miss Treen gave me some of the details of Singleton's dis-appearance." I passed them on to Brake, or at least enough of them to hold his co-operation in Bella City without being embarrassed by it in Arroyo Beach. I left the blonde woman out of it entirely.

Bored with my expurgated version, Brake snapped his metal armbands and fiddled with the papers in his "In" basket. Benning listened with close and nervous attention.

When I finished, the doctor rose abruptly, turning his hat

in his hand: " If you'll excuse me, men, I should look in at the hospital before church."

" Appreciate your coming in," Brake said. " Give the stiff a once-over if you like, but I don't think you'll find any hesitation marks. I never seen a suicide with a cut throat that didn't have hesitation marks. Or one that was cut so deep."

" Is she in the hospital morgue?"

" Yeah, waiting for autopsy. Just go right in and tell the guard I sent you."

" I'm on the staff of the hospital," Benning said with his sour private smile. He jammed his hat on his head and moved sideways to the door, his long legs scissoring awkwardly.

" Just a minute, doctor." I stood up and handed him the thermometer Mrs. Norris had given me. " This belonged to Lucy Champion. I'd like to see what you make of it."

He took the thermometer out of its case and held it to the light. " A hundred and seven, that's quite a temperature."

" Did Lucy have a fever yesterday?"

" Not to my knowledge."

" Isn't it standard practice to take a patient's temperature?"

He answered after a pause: " Yes, I remember now, I took Miss Champion's. It was in the normal range. She wouldn't have lasted long with a temperature of 107."

" She didn't last long."

Brake came around his desk and took the thermometer from Benning's hand. " Where did you get this, Archer?"

" From Mrs. Norris. She found it in Lucy's room."

" She could of hotted it up with a lighted match. Eh, doc?"

Benning looked puzzled. " That wouldn't make much sense."

" It does to me. She might of been trying to prove that Champion was delirious, killed herself when she was out of her head."

" I don't think so," I said.

" Wait a minute. Hold it." Brake banged his desk with a gavel-heavy palm. " Didn't Champion come here around the first of the month?"

" Two weeks ago to-day."

" That's what I thought. You know what the heat was here in the valley weekend before last? A hundred and seven. It wasn't Champion who had the fever, it was this bloody town."

"Is that right, doctor?" I said. "Does a mercury thermometer hold a reading like that?"

"If it's not disturbed. It happens to mine all the time, I should have remembered."

"There goes your clue," Brake said.

"And here go I," Benning added with lame whimsy.

When the door had closed behind him, Brake leaned back in his chair and lit a cigar. "You think there's anything in the doc's idea that Champion had a phobia?"

"He seems to know his psychology."

"Sure he does. He told me he wanted to specialise in it at one time, only he couldn't afford another five years of training. If he tells me the girl was psycho, I'm willing to take his word for it. He knows what he's talking about. The trouble is I don't." He blew a smoke ring and speared it with an obscene middle finger. "I'm all for physical evidence myself."

"Have you got much in that line?"

"Enough. You keep it under you hat and not go running to the defence?"

I caught him up on the word. "Aren't you jumping ahead of yourself a little?"

"I learned in this job to look a long way ahead."

He lifted a black steel evidence case from the bottom drawer of his desk, and raised the lid. It contained the bolo knife with the carved black wooden handle. The bloodstains on the curved blade had dried dark brown.

"I've seen that."

"You don't know who it belongs to, though."

"Do you?"

"I showed this bolo to Mrs. Norris last night, before she knew how Champion got killed. She identified it right off. Her husband sent it to Alex from the Philippines, about seven years ago. It's been in the kid's possession ever since. He had it mounted on his bedroom wall, and she saw it every morning when she went in to make his bed, right up to yesterday morning."

"Did she say that?"

"She did. So maybe Champion had hot psychological flashes like the doc said. Maybe there's a tie-up with the Singleton case that we don't know about. I'm not going to lose any sleep over it. I got enough evidence here to arraign *and* convict." He shut the lid of the evidence box, relocked it and replaced it in the drawer.

I had been trying to decide all morning whether to give Brake everything I knew. I decided not to. The frayed ends of several lives, Singleton's and his blonde's, Lucy's, and Una's were braided into the case. The pattern I was picking out strand by strand was too complicated to be explained in the language of physical evidence. Brake's understanding was an evidence box holding the kind of facts that could be hammered through the skulls of a back-country jury. It wasn't a back-country case.

I said: "Have you got the boy's side of it yet? He isn't stupid. He must have known the bolo could be traced to him. Would he use it to to do a murder and leave it lying there?"

"He didn't leave it lying. He started back for it. You saw him coming back. He even jumped you."

"That's not important. He thought I was messing with Lucy, and he got mad. The boy was under a strain."

"Sure he was. That's part of my case. He's the emotional type. I'm not claiming premeditation, see. I claim it's a crime of passion, second degree. He got hot pants and busted in on her. Or maybe he lifted the key from her purse when they were out riding. Anyway she wasn't having any. He ran wild and cut her and took off. Then he remembered the knife and came back for it."

"Your story fits the external facts. It doesn't fit your suspect." But I was thinking that if and when Brake discovered the jealousy motive, he would have a steamroller case.

"You don't know these people the way I do. I deal with them every day." He unbuttoned his left shirt-cuff and bared a heavy freckled forearm. A white scar ran jaggedly from the wristbone to the elbow. "The buck that gave me this was trying for my throat."

"So that makes Norris a slasher."

"There's more to it than that," Brake was on the defensive in spite of his honourable scar. The violent world he fought for and against didn't suit him or anybody else, and he knew it.

"I think there is more to it. Too many people were interested in Lucy. I wouldn't settle for the first suspect we stumble across. It isn't that easy."

"You took me up wrong," he said. "What I mean, the boy acts guilty. I been looking at their faces for thirty years, listening to them talk." He didn't have to tell me. The thirty years were marked clearly on him, like fire-traces on an old tree. "All right, I'm still in the minor leagues. All right. This is my league. Champion is a minor league killing."

"Consciousness of guilt is pretty tricky stuff. It's psychological, for one thing."

"Psychological hell. It's a plain fact. We try to hold him for questioning, he runs out. We catch him and bring him back and he won't talk. I tried to talk to him. He's sullen. Tell him the world was flat, he wouldn't answer yes or no or maybe."

"How have you been treating him?"

"Never laid a finger on him, neither did anybody else." Brake pulled down his shirt-sleeve and rebuttoned the cuff. "We got out own brand of psychology."

"Where is he?"

"Out at the morgue."

"Isn't that a little unusual?"

"Not by me. I get a killing a month in this town, sometimes two. And I solve them, see? Most of them. The atmosphere at the morgue will loosen a killer up faster than anything I know."

"Psychology."

"That's what I said. Now, you playing on my team or you want a crying towel to cry into? If you're on my team, we'll go on out there and see if he's ready to talk."

CHAPTER 20

The door was numbered 01. The room behind the door was windowless, low-ceilinged, concrete-walled. When the door sucked shut behind us, we might have been in a sepulchre far down under the earth. Brake's heel struck dully on the composition floor. His shadow spread across me as he approached the only light in the room.

It was a cone-shaded bulb that hung low on an adjustable pulley over a rubber-wheeled stretcher. Lucy's sheeted body lay on the stretcher under its white glare. Her head was uncovered and turned towards Alex Norris. He was sitting in a chair on the far side of the stretcher, looking steadfastly into the dead woman's face. His right wrist was linked to hers by twin rings of blue steel. The pumps of a cooling system hummed and throbbed like time running down in the concrete walls. Behind the paired glass doors of the refrigerator, the other sheeted bodies might have been waiting for judgment, dreaming a preview of hell. It was as cold as hell.

The uniformed policeman who had been sitting opposite Alex got to his feet, raising his hand in a slovenly salute. "Morning, lieutenant."

"What's good about it? You running a wake in here, Schwartz?"

"You told me not to mark him. Like you said, I been letting nature take its course."

"Well? Did nature take its course?" Brake stood over Alex, wide and impermeable against the light. "You want to make a statement now?"

Moving to one side, I saw Alex look up slowly. His face had thinned. The passage of the night had pared flesh from his temples and cheekbones. His wide carved lips drew back from his teeth and closed again without making any sound.

"Or you want to sit all day and hold hands?"

"You heard what the man said," Schwartz growled. "He ain't fooling. You sit here until you talk. In an hour or so the deputy coroner's gonna cut her up, finish the job you done. Maybe you want a ringside seat?"

Alex paid no attention to Brake or his subordinate. His gaze, incredulous and devoted, returned to the dead woman's head. Under the pitiless glare her hair shone like coiled steel shavings.

"What's the matter with you, Norris? You got no human feelings?" Brake sounded almost querulous in the subterranean stillness, almost feeble, as if the boy by accepting everything had turned the tables on him.

I said "Brake." The word had more force behind it than I intended.

"What's eating you?" He turned with a bewildered frown.

The dead cigar in the corner of his mouth was like a black finger pulling one side of his face crooked. I retreated to the door, and he followed his own diminishing shadow towards me: " You want that crying towel?"

I said in a low voice, but not too low for Alex to overhear: " You're handling him wrong. He's a sensitive kid. You can't treat him like a punchy thug."

" Him sensitive?" Brake removed his cigar and spat on the floor. " He's got a hide like a rhinoceros."

" I don't think so. Give me a chance at him anyway. Uncouple him and let me talk to him alone."

" My wife and me were going up in the mountains to-day," Brake said irrelevantly. " We promised the kids a picnic."

He sneered at the dead cigar in his hand, dropped it suddenly, and ground it under his heel. " Schwartz! Turn him loose. Bring him over here."

The click of the handcuffs opening was tiny but very important, like the sound of a moral weight shifting on its fulcrum.

Schwartz pulled Alex to his feet. They crossed the room together, Alex round-shouldered and hanging back, Schwartz roughly urging him. " Taking him back to the cell, lieutenant?"

" Not yet." Brake addressed the boy: " Mr. Archer here is a friend of yours, Norris. He wants a little chinfest with you. Personally I think he's wasting all our time, but it's up to you. Will you talk to Mr. Archer?"

Alex looked from Brake to me. His smooth young face had the same expression I had seen on the ancient Indian face of the woman in the alley, beyond the reach of anything white men could do or say. He nodded wordlessly, and looked back at Lucy.

Brake and Schwartz went out. The door pulled shut. Alex started back across the room. He walked uncertainly with his legs spraddled like an old man's. The concrete floor sloped gently to a covered drain in the centre of the room. He staggered down the barely perceptible slope and laboured up the other side to the stretcher.

Standing over Lucy with his head bowed, he asked her: " Why did they do it?" in a dry hard voice.

I reached past him and pulled the sheet up over her head. I took him by the shoulders, turned him to face me. Part of his weight hung on me for a moment, until his muscles tightened. "Straighten up," I said.

He was as tall as I was, but his head was drooping on his undeveloped neck. I pushed my closed right hand under his chin. "Straighten up, Alex. Look at me."

He flinched away. I held him with my other hand on his shoulder. Suddenly he tensed and knocked my hand away from his chin.

"Steady boy."

"I'm not a horse," he cried. "Don't you talk to me like I was a horse. Keep your hands off of me."

"You're worse than a horse. You're a stubborn mule. Your girl is lying dead, and you won't open your mouth to tell me who did it to her."

"They think I did it."

"It's your own fault if they do. You shouldn't have run out. You're lucky you didn't get shot."

"Lucky." The word was as blank as a hiccup.

"Lucky not to be dead. That's the one situation nobody can reverse. You think you've got it tough now, and you have, but that's no reason for turning into a dummy. One of these days you're going to snap out of it and really care what happened to Lucy. Only it'll be too late for you to do anything about it. You've got to help now."

I let go of him. He stood shakily, pulling at his fleshy lower lip with a bitten forefinger. Then he said: "I tried to tell them things at first, this morning when they brought me in. But him and the deputy D.A., they only had the one thing on their minds, to make me say I did it. Why would I kill my own fiancée?" The question rose up hard from his working chest. His face was blind with the effort of speaking, the more terrible effort of speaking as a man. He couldn't sustain it: "I wish I was dead like Lucy."

"If you were, you couldn't help us."

"Nobody asked for any help from me. Who wants any help from me?"

"I do."

"You don't believe I killed her?"

"No."

He looked at me for maybe half a minute, his gaze shifting in heartbeat rhythm from one of my eyes to the other. "She

didn't do it to herself, did she? Mister? You don't think
Lucy—cut her own throat?" He whispered the question so
as not to embarrass the dead woman behind him.

"It isn't likely. The suggestion has been made. What made
you think of it?"

"No reason, except she was scared. She was awful scared
yesterday. That's why I loaned her the knife, when she left
our house. She asked me for something to protect herself
with. I had no gun or anything to give her." His voice
dropped apologetically. "I gave her the knife."

"The one she was killed with?"

"Yes. They showed it to me this morning. It was a little
bolo knife that my father sent me from the South Pacific."

"She was carrying the knife?"

"Yessir, in her purse. She had a big purse. She put it in
her purse when I gave it to her, before she went away from
our house. If they caught her, she said she would leave her
mark on them." A frown of grief knitted his eyebrows.

"Who was she afraid of?"

"Men following her. It started Thursday, when she came
back on the bus from Arroyo Beach. She said this man got
off the bus and trailed her home. I thought at first she was
spinning me a tale, trying to be mysterious. Then the next
day I saw him myself when she came home from lunch. He
was lurking around our street, and that night he came and
visited her right in our house. I asked her about him yesterday, and she said that he was a crooked detective. That he
was trying to make her do something against her will, but
she wouldn't do it."

"Did she mention his name?"

"She said his name was Desmond. Julian Desmond. The
next day another man was after her. I didn't see him. Lucy
saw him, though. And there was the trouble at our house
and she moved out."

I swallowed the bitter taste of guilt in my mouth. "Was
she planning to leave town?"

"She couldn't make up her mind before she left. She said
she'd phone me. Then when she did phone, she was at the
station. There was no train out for a couple of hours, and
men were there spying on her. She said I should come with
the car. I picked her up at the station and we got away from

them, on the old airport road. We parked behind the airport fence, and we talked. She was shivering scared. Right there and then we decided to get married. I thought if we stayed together, I could defend her." His voice sank deep into his chest, almost out of hearing. " I didn't do so good."

" None of us did."

" She wanted to leave town right away. First we had to go back to the Mountview Motel to get her bags."

" Did she have her motel-key?"

" She said she lost it."

" Didn't give it to you?"

" Why would she give it to me? I couldn't go in there with her. Even if I was light enough to pass, like her, I wouldn't do it. She went in there by herself. She never came out again. Somebody was waiting in there for her, and took the knife away from her and used it on her."

" Who was waiting?"

" Julian Desmond maybe. She wouldn't do what he wanted. Or the other one that was after her."

I was ashamed to tell him that I was the other one. His shoulders were slumped, and the flesh around his mouth hung almost stupidly. His moral strength was running out again. I placed Schwartz's chair for him and eased him into it:

" Sit down, Alex. You've covered the big points against you. There are a few little points left. Money is one of them. What were you intending to marry on?"

" I have some money of my own."

" How much?"

" Forty-five dollars. I made it picking tomatoes."

" Not much to get married on."

" I aimed to get a job. My back is strong." There was a sullen pride in his voice, but he wasn't meeting my eyes. " Lucy could work too. She worked as a nurse before."

" Where?"

" She didn't tell me where."

" She must have told you something."

" No sir. I never asked her."

" Did she have any money?"

" I didn't ask her. I wouldn't take money from a woman anyway."

"If you earned it, though," I said. "Didn't she say she'd cut you in if you got her safe out of town?"

"Cut me in?"

"On the reward," I said. "The Singleton reward."

His black gaze climbed slowly to the level of my eyes, and quickly dropped. He said to the floor: "Lucy didn't have to pay me money to marry her."

"Where were you going to get married? Where were you going to drive to yesterday?"

"Las Vegas or someplace. It didn't matter. Any place."

"Arroyo Beach?"

He didn't answer. I had pushed him too fast and too far. Looking down at the locked round impenetrable skull, I understood Brake's routine and desperate anger after thirty years of trying to fit human truth into the square-cut legal patterns handed down for his use by legislators and judges. And thinking of Brake's anger, I lost my own.

"Listen, Alex. We're going back to the beginning again. Lucy was murdered. We both want to find the murderer and see him punished. You have more reason than I have to want that. You claim you were in love with her."

"I was!" The drill had struck the nerve.

"That's one reason, then. You have another reason: Unless we find the real killer, you'll be spending years of your life in jail."

"I don't care what happens to me now."

"Think about Lucy. When you were waiting for her at the motel, somebody took that knife and cut her throat with it. Why?"

"I don't know why."

"What did Julian Desmond want her to do?"

"Be a witness for him," he answered slowly.

"A witness to what?"

"I don't know what."

"A murder," I said. "Was it a murder?"

"Maybe. I don't know."

"It was a murder, wasn't it? He wanted her to help him collect the reward. But she thought she could go it alone, and get the reward money for herself. Isn't that the reason she was killed?"

"I didn't think it out, mister."

"But you knew about the reward money? You knew she hoped to collect it."

"I never hoped to share in it," he said doggedly.

"She went to Arroyo Beach on Thursday to see his mother, and lost her nerve at the last minute. Isn't that the truth?"

"Yes, sir, I gathered that."

"She was going to try again yesterday."

"Maybe she was. I had nothing to do with any murder. Lucy didn't either."

"But she knew what happened to Singleton."

"She knew something."

"And you know something, too."

"She let on about it to me. I didn't ask her. I didn't want to have any part of it. She told it to me anyway."

"What did she tell you, Alex?"

"A man shot him. A crazy man shot him and he died. She told me that."

CHAPTER 21

Schwartz was alone in the corridor. I asked him where Brake was.

"In his car. He got a radio call."

I started for the ambulance entrance, and met Brake coming in.

"Norris do any talking?"

"Plenty."

"Confess?"

"Hardly. He's ready to make a statement."

"When I'm ready. I got more important things right now. I'm going on a barbecue picnic in the mountains." He smiled grimly, and called along the corridor to Schwartz: "Take Norris back to his cell. Get Pearce in the D.A.'s office, if he wants to make a statement. I'll be back as soon as I can."

"Barbecue picnic?" I said.

"Yeah." He pushed out through the white metal-sheathed door and let it swing back in my face. I followed him out to his car and got in the right side as he got in the left.

"I thought you'd be interested, Archer," The car leaped

forward under us, its tyres whistling in the gravel of the hospital parking lot. "It was a man that got himself barbecued. A man."

"Who is it?"

"Not identified yet. His car went over the side of Rancheria Canyon early this morning, and caught fire. When they found it they didn't even know there was a body in it at first. Couldn't get into it until they brought up a pump-truck from the ranger station. By that time the guy inside was nothing more than a clinker."

"Torch murder?"

"Hallman seems to think so. He's the CHP Captain. They had it tabbed as an accident until they thought to take a look at the gas tank. It's intact, and that means the gasoline for the fire came from somewhere else."

"What kind of car?"

"1948 Buick sedan. Registration destroyed. They're checking the licence and engine number for ownership."

The last few jerry-built bungalows of the suburbs dropped behind. The speedometer needle moved steadily clockwise past fifty, sixty, and seventy, and hesitated near eighty. Brake flipped the siren switch. The siren began to moan in a low register.

I said before it drowned me out: "The car isn't two-tone green, is it? Singleton's car was a 1948 Buick. Is this one two-tone green?"

Brake pulled his hat off, leaving a red crimped line across his forehead, and tossed it into the back seat. "You've got Singleton on the brain. They didn't tell me the colour. But where does he come in?"

"Norris said he was murdered," I shouted above the siren. Brake switched it off. "What does Norris know about it?"

"Lucy Champion told him Singleton was shot."

"Only she don't make a very good witness. Don't let him string you, man. He'd tell you anything to wiggle his black neck out of the noose it's in."

The speedometer needle pushed on past eighty. At the top of a slight rise, the car lifted under us and almost took flight. I felt as if the speed had lifted us out of the world, pulled Brake loose from his roots in Bella City's broken pavements.

" Don't you think it's about time you admitted you made a mistake?"

He looked at me narrow-eyed. The speeding car wavered slightly with his attention before he turned back to the road.
" When I got the weapon, his own knife?"

" She borrowed it from him for self-protection. She had it in her purse."

" Can he prove that?"

" He doesn't have to. You're the proof department."

" Hell, you're talking like a shyster lawyer. I hate those mealy-mouthed shysters that try to block the law."

" That's quite a mouthful."

" Chew on it."

The county blacktop we were on curved in to join a concrete highway running east and west across the valley. Brake went through a red sign and took the turn on squealing tyres.

" What do I do when they go around cutting each other with knives, setting fire to each other? Pat them on the back and tell them to go to it? I say stop them, put them away."

" Put the right one away, though. You can't solve these killings separately, hang Lucy's on Alex and this new one on somebody else."

" I can if they're not connected."

" I think they are connected."

" Show me proof."

" I'm not going up for the fresh air."

The road had begun to climb through dried clay cutbanks marked with yellow Slide Area warnings. Even with the gas-pedal floorboarded under Brake's toe, the speedometer needle stuck at seventy like the hand of a stopped clock. The folded blue slopes of the eastern range were framed in steep perspective by the windshield. They looked near enough to touch. A minute later, a mile nearer, they looked just as far away. I began to feel the altitude in my ears. As we rose into new perspectives, a few small white clouds burst out like ripe cotton behind the peaks. Away behind and down, Bella City stood in its fields like carelessly grouped chesspieces on a dusty board.

Five miles farther on, a thousand feet higher, we came to a semicircular gravel turnout on the left side of the highway. Several cars, a tow-truck and a red pump-truck were parked in the turnout. A group of men stood at its outer edge, looking down. Brake pulled up behind a new Ford with Highway Patrol markings. An officer in olive-drab whipcord detached himself from the group and came towards us:

" Hello, Brake. I told the boys to leave everything the way it was down there after they put out the fire. We even took pictures for you."

" You people are learning. I'd paste a gold star on your forehead if I had one. Like you to meet Lew Archer here, the thinker. Captain Hallman."

The captain gave me a puzzled look and a hard hand. We moved to the low log fence that rimmed the edge of the turnout. Below it the canyon-side slanted down to a gravel creek-bed overgrown with live oaks. From our height the September creek looked like a winding pebble-path dotted with occasional mud puddles. A toy automobile lying on its bank sent up tendrils of steam to vanish in the sun. It was a Buick, painted two shades of green.

A trail of broken bushes, some of them charred, showed where the Buick had left the road and rolled down into the gorge. Brake said to Hallman:

" Find anything on the road?"

" The tyreprints on the shoulder. It wasn't rolling fast, and that's what made me suspicious in the first place. No skid marks. Somebody set fire to it and just took off the emergency and let her roll." Hallman added in dead earnest: " Whoever poured that gasoline and ignited it out here has got more than murder against him. It was just good luck it didn't start a forest fire. No wind."

" When did it happen?"

" Must have been before light this morning. The headlights were turned on. I didn't get a report until after eight o'clock. Then when I figured it for murder, I left the guy for you the way we found him."

" You still don't know who he is?"

" Wait until you see him. Like looking for a brand on a cooked hamburger. We should get a fast answer on the engine number, though."

" It's Singleton's car," I said to Brake.

" You might be right at that." He sighed. " Well, if I got to go down there, I got to go down."

"Feeling your age?" Hallman said. "You've packed a buck out of deeper holes than this. I'd go with you, but I been down twice already. I left a couple of the boys on guard."

I could see them sitting on a boulder behind the smashed car. In the telescopic air it was almost possible to read the conversation off their moving lips.

Brake stepped over the log barrier and started down. I followed him, using the zigzag trail he improvised and braking my descent by holding on to the branches of stunted trees. We were both breathing hard when we reached the bottom. The two highway patrolmen led us along the creekbed to the wreck.

It rested on its right side. The hood and top and radiator grille looked as if a sledgehammer crew had been working on them. All four tyres had blown out. The left door was sprung.

"I'm afraid it isn't salvageable," one of the patrolmen said. "Even if there was any way of getting it out."

Brake turned on him savagely: "That's too bad. I was planning to take it for a spin."

He climbed onto the upper side of the car and wrenched the sprung door open as wide as it would go. I looked past him into the fire-gutted, water-soaked interior. Against the right front door, which rested on the ground, a human shape lay curled with its face hidden.

Brake lowered himself through the opening. Supporting himself with one hand on the steering column, he reached for the black shape with his other hand. Most of the clothes had burned away, but there was still a belt around the middle. When Brake took hold of the belt and heaved, it snapped in his hand. He passed it up to me. The blackened silver buckle bore the initials C A S.

CHAPTER 22

rang three times at long intervals. Sunday bells tolled antiphonally in the silences. Mrs. Benning finally came to the door. A bathrobe of rough brown wool was pulled high around her throat. Her face was marked by sleep, as if she had been battling dreams all morning.

"You again."

"Me again. Is the doctor in?"

"He's at church." She tried to shut the door.

My foot prevented her. "That's fine. I want to talk to you."

"I'm not even dressed."

"You can dress later. There's been another killing. Another friend of yours."

"Another?" Her hand covered her mouth, as if I had slapped her.

I pushed into the hallway with her and closed the door. Sealed off from the noon glare and the slow Sunday noises, we stood close and looked into each other's faces. It seemed to me that we shared a twilight understanding. She turned away, her long back swaying from the waist. I kept my hands from reaching out to hold her still.

She spoke to the mirror: "Who was killed?"

"I think you know."

"My husband?" In the mirror her face was masklike.

"That depends on who you're married to."

"Sam?" She whirled, in a dancer's movement, ending plumb. "I don't believe it."

"It occurred to me as a possibility that you were married to Charles Singleton."

She laughed unexpectedly. It wasn't pleasant laughter, and I was glad when it broke off.

"I've never heard of Singleton. Is that the name—Singleton? I've been married to Sam Benning for over eight years."

"That wouldn't prevent you from knowing Singleton, knowing him intimately. I have evidence that you did. He was murdered this morning."

She recoiled from me, breathing hard. Between breaths, she said: "How was he killed?"

"Somebody hit him with a hammer or some other heavy weapon. It made an inch-deep dent in his skull, but it didn't kill him. Then he was driven up into the mountains in his own car, soaked with gasoline, and set fire to. The car was pushed over a three-hundred-foot bank and left to burn, with Singleton inside it."

"How do you know it was his car?"

"It's a 1948 Buick two-door with a dark green body and a light green top."

"You're sure it was him inside?"

"He's been identified. Most of his clothes were burned off him, but his belt buckle has his initials engraved on it. Why don't you come down to the morgue and make a formal identification?"

"I told you I don't even know him."

"You're showing a lot of interest in a stranger."

"Naturally, when you come here and practically accuse me of murdering him. When did all this happen, anyway?"

"Before dawn this morning."

"I've been in bed all night and all morning. I took a couple of nembutals, and I'm still groggy. Why come to me?"

"Lucy Champion and Charles Singleton were both friends of yours. Weren't they, Bess?"

"They were not." She caught herself. "Why did you call me Bess? My name is Elizabeth."

"Horace Wilding calls you Bess."

"I never heard of him, either."

"He lives on the Sky Route near Singleton's studio. He says Singleton introduced him to you in 1943."

"Wilding is a liar, he always has been a liar." She caught her lower lip in white teeth and bit it hard.

"You said you didn't know him."

"You're doing the talking. Talk yourself to death."

"Is that what Lucy did?"

"I don't know what Lucy did."

"She was a friend of yours. She came here to this office to see you."

"Lucy Champion was my husband's patient," she said flatly. "I told you that last night."

"You were lying. This morning your husband lied to cover you. He went into an explanation of why he had no records on her, and then he had to explain what he was treating her for. Any real disease would show up in an autopsy, and he knew that. So he had to make her a hypochondriac, a patient whose sickness was caused by fear. There's no post-mortem test for a phobia."

"She was a hypochondriac. Sam told me she was."

"I never knew a hypochondriac who didn't take his

temperature once a day at least. Lucy hadn't touched her thermometer in two weeks."

"Wouldn't that sound good in court, though, against the word of a professional man and his wife?"

"It's good enough for me. And this is as close to court as you want to get."

"I see. You're judge and jury and everything else. Those are a lot of things for one little man to be."

"Don't stretch my patience. If I get tired of this, what happens to you? See what kind of a judge you draw down town. I'm giving you a chance to talk before I hand my evidence to the cops."

"Why?" Deliberately, she made me conscious of her body. She turned slightly and raised one hand to her head so that one of her breasts was lifted asymmetrically under the wool. The wide sleeve fell away from her round white forearm, and her white face dreamed upward. "Why go to all that trouble for poor little me? Poor little old incendiary me?"

"It's no trouble at all," I said.

She laid a cool hand on my cheek and let it trail onto my shoulder before she withdrew it. "Come out to the kitchen. I was making coffee. We can talk there."

I followed her, not certain which of us was doing what the other wanted him to do. The kitchen was large and poorly lit by a window over the sink. The sink was piled with dishes. I sat down at a chipped enamel table and watched her pour two cups of coffee from an automatic glass maker. When she had finished pouring, I pushed my full cup across the table to her and took hers.

"You don't trust me as far as you can see me, Mr. Man. What did you say your name was?"

"Archer. I'm the last of my branch of the Archer family. I'd hate to see it die out suddenly by poison."

"No children? Wife?"

"None of those things. Are you interested?"

"I could be." She pushed out her lips, which were fleshy and well-moulded. "It happens I'm already fixed up with a very satisfactory—husband."

"You find him satisfactory?"

Her eyes, which had not gone soft with the rest of her face, narrowed to cool blue slits. "Leave him out of it."

" Because you've been playing him for a sucker?"

" I said leave him out of it. Unless you want hot coffee in the face." She reached for her cup.

" What about hot gasoline?"

Her cup rattled on the table, slopping some of its contents over the rim. " Do I look like a murderer to you?"

" I've seen some fine-looking ones. You can't deny that you're a hard girl."

" I came out of a hard school," she said. " Do you know the mill section of Gary, Indiana?"

" I've passed through."

" I graduated from it with honours." A queer pride glinted in her smile. " That doesn't make me a criminal, though. I might have turned into one if Sam hadn't taken me out of it. I was on probation when he married me."

" What for?"

" Nothing much. I guess I was what you call a juvenile delinquent. I didn't feel like one. My old man was a hunkie, see, a real old-country hunkie. He had the grand old hunkie idea of tying one on and beating the womenfolk every Saturday night. I got tired of hiding under the bed, so I went out on my own. Out into the great world, ha. I waited table for a while and then I made a connection. My connection gave me a hat-check concession in one of the east side clubs. It wasn't much of a joint but by the time I was sixteen I was making more in tips than my old man ever made sweating it out in the mills. Only my luck went sour. There was gambling in the place I worked, somebody fluffed the protection, and I got picked up in a raid. I copped a plea and they put me on probation. The sourpuss judge set it up so I couldn't work in the clubs any more. That wasn't the worst of it. I had to go home and live with the family."

The dreams she had been battling with in her sleep were taking over her waking mind. I didn't say a word.

" Naturally I took the first chance I had to get out of that stinking flat with the arguments. The social workers were snooping on me, making me stay in at nights where the old man could get at me. Sam saved my life. He picked me up in a movie one day. I thought he was a wolf at first, but he was innocent. It was really funny to see a doctor so innocent. Sam was a Navy medico then, stationed at Great Lakes. He was the first man that wanted to marry me, and I took him up on it. He had his orders to California and he was leaving the next week. We came out here together."

"Did he know what he was getting?"

"He could see me," she said levelly. "I admit I didn't tell him I was jumping probation. But let's get one thing straight about Sam and me, before we drop the subject. I was the one that was doing him the favour. I always have been."

Looking at her and thinking of her husband, I believed her. "It's a pretty colourful background for a small-town doctor's wife. And I don't imagine you've told me the half of it."

"I don't imagine I have. More coffee?"

"More information. When did you and Benning come out here?"

"The spring of 1943. They gave him duty at Port Hueneme because it was near his home here. We rented a cottage in Arroyo Beach for six months. Then he was shipped out. The next two years he was at sea, medical officer on a big transport. I saw him a few times when it came into San Francisco."

"Who else were you seeing?"

"That's a hell of a question."

"A hell of an answer. Why did you leave Benning two years ago?"

"You've really been snooping, eh? I had my private reasons."

"You ran away with Singleton, didn't you?"

She had started to rise from the table, and froze for an instant, leaning on it, with her face averted. "Why don't you mind your own business?"

"Singleton was incinerated this morning. I've made it my business to find out who struck the match. It's a queer thing you're not interested."

"Is it?"

She poured herself another cup of coffee, with steady hands. Somewhere in the Chicago wilderness, or beating around the country in wartime and peacetime, she had gathered strength and learned balance. I looked at her firm white legs. She caught my look and returned it in a slow curve. To a window-peeper it could have seemed like a pleasant domestic scene on a Sunday morning. I almost wished it was.

I got up and looked out of the window. The backyard was overgrown with brown weeds and cluttered with the detritus of years. At its rear a small ramshackle barn sagged in the shade of a pepper tree.

She came up behind me. I felt her breath on my neck. Her body touched my back:

"You don't want to make trouble for me, Archer. I've had plenty of trouble. I could use a little peace in my old age."

I turned, softly ambushed by her hips. "How old are you?"

"Twenty-five. Church lasts a long time in these parts. He usually stays for Sunday school, too."

I took her head in my hands. Her breasts were full and strong between us. Her hands moved on my back. I was looking at the part-line that ran white through her dull black hair. Where the part divided it there were narrow vestiges of blondeness at the roots.

"I've never trusted blondes, Bess."

"I'm a natural brunette," she said thickly.

"You're a natural liar, anyway."

"Maybe I am," she said in a different voice. "I feel like nothing at all. This business has torn me in half, if you want the truth. I'm only trying to hold myself together and stay on this side of the walls."

"And keep your friends out of trouble."

"I have no friends."

"What about Una Durano?"

Her face went stupid, with ignorance or surprise.

"She bought you a hat last spring. I think you know her well."

Her mouth twisted in a grimace which threatened to turn to crying. She was silent.

"Who killed Singleton?"

She wagged her head from side to side. The short black hair fell over her face. Her face was grey and wretched. I felt ashamed of what I was doing to her, and went on doing it:

"You were with Singleton when he left Arroyo Beach.

Was it a snatch? Did you finger him for a mob, and the
have to kill him? Did you have to kill him because Luc
got big ideas? Did Lucy dream a five-grand dream and hav
to die before it came true?"

"You've got it all wrong. I didn't finger Charlie Singletor
I wouldn't do anything to hurt him, or Lucy either. She wa
a friend of mine, like you said."

"Go on."

"I can't," she said. "I'm not a squealer. I can't."

"Come down to the morgue and have a look at Charlie
You'll talk then."

"No." The word was like a retching in her insides. "La
off me a little. Promise to lay off me, and I'll tell you some
thing you don't know. Something important."

"How important?"

"Will you lay off me? I swear I'm absolutely clean."

"Let's have the one big fact."

Her head was down, but her slant blue gaze was on my
face. "It isn't Charlie Singleton in the morgue."

"Who is it?"

"I don't know."

"Where is Singleton?"

"I can't answer any more questions. You promised you'd
let me alone."

"How do you know it isn't Singleton?"

"That wasn't in the bargain," she said faintly. Behind
fluttering eyelids, her blue gaze jumped like an unsteady gas
flame.

"I'll put it as a hypothetical question. You know it
wasn't Singleton this morning, because he was killed two
weeks ago. He was shot and you saw it happen. Yes or no?"

She didn't answer at all. Instead she fell forward against
me, heavily. Her breath came fast as a small animal's. I had
to hold her up.

CHAPTER 23

A high-pitched voice flicked at my back: "Take your hands
off my wife."

Dr. Benning was standing just inside the kitchen door,

with one hand on the knob. A black leather Bible was under his arm and his hat was on his head. I moved between him and his wife. "I was waiting to see you, doctor."

"Filth," he cried. "Ordure. I come home from the House of God——" The trembling of his mouth ruined the sentence.

"Nothing happened," the woman said behind me.

Benning had the eyes of a pole-axed steer. His hand on the doorknob and his shoulder against the jamb were supporting his weight. His body vibrated grossly like a tuning fork: "You're lying to me, both of you. You had your hands on her. Carnal knowledge——" The words knotted in his throat and almost choked him. "Like dogs. Like two dogs in the kitchen of my home."

"That's enough." The woman stepped around me. "I've heard enough from you, after I told you nothing happened. What would you do if it had?"

He answered diconnectedly: "I gave you a helping hand. I lifted you out of the gutter. You owe everythng to me." The shock had sprung a booby-trap of clichés in his head.

"Good grey doctor Good-Samaritan! What would you do if anything had happened?"

He choked out: "A man can take so much from a woman. I have a gun in my desk——"

"So you'll shoot me down like the dog I am, eh?" She planted herself firmly on braced legs. Leaning towards him in a fishwife attitude, her body seemed to be revelling in its power, drawing terrific energy from his weakness.

"I'll kill myself," he cried on a high note.

A few tears squeezed from his eyes and ran down into the failure marks that dragged from the wings of his nose. He was the suicidal man who never quite nerved himself to suicide. I realised suddenly why his description of Lucy's fears had sounded so convincing. They were his own.

His wife said: "Go ahead. Don't let me stop you. Maybe that isn't such a bad idea." She moved in on him with her hands on her hips, flailing him with words.

He cringed away from her with one hand stretched towards her, asking for mercy. His hat caught on the end of a towel-rack and fell to the floor. He looked as if he were disintegrating.

"Don't, Bess," he said so rapidly that I could barely catch

the words. "I didn't mean it. I love you. You're all I've
got."

"Since when have you got me?"

He turned to the wall, stood with his face against the
rough plaster, his shoulders heaving. His Bible dropped to
the floor.

I took her by the elbows from behind: "Leave him
alone."

"Why should I?"

"I hate to see any man broken down by any woman."

"You can leave."

"You're the one that's leaving."

"Who do you think you're talking to?" She was still
showing fire, but it was warmed-over fire.

"Singleton's girl friend," I said into her ear. "Now get
out of here. I want to ask your husband a couple of
questions."

I pushed her through the doorway and closed it after her.
She didn't try to come back into the kitchen, but I could
feel her presence behind the door.

"Dr. Benning."

He was quieting down. After a while he turned to face
me. In spite of his baldness, his middle age, his beaten air,
he looked like a heartbroken adolescent in disguise.

"She's all I've got," he said. "Don't take her away from
me." He was slipping rung by rung into a hell of self-
abasement.

I lost patience: "I wouldn't take her as a gift. Now if you
can concentrate for a minute, where was your wife between
five and six yesterday afternoon?"

"Right here, with me." A grief-stricken hiccup made a
cæsura between the phrases.

"Where was she between twelve last night and eight this
morning?"

"In bed, of course."

"Will you swear to it, on the Bible?"

"Yes, I will." He picked up the Bible and held it with his
right hand flat on the cover: "I swear that my wife Elizabeth
Benning was in this house with me yesterday afternoon between five and six and all last night from midnight until
morning. Does that satisfy you?"

"Yes. Thank you." I wasn't satisfied, but this was the best I could hope for until I found more evidence.

"Is that all?" He sounded disappointed. I wondered if he was afraid to be left alone in the house with her.

"Not quite. You had a servant until yesterday. Florie?"

"Florida Guiterrez, yes. My wife discharged her for incompetence."

"Do you know her address?"

"Of course. She'd been in my employ for nearly a year. 137 East Hidalgo Street, Apartment F."

Mrs. Benning was standing outside the door. She flattened herself against the wall to let me go by. Neither of us spoke.

The long one-storied frame building stood at right angles to Hidalgo Street, facing a littered alley. Across the alley, a high wire fence surrounded a yard of piled lumber. I could smell cut white pine when I got out of my car.

At the head of the roofed gallery that ran along the building, a very fat Mexican was propped in a chair against the wall. He had on a bright-green rayon shirt that showed every fold of his stomach and chest.

I said: "Good morning."

"Good afternoon, I think."

He removed a brown cigarette from his mouth and shifted his weight, bringing his slippered feet onto the floor. There was a grease-spot on the wall where his iron-grey head had rested. The open door beside him was lettered amateurishly with a large red A.

"Good afternoon then. Where is Apartment F?"

"Second last door." He gestured with his cigarette towards the rear, where a few dark men and women in their Sunday clothes were sitting in the shadow of the gallery, watching the lumberyard. "Florida ain't here, if it's her you're looking for."

"Florida Guterrez?"

"Gutierrez." He repronounced the name for me, with the accent on the second syllable. "She went away."

"Where to?"

"How do I know where to? She told me she was going to live with her sister in Salinas." His brown eyes were gently cynical.

"When did she go?"

"Last night, about ten o'clock. She was five weeks behind in her rent. She came in with a handful of bills and said: 'how much do I owe? I am moving out, to live with my sister in Salinas.' I saw the main waiting outside in the big automobile and I said: 'Florida, your sister has changed in appearance.' She said: 'He is my brother-in-law.' And I said: 'You're a lucky young woman, Florida. Ready to join the starvation army this morning, and to-night driving off with your brother-in-law in a Buick automobile'." He set the cigarette between his smiling white teeth and blew a plume of smoke.

"Did you say Buick?"

"A fine big Buick," he said, "with holes in the side. And a foolish girl riding away in it, with holes in her head. What could I do?" He spread his hands in cheerful resignation. "She is not a member of the Martinez family. *Gracias á Dios,*" he added under his breath.

"Did you notice the colour of the car?"

"I couldn't tell for sure. It was dark night. Blue or green, I would say."

"And the man?"

He studied me with noncommittal eyes. "Florida is in trouble? You are from the police?"

I showed him my photostat and listened to him spell it out. "I thought it was trouble," he said quietly.

"Was the man young and good-looking?"

"He was a man of middle age. He didn't leave the automobile, even when Florida carried out her bags. No manners! I didn't like his looks."

"Can you describe him?"

"I didn't see him too well."

"I have a man in mind," I said. "Short brown hair, fattish, shifty-looking, wino eyes, panama hat, light tan jacket. Calls himself Julian Desmond."

He snapped his fingers. "That is the man. Florida called him Julian. Is he truly her brother-in-law?"

"No. You were right about him. I guess you know this town pretty well, Mr. Martinez."

The suggestion seemed to exhilarate him. "For sixty-three years! My father was born here."

"Here's a question you should be able to answer. If you were Julian, and you wanted to take Florida to a hotel for the night, which one would you go to?"

"Any of them in the lower town, I guess."

"Name the most likely ones, will you?" I took out my notebook.

He regarded it unhappily, disturbed by the notion of having anything he said committed to writing. "This trouble, is it serious?"

"Not for her. She's needed as a witness."

"A witness? Is that all? What kind of a witness?"

"The Buick she left in was involved in an accident this morning. I'm trying to identify the driver."

The old man sighed with relief. "I will be glad to help."

When I left him, I had the addresses of several hotels: the Rancheria, the Bella, the Oklahoma, the California, the Great West, the Pacific, and the Riviera. I was lucky on my third try which happened to be the Great West.

CHAPTER 24

It was an old railroad hotel on Main Street between the tracks and the highway. Its narrow-windowed brick face was lugubrious, as if the big trucks going by for years had broken its steam-age spirit. There were battered brass spittoons on the floor of the lobby, old Union Pacific photogravures on the walls. Four men were playing contract at a card table near the front window. They had the still faces and satisfied hands of veteran railroaders growing old on schedule.

The clerk was a skinny old man in a green eyeshade and a black alpaca coat. Yes, Mr. and Mrs. Desmond were registered: 310, on the third floor. No phone, I could just go up. The bell-hop was off on Sundays, he added whiningly.

I started for the elevator. The clerk called me back: "Wait a minute, young fellow, since you're going up anyways. This wire came in for Mr. Desmond this morning. I didn't like to disturb him." The eyeshade suffused his face with a green cadaverous flush.

I took the sealed yellow envelope. "I'll give it to Mr. Desmond."

"The elevator isn't working," he whined. "You'll have to use the stairs."

The second floor was hotter than the first. The third floor was stifling. At the end of a windowless corridor lit by twenty-watt bulbs I found the door I was looking for. A cardboard DO NOT DISTURB sign dangled from the knob.

I knocked. Bedsprings groaned. A woman called out drowsily: "Who is it? Julian?"

I said: "Florie?"

Unsteady footsteps approached the door. She fumbled at the lock. "Just a minute. I'm blind this morning."

I slipped the telegram into the breast pocket of my jacket. The door opened inward and I went in with it. Florie looked at me dumbly for five or six long seconds. Her black hair was matted and frizzled. Her eyes hung heavy and dark under heavy lids. In the frightened attitude her body had assumed, her hips and breasts seemed strangely irrelevant. The rouge-stained mouth in her sallow face was like a wilted red rose stuck in plasticine.

She made an erratic rush for the bed, and covered herself with a sheet. Her mouth fell open. I could see her pale lower gums. She brought it closed with an effort. "What do you want?"

"Not you, Florie. Don't be scared."

The air in the room was stale, spiked with cheap alcohol and perfume. A half-empty half-gallon jug of muscatel stood on the floor by her bed. Her clothes were scattered on the floor and chair and dresser. I guessed she had taken them off in a staggering fury before she passed out.

"Who are you? Did Julian send you?"

"I was hired by the hotel association to check on false registration." I didn't mention that my work in that field had ended ten years ago.

She chattered over the taut edge of the sheet: "I didn't register. He did. It was all his fault. Besides, we didn't do nothing. He brought me up here last night and parked me with a jar of muscadoodle. Then he went away and I haven't seen him since. I waited up for him half the night. He never did come back. So how do you have anything on me?"

"I'll make a bargain with you. No charges if you co-operate."

Suspicion darkened her face. "How do you mean, co-operate?" Her body wriggled uneasily under the sheet.

"Just answer my questions. Desmond's the one I want. It looks as if he ran out on you."

"What time is it?"

"One-thirty."

"Sunday afternoon?"

"Uh-huh."

"He did run out! He promised to take me on a trip." She sat up on the bed, holding the sheet across her excessive bosom.

"How did you meet him?"

"I didn't meet him. He come to the office one night last week, Thursday night it was. I was just finishing up my cleaning. The doctor was out already, over at the library or someplace, and I was all alone in the office."

"Where was Mrs. Benning?"

"She was upstairs, I guess. Yeah, she was upstairs with that coloured girl friend of hers."

"Lucy Champion?"

"That's the one. Some people have funny friends. This Lucy woman came to visit her and they went upstairs to talk. Julian Desmond said it was me he wanted to see. He fed me a line how he was recruiting nurse's aides for Hawaii at four hundred dollars a month! I was a sucker, I guess. I let him pump me about who I worked for and he took me out that night and got me plastered and asked me a bunch of questions about Mrs. Benning and that Lucy. I told him I didn't know Lucy from a hole in the ground, or Mrs. Benning either for that matter. He wanted to know when she came back to her husband and if her hair was dyed and if they were really married, stuff like that."

"What did you tell him?"

"I told him how she came back over the weekend, two weeks ago it was. When I walked in on Monday morning there she was. Doctor says: 'Meet my wife. She's been in a sanitarium.' She didn't look like san stuff to me——" Florie broke off suddenly. Her mouth clamped shut. "That was all I said. I caught on what he was up to, and you don't catch me playing blackmailers' games."

"I can see that. What else was there to tell?"

"Nothing else, not a thing. I don't know nothing about Mrs. Benning. She's a mystery woman to me."

I changed the direction of my approach: "Why did she fire you last night?"

"She didn't fire me."

"Why did you leave?"

"I didn't want to work for her any more."

"You worked for her yesterday, though."

"Yeah, sure, that was before she fired—I mean I left."

"Were you in the house all Saturday afternoon?"

"I was until six. I get off at six unless there's extra cleaning. I mean I did."

"Was Mrs. Benning there all afternoon?"

"Most of it. She went out in the late afternoon, said she was going to shop for Sunday."

"What time did she go out?"

"Around five, a little before five."

"What time did she come back?"

"I left before she came back."

"And the doctor?"

"He was there, far as I know."

"He didn't go out with her?"

"No, he said he was going to take a siesta."

"When did you see her after that?"

"I didn't."

"You saw her in Tom's Café around eight."

"Yeah. Yeah, I forgot about that." Florie was getting rattled.

"Did she give you money?"

She hesitated. "No." But she had to turn and look at the red plastic purse on the dresser.

"Why did she give you money?"

"She didn't."

"How much money?"

"Just my back pay," she stammered. "They owed me back pay."

"How much back pay?"

"Three hundred dollars."

"That's a lot of back pay. Isn't it?"

She lifted her heavy gaze to the ceiling and brought it

down again to the red purse on the dresser. She watched the purse intently, as if it was alive and struggling to take flight. " It was a bonus." She had found a word. " She gave me a bonus."

" What for? She didn't like you."

" *You* don't like me anyway," she said in a childish voice. " I didn't do anything bad. I don't see how you have to jump on me."

" I like you fine," I lied. " Only it happens I'm trying to solve some murders. You're an important witness."

" Me?"

" You. What did she pay you to keep quiet about?"

" If I'm a witness, do I have to give the money back? The bonus?"

" Not if you keep your mouth shut about it."

" You won't tell?"

" I couldn't be bothered. What did she buy from you, Florie?"

I waited, listening to her breathing.

" It was the blood," she said. " I found some dried drops of blood on the floor of the examination room. I cleaned it up."

" When?"

" Monday two weeks ago, the first day I saw Mrs. Benning. I asked the doctor about the blood and he said he had an emergency over the weekend—a tourist that cut his finger. I didn't think of it again until Mrs. Benning brought it up last night."

" Like the woman who urged her children not to put peas in their noses."

" Who was she?" Florie asked almost brightly.

" It's a story. The point is that the children put peas in their noses as soon as she turned her back. I'll bet a nickel you told Desmond about the blood the minute Mrs. Benning turned hers."

" I did not," she said, with that peculiar whining intonation which means guilty as charged but I can't help it if people are always leading me astray.

She introduced a diversion:

" Anyway, his name isn't Desmond. It's Heist or something like that. I caught a glimpse of his driver's licence."

" When?"

" Last night in the car."

" The Buick?"

" Yeah. Personally I think he stole it. I had nothing to do
with it. He already had it when he came to move me out of
the apartment. He tried to tell me he *found* it, can you
imagine. He said it was worth five thousand, probably more.
I told him that was a lot of money for a second-hand Buick,
but he just laughed."

"Was it a green 1948 two-door sedan?"

" I don't know the years. It was a two-door Buick, and
that was the colour. He stole it, didn't he?"

" I think he found it all right. Did he say where?"

" No. It must have been in town, though. He had no car
at suppertime and then at ten o'clock when he picked me up
at the apartment, he was driving this Buick. Where would a
guy find a Buick?"

" It's a good question. Put on your clothes, Florie. I'll
look away."

" You're not going to arrest me? I didn't do nothing
wrong—anything wrong."

" I want you to try to identify somebody, that's all."

" Who?"

" That's another good question."

I went to the window and tried to open it. I could hardly
breathe the hot foul air sealed in the little room. The window
rose four inches and stuck for ever. It faced north towards
the City Hall and the Mission Hotel. In the sun-stopped
streets a few pedestrians trudged, a few cars crawled and
snored. Behind me I heard the twang of a snagged comb,
Florie's quiet swearing, the pull and snap of a girdle, the
slither of silk stockings, heels on the floor, water running in
the sink.

At the rear of a bus depot below the window, a dusty blue
bus was loading passengers: a pregnant Mexican woman
herding half-naked brown children, a fieldworker in overalls
who might have been the father of the children, an old man
with a cane casting a tripod shadow on the asphalt, two
young soldiers looking bored with any possible journey
through any valley under any sky. The line moved forward
slowly like a coloured snake drunk with sun.

"Ready," Florie said.

She had on a bright red jacket over the batiste blouse. Her hair was combed back from her face, which looked harder under a white and red cosmetic mask. She peered at me anxiously, clutching the red plastic purse.

"Where are we going?"

"To the hospital."

"Is he in the hospital?"

"We'll see."

I carried her cardboard suitcase down to the lobby. Heiss had paid for the room in advance. The aged clerk didn't ask me about the telegram. The contract players followed our progress across the lobby to the street with knowing looks.

In my car, Florie relaxed into hangover somnolence. I drove across town to the county hospital. Obscured by the dust and insect splashes on the windshield, wavering in the heat, the streets and buildings were like an image of a city refracted through Florie's mind. The asphalt was soft as flesh under the wheels.

It was cold enough in the morgue.

CHAPTER 25

She came out shivering, holding the red purse against her breast like an external heart that wouldn't hold still. I supported her elbow. At the ambulance door she pulled away from me and went out by herself to the car. She stumbled on high heels across the gravel, dazed by too much light.

When I got in behind the wheel she looked at me with horror as if my face had been scorched, and slid far over against the opposite door. Her eyes were like large marbles made of black glass.

I took the yellow Western Union envelope out of my inside pocket: Mr. Julian Desmond, c/o Great West Hotel, Bella City, California. As long as Heiss was alive, it was a crime to open it. Since he was dead, it was legitimate evidence.

It contained a night letter sent from Detroit by someone who signed himself "Van":

ONCEOVER LIGHTLY DURANOS AIRMAIL REPORT FOLLOWS. LEO ARRESTED FELONIOUS ASSAULT 1925 AGE TWENTY SERVED SIX ARRESTED 1927 KIDNAPPING NO CASE ALLEGED MEMBER OR PROTECTEE PURPLE GANG ARRESTED 1930 SUSPICION MURDER NOLLE PROSSED NO WITNESSES 1932 MURDER AIRTIGHT ALIBI ACQUITTED. BREAKUP PURPLE GANG LEO TO CHICAGO RAN GOON SQUAD THREE-FOUR YEARS THEN SYNDICATE TIEUP LEGIT FRONT HATCHECK CONCESSIONS. ARRESTED CONTRIBUTING DELINQUENCY MINOR EARLY 1942 COMMITTED STATE HOSPITAL DIAGNOSIS UNKNOWN RELEASED OCTOBER 1942 GUARDIANSHIP SISTER UNA PUBLIC STENOGRAPHER AND BOOKKEEPER. ENFORCER FOR NUMBERS RING ATTEMPTING TAKEOVER ROUGE AND WILLOW RUN PLANTS BROKEN UP 1943. 1944 LEO AND UNA ORGANISED DETROIT-BASED NUMBERS RING STILL GOING GOOD PROTECTION ESTIMATED WEEKLY NET TWO TO THREE GEES. LEO AND UNA NOT SEEN MICHIGAN SINCE JANUARY YPSILANTI HOUSE CLOSED BANKS BEING RUN BY WILLIAM GARIBALDI ALIAS GARBOLD OLDTIME PURPLE ALUMNUS. NO RECORD ELIZABETH BENNING LEO LIVING WITH BESS WIONOWSKI PRIOR DEPARTURE MICHIGAN. DO I DIG DEEEPER.

"I should go some place and lie down," Florie said in a small voice. "You didn't tell me he was dead. You didn't tell me they blowtorched him. A shock like that is enough to kill a girl."

I put the telegram away. "I'm sorry. I didn't know who it was until you identified him. What makes you so positive?"

"I worked for a dentist one time. I notice teeth. Julian had bad teeth. I could tell it was him by the fillings." She covered her glassy black eyes with her hand. "Won't you take me where I can lie down?"

"First the police."

Brake was sitting at his desk with a deeply bitten sandwich in his hand. The bite he had taken was pouched in his cheek, rolling rhythmically with his chewing. He said around it:

"The wife put up enough sandwiches to feed an army before I remembered to call off the picnic. I told her to bring some down here, save me lunch money. Lunch money mounts up."

" Even with all this overtime? "

" I'm saving the overtime to buy a yacht." Brake knew I knew that no cop ever was paid for overtime.

" Miss Gutierrez here has just made a positive identification on your torch victim." I turned to her. " This is Lieutenant Brake."

Florie, who had been hanging back in the doorway, took a timid step forward. " Pleased to meet you. Mr. Archer convinced me to do my duty."

" Good for him." Brake popped the remnant of his sandwich into his mouth. Whatever was about to happen or be said, he would have finished his sandwich. " Does she know Singleton? "

" No. It isn't Singleton."

" The hell it isn't. The licence was issued to Singleton, and the engine-number checks." He tapped a yellow telegram flimsy on top of the pile in his " In " basket.

" It's Singleton's car but not his body in it. The body belongs to Maxfield Heiss. He was a Los Angeles detective. Florie knew him well."

" I didn't know him so well. He made advances to me, trying to pump me about my bosses."

" Come inside, Miss Gutierrez, and shut the door behind you. Now tell me, who are your bosses? "

" Dr. and Mrs. Benning," I said.

" Let her do her own talking. What was he trying to find out about them, Miss Gutierrez? "

" When Mrs. Benning came back and if she dyed her hair and all like that."

" Anything about murder? "

" No sir. Julian didn't say nothing about a murder."

" Julian who? "

" Heiss was using an alias," I said. " We should get over to Benning's."

I turned to the door. There was a cork bulletin board beside it, with a number of frayed Wanted circulars thumb-tacked to it. I wondered how Mrs. Benning would look in that crude black-and-white.

Brake said: " Can you swear to the identification, Miss Gutierrez? "

" I guess, if you insist."

"What do you mean, you guess?"

"I never like to swear, it ain't ladylike."

Brake snorted and stood up and left me standing in the room with Florie. He returned with a uniformed police-woman, white-haired and granite-eyed:

"Mrs. Simpson will stay here with you, Miss Gutierrez, until I get back. You're not in custody, understand."

Brake and I climbed the ramp to the parking lot.

"We'll take my car. There's something I want you to read." I handed him the night letter from Detroit.

"I hope it makes more sense than that little dame. She's a moron."

"She can see and remember."

He grunted as he climbed into the car. "What did she see?"

"Blood. Dried blood on the floor of Benning's examination room. It was her job to clean it."

"When? Yesterday?"

"Two weeks ago. The Monday after the weekend that Singleton was shot."

"You definitely think he was shot?"

"Read the telegram. See what it means to you." I started the car, and turned on a crosstown street in the direction of Benning's house.

Brake looked up from the yellow paper. "It don't mean a great deal to me. It's mostly a rap sheet on a mobster I never heard of. Who is this Durano?"

"A Michigan numbers racketeer. He's in California now. His sister Una is the one who hired me in the first place."

"Why?"

"I think her brother shot Singleton. Lucy was a witness, and Una Durano was trying to find her and silence her.'"

"Where is he now?"

"I wouldn't know." But the blasted man with the toy gun was vivid behind my eyes.

"Funny you didn't pass on this stuff to me."

I said, a little disingenuously: "I couldn't tell you what I didn't know. I just got hold of the telegram, at the hotel where Heiss was staying."

"You're building a pretty big story out of a little bit of a telegram. And it ain't even evidence, unless you have your mits on the guy that sent it. Who's this Van?"

"Sounds like an undercover man for a Detroit agency."

"Agency work costs money. Was Heiss a bigtimer?"

"Hardly, but he kept hoping. He thought he saw big money in this case, starting with the Singleton reward."

"What was he doing with Singleton's car?"

"He told Florie he found it. It was evidence, to help him collect the reward. Before that he tried to get Lucy to be a witness for him. But the Singleton reward was only a beginning for him. He had bigger money on his mind."

"Blackmail? From Durano?"

"So you think those mobsters torched him."

"That's possible, too."

We had reached Benning's block. I parked in front of the barber shop beside his house. Brake made no move to get out of the car. "Do you know any of these things that you say are possible?"

"I don't know anything for sure. It's a peculiarity of this case. We've got damn little physical evidence and damn few honest witnesses. There's no single detail strong enough to hang your hat on. But I have got a *Gestalt* on the whole picture."

"A what?"

"Call it a hunch, about how the case hangs together. There are a lot of people in it, so it can't be simple. Even with two people, actions are never simple."

"Cut the philosophy. Come down to cases again. If these are gang killings, what are we doing here? Mrs. Benning doesn't come into it at all."

"Mrs. Benning is the central figure in the picture," I said. "She had three men on the string: Durano, Singleton, Benning. Durano shot Singleton over her. She couldn't face an investigation so she skipped out and came back to Benning for help."

"What did she do with Singleton?"

"We better ask her."

CHAPTER 26

Blinded and grey-sided, Benning's house seemed to exhale its own shabby twilight. The doctor was pale and blinking like a twilight creature when he came to the door:

"Good afternoon, lieutenant."

He looked at me without speaking. Brake flashed his buzzer to indicate this wasn't a social call. Benning backed up abruptly, reaching for his hat on the hall rack and setting it on his head.

"You going somewhere, doctor?"

"Why no, I wasn't. I often wear a hat in the house." He gave Brake a sheepish smile.

The hallway was dim and chilly. An odour of rotting wood, which I hadn't noticed before, underlay the other odours. Men with a sense of failure like Benning had a knack of choosing the right environment for failure, or creating it around them. I listened for the sound of the woman in the house. There was no sound except the drip of a tap somewhere like a slow internal hæmorrhage.

Brake said in formal tones: " I want to see the lady known as Mrs. Benning."

"Do you mean my wife?"

"I do."

"Then why not say so?" Benning spoke with acerbity. He was pulling himself together under the hat.

"Is she here?"

"Not at the moment, no." Biting at the inside of his long upper lip, the doctor resembled a worried camel chewing a bitter cud. "Before I answer any question, no matter how charmingly phrased, I'd like to know if you're here in an official capacity. Or do you simply derive a puerile pleasure from displaying your badge?"

Brake turned dull red. "There's no pleasure in it, doctor. I got two murders on the book, another one floating."

Benning swallowed several times, his adam's-apple bobbing like a distorted yo-yo in his throat. "You're not seriously suggesting that there's any connection." The words fell into a silence that seemed to disturb him. He filled it by adding: "Between my wife and these murders?"

"I'm asking for your co-operation, doctor. You gave it to me this morning. I can't keep down crime without the co-operation of the citizenry."

The two men faced each other in silence for a minute. Brake's silence was heavy, persistent, thick, like a tree-stump's. Benning's was tense and alert. He might have been listening to a sound too high for our ears to catch.

He cleared his throat. The distorted yo-yo bobbed. "Mrs. Benning has gone to San Francisco for a few days. It's been hard for her to readjust to Bella City and—marriage. After the unpleasantness of the last two days—well, we both thought she needed a rest. She left town about an hour ago."

I said: "Where is she going to stay in San Francisco?"

"I'm sorry, I don't know the address. Bess makes a point of enjoying the utmost personal freedom, and I make a point of allowing it." His pale eyes were watching me, daring me to mention our last meeting.

"When is she coming back?"

"I assume in a week or so. It will depend partly on the friends she's staying with."

"What friends?"

"I can't help you there, either. I don't really know my wife's friends. We've been living apart for the past two years."

He was choosing his words very carefully, as if the slightest mishandling might jar out of them a blast of meaning that would destroy him and his house. It struck me that Bess had left him and wasn't coming back. This was the fact he was concealing from me and Brake, and possibly from himself.

"Why did she come back after those two years?"

"I believe she realised that she had made a mistake in leaving me. Not that you have any licence to ask me."

"The doctor's right," Brake said. "Absolutely right. How's she travelling, by the way?"

"By car. She took my car." He added stiffly: "She had my permission to take it."

"Let's see, that's a Chevvie sedan, isn't it, doctor?"

"A 1946 blue Chevrolet sedan."

" And the licence?"

" 5T1381."

Brake made a note of it. " What route is she taking?"

"I have no idea. Surely you're not proposing to have Mrs. Benning picked up on the highway?"

" First I want to make sure she isn't here."

" You think I've been lying to you?"

" Not a bit. I'm just doing my job. May I have your permission to look through the house?"

" Do you have a search warrant?"

"I do not. I took it for granted you had nothing to hide." Benning managed to smile. " Of course. I was merely curious." He swung his arm in a quarter circle that ended with his knuckles thumping the wall. " Make free with my demesne, gentlemen."

Brake started up the stairs that rose at the end of the hallway. I went through the outer rooms with Benning, and paused in the examination room. He spoke quietly from the doorway:

"I know my enemies, Mr. Archer, and my wife's enemies. I understand your type, the appetitive man. What you can't have you seek to destroy." His voice was rising like an ill wind, carrying echoes of our previous meeting.

" Why did your wife come back to you?" I said.

" She loved me."

" Then why did she leave you again to-day?"

" She was afraid."

" Afraid of the Duranos? The police?"

" She was afraid," he repeated.

I looked around the shabby oilcloth walls and the scrubbed linoleum floor. The faucet was still leaking drop by drop into the sink.

" Is this the room where Florie found the blood, doctor?"

" Blood?" he said. " Blood?"

" The day after your wife came back there were spots of blood on the floor. According to Florie."

" Oh, yes. I had an emergency patient that Sunday. Cut finger."

"I suggest that your emergency patient came here late Saturday night. Mrs. Benning brought him to you for treatment. He had a slug in his body instead of a cut finger. His name was Singleton. What happened to him, doctor, did he die on your hands?"

"I had no such patient."

"I suggest that you performed an unreported operation on a dying man, and couldn't save him."

"Have you made that suggestion to Brake?"

"No. I'm not your enemy. I'm not interested in breaches of medical ethics. I'm after a murderer. But I haven't even been able to prove that Singleton was murdered. Was he?"

Our glances met and locked, until Benning disengaged his. "It's not myself I'm concerned about," he said falteringly.

"Your wife? Did she do the shooting?"

He failed to meet my eyes again. Both of us were listening to Brake's unaccompanied footsteps coming down the stairs and through the house.

Brake saw the tension between us as soon as he entered the room:

"What goes on?"

"Very little," I said.

Benning looked at me with gratitude, and drew himself up visibly. "Did you look under all the beds, lieutenant?"

"I did. No women's clothes in the closets, either. You sure your wife isn't planning to stay away?"

"She hasn't many clothes."

Brake crossed the room to the locked chest which I had broken into the night before. He shook the knob with the violence of frustration. "You check this room in here, Archer?"

"It's only a closet," Benning said. "There's nothing inside but my skeleton."

"Your what?"

"It's an anatomical specimen."

"Open up."

Benning went to the closet door with a key-ring jingling in his hand. As he unlocked it, he gave us a bright bitter smile over his shoulder. "You don't seriously think I've locked my wife in here?"

He swung the door open. The sparse head grinned steadfastly, superciliously, from its refuge beyond time. Benning stood back, watching us for signs of shock or surprise. He seemed disappointed when we showed none.

" Mr. Macabre," I said. " Where did he come from?"

" I got him from a medical-supply house." He pointed out a rectangular brass tag attached to one of the ribs: Sunset Hospital Equipment Co., Ltd. I had missed it the night before.

" Not many doctors have these any more, do they?"

" I keep him for a special reason. I worked my way through medical school, and I never received an adequate grounding in anatomy. I've been studying it on my own, with the help of this old boy." He poked the varnished cage of ribs with his finger, and set the whole thing swaying. " Poor old boy. I've often wondered who or what he was. A convicted felon, or a pauper who died in a charity ward? *Memento mori.*"

Brake had been fidgeting. " Let's go," he said suddenly. " I've got work to do."

" There are a couple of other points I want to take up with Dr. Benning."

" Make it fast, then." Brake seemed to have broken through the thin ice, and contracted a case of cold feet. He moved out through the waiting-room as if to detach his authority from me.

The doctor followed Brake, emphasising the realignment that was taking place. It had been two against him. Now it was two against me.

" I don't really mind, lieutenant. I'd like to satisfy Mr. Archer completely and have it over with. If Mr. Archer can be satisfied." Benning turned to face me in the waiting-room like an actor who has been groping for his part and finally begun to live it.

" There's a conflict of testimony," I said. " Florie Gutierrez says that your wife and Lucy Champion were friends. You claim they weren't. Florie says your wife was out of the house when Lucy was killed yesterday afternoon. You claim she was here with you."

" I can't pretend to be objective in this matter, with my wife's reputation at stake. I'll tell you my own experience of Florida Gutierrez. She's an unmitigated liar. And when my wife discharged her last night——"

" Why did your wife discharge her?"

" Incompetence. Dishonesty and incompetence. The

Guiterrez woman threatened to get even, as she put it. I knew she'd go to almost any lengths to damage us. But the lengths she's gone to have surprised even me. There seems to be no limit to human malice."

"Was your wife in the house between five and six yesterday?"

"She was."

"How do you know? You were taking a siesta."

He was silent for nearly half a minute. Brake was watching from the doorway with the air of a disinterested spectator.

"I didn't sleep," Benning said. "I was conscious of her presence in the house."

"But you couldn't see her? It might have been Florie? You can't swear it was your wife?"

Benning took off his hat and inspected its interior as if for a missing idea. He said slowly and painfully: "I don't have to answer that question, or any other question. Even if I were in court—you can't force a man to testify against his wife."

"You volunteered an alibi for her. Incidentally, you haven't proved she is your wife."

"Nothing could be easier." He strode ino his consultation room and came back with a folded document that he handed to Brake.

Brake glanced at it, and passed it to me. It was a marriage certificate issued in the State of Indiana on May 14, 1943. It stated that Samuel Benning, aged 38, had been married on that date to Elizabeth Wionowski, aged 18.

Benning took it out of my hands. "And now, gentlemen, it's about time I insisted that my private life, and my wife's is no affair of yours. Since she isn't here to defend herself, I'll remind you that there are libel laws, and false arrest is actionable in the courts."

"You don't have to remind me." Brake stressed the personal pronoun. "There's been no arrest, no accusation. Thank you for your co-operation, doctor."

Brake slung a look from the door which tightened on me like a rope. We left Benning in the hallway, leaning like a flimsy buttress against the rotting wall. He was pressing the marriage certificate to his thin chest as if it was a love token or a poultice or a banknote, or a combination of all three.

The interior of my car was furnace-hot. Brake pulled off his coat and folded it on his knees. His shirt was blotched with sweat.

"You went too far, Archer."

"I think I didn't go far enough."

"That's because you don't have my responsibility."

I admitted that that was true.

"I can't take chances," he went on. "I can't act without evidence. I got nothing to justify a warrant for Mrs. Benning."

"You've got just as much on her as you have on Alex Norris. He's still in jail."

Brake answered doggedly: "He's being held without charge for twenty-four hours. It's legal. But you can't do that with people like Mrs. Benning. She's a doctor's wife, remember. I stuck my neck out going to Benning at all. He's lived all his life in this town. His father was the high-school principal for twenty years." He added defensively: "Anyway, what have we got on her?"

"You noticed her maiden name in the marriage certificate? Elizabeth Wionowski. The same name as the one in the telegram. She was Durano's woman."

"That don't prove anything about Singleton, even if it was evidence, which it isn't. What I don't see in your story is this idea of a woman changing partners back and forth like a bloody square dance. It don't happen."

"Depends on the woman. I've known women who kept six men on the string at the same time. Mrs. Benning has been alternating three. I have a witness who says she was Singleton's mistress for seven years, off and on. She came back to Benning because she needed help——"

Brake brushed the words like mosquitoes away from his head. "Don't tell me any more. I got to take this careful and slow or I'm up the crick without a paddle."

"You or Norris."

"And don't needle me. I'm handling this case the way I have to. If you can bring in Mrs. Benning to make a statement, okay, I'll listen. But I can't go out and bring her in myself. I can't do anything to the doctor just because his wife went on a trip. Nobody told her not to."

The sweat was running down his slant low forehead, gathering in his eyebrows like dew in a thicket. His eyes were bleak.

"It's your town, lieutenant."

I dropped him at the rear of the City Hall. He didn't ask me what I intended to do next.

CHAPTER 27

It was late afternoon when I drove through Arroyo Beach to the ocean boulevard. The palm-lined sand was strewn with bodies like a desert battlefield. At the horizon sea and sky merged in a blue haze from which the indigo hills of the channel islands rose. Beyond them the sun's fire raged on the slopes of space.

I turned south into traffic moving bumper to bumper, fender to fender, like an army in retreat. The arthritic trees cast long baroque shadows down the cemetery hill. The shadow of Durano's house reached halfway across its wilderness of lawn towards the iron fence. I pulled out of the traffic into the entrance to the drive.

The gate was still chained and padlocked. There was a button set in the gatepost under a small weathered sign: RING FOR GARDENER PLEASE. I rang three times, without audible effect, and went back to my car to wait. After a while a small figure came out of the house. It was Una. She moved impatiently down the drive, chunky and squat between the slender coconut palms.

Her gold lamé coat gleamed like mail through the bars of the gate. "What do you want, you?"

I got out of the car and approached her. She looked at me, and at the house, as if invisible wires were jerking at her alternately from each direction. Then she right-about-faced and started away.

"I want to talk about Leo," I said above the traffic noises.

Her brother's name pulled her back to the gate: "I don't understand you."

"Leo Durano is your brother?"

"What if he is? I thought I fired you yesterday. How many times do I have to fire you before you stay fired?"

F

"Was that the trouble with Max Heiss, that he wouldn't stay fired?"

"What about Max Heiss?"

"He was killed this morning, murdered. Your labour turnover is rapid, and all of your ex-employees are ending the same way."

Her expression didn't change, but her diamonded right hand reached for one of the bars and gripped it. "Heiss had a lot of drunky ideas. If somebody cut him down, it's no affair of mine. *Or* my brother's."

"It's funny," I said, "when I saw Heiss in the morgue I thought of you and Leo. Leo has quite a record in that line."

Her hand left the bar and jumped like a brilliant crustacean to her throat. "You've seen Bess Wionowski."

"We had a little chat."

"Where is she?" Una spoke as if her throat was hurting her.

"Blown again," I said. "You might as well open the gate. We can't talk here."

"I might as well."

She groped in the wide square pocket of her gold coat. I had my finger hooked in the trigger guard of my gun. All she brought out was a key, with which she opened the padlock. I unchained the gate and pushed it open.

Her hand closed on my arm: "What happened to Max Heiss? Did he get sliced, like Lucy?"

"He was put to the torch like Joan of Arc."

"When?"

"Early this morning. We found him in the mountains, in a wrecked car. The car belonged to Charles Singleton, and Heiss was wearing Singleton's clothes."

"Whose clothes?"

Her fingers were biting into me. Contact with her was unpleasant and strange, like being grabbed by the branch of a small spiny tree. I shook her hand off.

"You know him, Una, the golden boy Bess was running with. Somebody blowtorched Heiss and dressed him in Singleton's clothes to make it look as if Singleton died this morning. But we know better, don't we?"

"If you think Leo did it, you're crazy."

"I'm surprised you still use that word in your family."

Her gaze, which had been steady on my face, swerved away. She said with her head down: "Leo was home in bed this morning. I can prove it by his nurse. Leo is a very sick man."

"Paranoia?" I said distinctly. "G.P.I.?"

Her rigid calm tore like a photograph. "Those lying saw-bones at the clinic! They promised me they kept professional secrets. I'll professional-secret them when they send me their next bill."

"Don't blame the clinic. I've seen enough commitment trials to recognise paranoid symptoms."

"You've never seen my brother."

I didn't answer the unasked question. "I'm going to see him now, with you."

"I've taken good care of Leo," she cried suddenly, "with trained nurses all the time, the best of care! The doctor comes every day to see him. I work and slave for that man, making him things he likes to eat, spumoni, minestrone. When I have to, I feed him with my own hands." She choked back the running words and turned away from me, ashamed of the solicitous old woman jostling her other selves.

I put one hand on her stiff elbow and propelled her towards the house. Its red-tiled upper edge cut off the sun. I looked up at the barred window behind which Leo Durano had been receiving the best of care, and heard a silent word repeated like an echo from the wall many times.

Inside the front door, an iron stairway curved in a spiral to the second floor. Una climbed it and preceded me along a dust-littered hallway. Near its end, the large young man in the white smock sat in an armchair beside a closed door.

My presence startled him. "Doctor?" he said to Una.

"Just a visitor."

He shook his cheeks at her. "I wouldn't do it, Miss Durano. He's been hard to handle this afternoon. I had to restrain him."

"Open the door, Donald." Una said.

He produced a key from his tentlike smock. The room contained a bare iron cot and a disembowled platform-rocker bolted to the floor. A few shreds remained of the drapes that had hung at the barred window. Beside the window, the plaster wall showed handprints, and indentations that could have been made by fists. The inner side of the oak door had been splintered, and repaired with bare oak boards.

Durano was sitting on the floor against the wall in the far corner by the window. His arms, folded in his lap, were sheathed in a brown leather restrainer on which toothmarks were visible. He looked up at us through soiled black hair that straggled over his forehead. His bleeding mouth opened and closed, trying to trap a word.

The word sounded like: " Forgive."

Una ran across the room to him and went down clumsily on her trousered knees. " We don't treat you good, Leo. Forgive me." She drew his head against her metal torso.

" Forgive," he answered brokenly. " I forgive me. Released without charge. I told the ragpickers you can't vag an honest man or the son of an honest man, told them I was doing my father's business."

Clasping the mumbling head in both arms, Una looked up at me scornfully. " This is the poor little fellow who committed a murder this morning, eh? Tell him, Donald, where was Leo this morning?"

Donald swallowed painfully. " Police?"

" Close enough," I said.

" He was right in this room. All night and all morning. Every night and morning. Durano don't get around much any more."

" Shut up, you." Una left her brother and advanced on Donald. " No smart cracks, fat boy. He's a better man right now than you'll ever be. You'd still be emptying bedpans for sixty a month if it wasn't for Leo Durano. Mister to you."

He backed away from her, flushed and cowering like a browbeaten German wife. " You ask me a question, Miss Durano."

" Shut up." She passed him like a small cold wind, and hustled off down the corridor.

I said: " Donald. What about Saturday night two weeks ago? Was Durano in his room?"

" I wasn't here. We usually get Saturday nights off."

" We?"

" Me and Lucy before she left. Miss Durano paid me extra to stay last night. He was bad last night."

" You coming?" Una called from the head of the stairs. She took me to the room with the picture window at the rear of the house. The sun's fires had blazed out of control across the whole western sky and were eating at the sea's edges. Along the shore where the beach curved, a few late swimmers were tossed like matchsticks in a bloody froth of surf. I sat down in a chair against the side wall where I could watch the whole room and its doors and windows.

Seen from inside by daylight, the room was spacious and handsome in an old-fashioned way. Kept up, it might have been beautiful. But the carpets and the surfaces of the furniture were grey with dust, strewn with the leavings of weeks: torn magazines and crumpled newspapers, cigarette butts, unwashed dishes. A bowl of rotting fruit was alive with insects. The wall plants had drooped and died. Cobwebs hung in shabby strands from the ceiling. It was a Roman villa liberated by Vandals.

Una sat down at the card-table by the big window. The cards with which she and Donald had been playing the night before lay scattered across the table, mixed with a confetti of potato chips. A pair of clouded glasses sat on its edge. Una's hand crept out onto the table and began to gather the cards.

" How long has Leo been insane?" I said.

" What does it matter? You know he didn't kill Heiss."

" Heiss isn't the only one."

" Lucy Champion, then. He wouldn't hurt Lucy. They got along swell till she left. She was a damn good nurse, I'll give her that."

" That isn't why you were so anxious to get her back."

" Isn't it?" She smiled a keen half-smile, as bitter as wormwood.

" How long has he been insane, Una?"

" Since the first of the year. He blew his top for keeps at a New Year's party in the Dial, that's a night spot in Detroit. He was trying to make the orchestra play the same piece over and over, some piece from an opera. They played it three times and quit. Leo said they were insulting a great

Italian composer. He was going to shoot the orchestra leader. I stopped him.

"It was New Year's Eve and everybody thought he was loaded. I knew different. I'd been watching him since summer. He had bad headaches all last year, and along in the fall he was flying off the handle every day. It was Bess set him off, he never should have taken her back. They fought like wildcats all the time. Then he started to lose his memory. He got so he didn't even know his collectors' names."

"Collectors?"

Her hand became still among the half-gathered cards. She uncrossed and recrossed her legs. "He runs a collection agency."

"With a gun?"

"Leo always carried large sums. The gun was for protection. I didn't realise he was dangerous until he tried to use it on that musician. The doctor in Detroit said he was in a hopeless state, he wouldn't live long. I saw I had to get him out of Michigan. I wasn't going to have my brother committed."

"Again."

"*Again*, God damn you, if you know so much."

"So you hired a couple of nurses and moved to California. No doubt reasoning that Californians were expendable, in case he tried to shoot somebody else."

She turned from the card-table to look at my face, try to assess my meaning. "California was *her* idea. Anyway, I don't see why you go on about killing. I keep him under close guard. The idea that Leo did these murders is ridiculous."

"You didn't take it so lightly when I brought it up. You've worked like a dog since I got here to build up his alibi. On top of that you've outlined his defence on a plea of not guilty by reason of insanity, complete with medical witnesses."

"I've been showing you that Leo can't be tried for murder, let alone convicted."

"Why go to all that trouble if the idea is ridiculous?"

She bent forward stiffly in her chair, planting her feet on the floor: "You wouldn't want to harass a poor sick guy. What happens if you tip the cops in? They'll pin a bum rap on him, with his record, or if that doesn't work they'll send him away."

"There are worse places than a state hospital." I was sitting in one.

"I can't face it," she said. "He was in before and I saw how they treated him. He's got a right to spend his last days with somebody that loves him."

Though she said them with great intensity, the words fell flat. I studied her head, slanting square and hard out of the gold coat. On the window side the sun cast her face in rosy relief. Its other side was in shadow so deep by contrast that she looked like half a woman. Or a woman composed half of flesh and half of darkness.

"How long do the doctors give him?"

"Not more than a year. You can ask them at the clinic. Two years at the outside."

"Anywhere from one hundred to three hundred grand."

"What the hell do you mean by that?"

"My information is that Leo draws two to three grand a week from a numbers ring in Michigan. That adds up to a possible total of three hundred grand in two years, before taxes if you pay taxes."

"I don't know what you're talking about."

"Money," I said. "Don't tell me you're not handling Leo's money. I wouldn't believe it."

An irrepressible faint smile appeared on her mouth, as if I had flattered her subtly. "I have big expenses, very big expenses."

"Sure you have. Mink, diamonds, an ocean-front estate. They all cost money."

"Medical expenses," she said, "you wouldn't believe."

"Sure. You've got to keep him alive. The income lasts as long as he does. As long as you keep him under wraps, he's a boss racketeer on Sabbatical leave drawing his weekly take. But when he dies, or the cops lock him up, or news of his condition gets back to Michigan, it's finished for you. You're a pretty hard type but I don't see you going back to Michigan and fighting a war of succession with his mob. If you could do that, you wouldn't have come to me in the first place."

She sat in silence, shivering a little inside the metal coat.

Then she took up the gathered half of the deck and flung it down at random on the table. Brushed by her sleeve, a glass fell to the floor and broke.

"You didn't figure this out for yourself," she said in cold still anger. "It was Bess Wionowski put you onto it."

"She may have helped."

"That's Wionowski's gratitude." A hard pulse kicked like a tiny animal tangled in the veins of her left temple. "She was on her uppers, last year when Leo took her back. We ransomed her out of a cell in Detroit city jail and treated her like a queen. When we came out here to Cal, we even let her choose the town to live in. I might of known she had a reason for picking this place."

"Singleton," I said.

The name acted on Una like an electric shock. She jumped to her feet, kicking out at the shards of glass on the floor as if she hated everything actual. "The filthy disloyal filly. Where is she now? Where is she? If you got her hid out waiting for her cut, you can go back and tell her I don't pay off to squealers."

She stood above me in a spiteful rage, less than half a woman now, a mean little mannish doll raving ventriloquially.

"Come down to earth," I said. "You'll give yourself a migraine. Neither of us wants your dirty money."

"If my money's so dirty, what are you sucking around for?"

"Just the truth, sweetheart. You know what happened to Singleton, if anybody does. You're going to tell me."

"And if I don't?"

"You tell the cops. I'll have them here before dark."

She sat on the edge of her chair and looked out at the setting sun. Half down on the horizon, its red hemisphere was like a bird's giant eye on which the inflamed blue underlid was shutting slowly.

"How did it happen?" I said.

"Give me a chance to think——"

"You've had two weeks. Now talk."

"It was all Bess Wionowski's fault. The big estate and the high living weren't good enough for that Chicago

chippie. Way last spring she started dating this guy from
the Hill, this Singleton scion. I figured she knew him from
when she lived here during the war. Before long she was
spending nights with him. I tried to keep it from Leo but
he found out about it some way. He has his lucid times,
anyway he had until two weeks ago. It was a Saturday
night, and Bess was up the mountain with her highfalutin
boy friend, set to make beautiful music. Leo found out
where she was, from Lucy Champion, I guess. Lucy was supposed to be looking after him that night. When he blew off,
she couldn't handle him. Lucy called a taxi and went up
the hill to warn the—lovers." The word had an obscene
sound in Una's mouth.

"Where were you?"

"Downtown. When I got back Leo was waiting for me
with a gun. He'd taken the springs off his bed and broken
the door down and found the gun in my room. He made
me drive him up to Singleton's studio, forced me at gun-
point to do it. Singleton came out of the door, and Leo
shot him in the guts. I grabbed Leo from behind as soon as
he turned that gun away from me. It took all four of us to
tie him."

"All four?"

"Me and Bess and Lucy. Lucy was there. And Singleton."

"Singleton was shot, you said."

"He could still navigate, the last I saw of him. I left right
away when we got Leo under control. I had to get Leo
home."

"So you don't know what happened to Singleton?"

"No. They all three dropped out of sight. I hired Max
Heiss to find out if Singleton was alive or dead. He
watched the Singleton house all last week. On Thursday
Lucy turned up there, sniffing around for the reward I
guess. Heiss rode the bus back to Bella City with her and
found out more than he ever turned in to me. Friday night
he reported to me and claimed he lost Lucy in Bella City.
I knew he was crossing me because he dropped a hint about
the shooting. He was going to let me buy him off and then
collect the Singleton reward besides."

"So you killed him for being greedy."

"Think again."

"You were the one with everything to lose. Lucy and Heiss were the ones to lose it for you."

"I still have everything to lose. Would I hand you all this on a silver platter if I wasn't clear?"

"Who else had a reason to kill them?"

"Bess," she said harshly. "Lucy was in touch with Bess in Bella City, I could tell by talking to Lucy. Max Heiss was on her track. How do I know what Bess did with Singleton? Maybe he died on her hands and that made her accessory. Bess couldn't stand a police investigation. Bess has a record going back ten years."

I stood up and moved towards her and stood over her: "Did you remind Bess of her record, up at Singleton's cabin, after your brother shot him? Is that why she dropped out of sight and took Singleton into hiding?"

"Figure it out for yourself."

"You scared her into hushing it up, didn't you? Purely out of sisterly devotion, of course, to protect your brother, and his income."

She shifted restlessly in the chair, doubling her legs under her to tighten her defences. "What other reason would I have?"

"I've been casting around for one," I said. "I thought of something that happened in Los Angeles about fifteen years ago, to a man and his wife and their son. The son was a Mongolian idiot, and the man hated his wife for giving him that son. When the boy was ten or twelve years old, his father bought a shotgun and took him out on the desert and taught him to shoot. The boy had brains enough to pull the trigger of a shotgun. One night the father handed him the gun and told him to shoot his mother. She was asleep in bed. The boy blew her head off, being eager to please. He wasn't prosecuted. But his father was, though he hadn't physically committed the murder. He was convicted on a first-degree charge and put away with cyanide."

"Too bad for him."

"Too bad for anybody who tries to do murder by proxy. If you incite an insane person to commit a crime you're legally guilty of it. Did you know that was the law when you drove your brother up the mountain to Singleton's cabin and handed him a gun?"

She looked up at me with loathing, the muscles weaving and dimpling around her mouth. On the left side of her head where the knotted veins jerked, her face had swelled lopsided, as if moral strain had pushed or melted it out of shape. The light from the window fell on her like a visible heat from an open furnace-door.

"You'll never bum-rap me," she said. "You haven't even got a body. You don't know where golden boy is any more than I do."

Her statement turned at the end into a question. I left the question turning like a knife in her brain.

CHAPTER 28

Lights shone like wit in a dowager behind the windows of the Palladian villa. The green spectrum of its lawns and trees was deepening around it into solid green darkness. I parked under the porte-cochere and yanked at the old fashioned bell-pull that hung by the side entrance.

A stout woman in an apron opened the door. Her hand left a deposit of white flour on the doorknob. "What is it?"

"Is Miss Treen in?"

"I think she's busy. Who shall I say is calling?"

"Mr. Archer."

She premitted me to enter the hallway. I started to sit down on an elegant bowlegged chair, caught her backward look of disapproval, and remained standing. The Chinese gentleman with the wise earlobes was pursuing his timeless journey along the wall, from the lowlands across a river valley into the highlands and up the snowcapped mountain to his shrine. There were seven of him, one for each stage of the journey. There was only one of me, and my earlobes felt inadequate.

Sylvia appeared at the end of the hall, pale and absent-looking in a black suit like a uniform. "I'm so relieved you've come."

"How's Mrs. Singleton?"

"Not well, I'm afraid. This afternoon was too much for her. The police phoned from Bella City to say that Charles's car had been found with his body in it. They wanted her to make a formal identification. Before she was ready to leave they called again. The body had been identified as someone else, some detective. I'm so glad it wasn't you."

"So am I. It was Max Heiss."

"Yes. I found that out. Why was he killed, do you know? Why was he dressed in Charles's clothes?"

"Somebody wanted to have it appear that Charles died in an accident this morning. The body was burned to make it hard to identify."

Her mouth was pulled thin across her teeth in horror. "There are such dreadful things in the world. Why?"

"There are dreadful things in people's heads. This one is easier to explain than some. If Charles died in an accident this morning, he couldn't have died in a shooting two weeks ago."

"You mean that he did die two weeks ago? You can't mean that," she softly prompted the irreversible facts.

"Charles is probably dead, Sylvia. I know he was shot. I think he died of it."

"Who would shoot Charles?"

"He was mixed up with a woman named Bess. She had other lovers. One of them caught Charles with her in his studio, and shot him. Bess had a police record, and she was forced to cover up the shooting. She took Charles to her husband, who is a doctor in Bella City. Charles died, apparently. No one has seen him since."

"*She* has," Sylvia whispered.

"Who?"

"The woman, Bess. She phoned here a little while ago. I'm certain it was the same woman."

"You spoke to her?"

"Yes. She insisted on talking to Mrs. Singleton, but Mrs. Singleton was in no condition. The woman didn't identify herself. She didn't have to. I knew from what she said that she was—Charles's mistress."

"What did she say?"

"That she could give us information."

" Five thousand dollars' worth?"

" Yes. She claimed to know where Charles is."

" Did you arrange to meet her?"

" I invited her to come here, but she wouldn't. She said she'd phone again at seven to fix a meeting-place. We must have the money ready for her in cash, in unmarked bills. Fortunately Mrs. Singleton has the cash on hand. She's been holding it in readiness ever since she posted the reward."

" Mrs. Singleton's going through with this, then."

" Yes, I advised her to. I may be wrong. I've had no one to turn to. The woman particularly warned me not to call in the police or Mrs. Singleton's detective agency or her lawyers. She said that if we did, the deal was off."

" She didn't mention me, though."

" If only you would stand by, Mr. Archer. I'm not equipped to handle this kind of transaction. I wouldn't even know what to ask for in the way of proof."

" What sort of proof did she offer?"

" Proof that she knows where Charles is. She didn't describe its nature and I hadn't the presence of mind to question her about it. The whole thing took me by surprise. I lacked the wit, even, to ask her if Charles was dead." She hesitated, then said in a rush of feeling: " Of course I meant to ask her. I was afraid to, I suppose. I put it off. Then the operator asked her to deposit more money, and she hung up."

" It was a long distance call?"

" I had the impression it was from Los Angeles."

" How much did the operator ask for?"

" Forty cents."

" Probably Los Angeles. Bess didn't give her name?"

" No, but she called him Charlie. Not many people did. And she knew my name. Charles told her about me, I guess." She bit her lip. " When I realised that, I felt sort of let down. It wasn't simply her calling me by my first name. She *condescended* to me, as if she knew all about me— how I felt about Charles."

" You'd feel better if you knew all about her."

" Do you?"

" Nobody does. She's crowded several lives into her first twenty-five years."

"Is that all she is, twenty-five? I imagined she was much older, older than Charles."

"Bess grew up early and fast. She was married in her teens to a man twice her age. He brought her out here during the war. She met Charles here in 1943."

"So long ago," she said desolately. Her loss of Charles was final, and retroactive. "Long before I knew him."

"Wilding saw her with Charles in 1943."

"He didn't tell me."

"He wouldn't. Since then she's been back and forth across the country, in and out of jail——"

"You said she had a husband. What about him?"

"She broke his spirit years ago. She uses him when she has to, when she has nothing better to do with herself."

"I don't—I can't understand—Charles's taking up with such a woman."

"She's a fine-looking wench. And she was safely married to a man who wouldn't divorce her."

"But he's such an idealist. His standards are so high. Nothing was ever good enough for Charles."

"It's possible he was out of touch with his own standards. I never met Charles, but he sounds flawed to me—a man trying all his life to get hold of something real and not succeeding." I didn't know for sure whether my candour came from concern for the living girl or jealousy of the dead man: "That bullet in the guts was probably the realest thing that ever happened to him."

Her hazel eyes were troubled, but transparent as water in a well. "You mustn't speak of him in that way."

"Speak no ill of the dead?"

"You don't know that he is dead." She cupped her left breast gravely in her right hand. "I feel, here, that he is alive."

"I interviewed a witness to-day who saw him shot."

"How can I feel so strongly that he is alive?"

"He may be," I said without conviction. "My evidence isn't conclusive."

"Yet you won't let me have any hope. I think you wish him dead."

I touched the back of her hand, which still lay over her breast. "I never saw a girl with more goodness. I'd hate to

see you waste it all on the memory of a guy who never gave
a thought to anybody but himself."

"He wasn't like that!" She was flushed and radiant with
anger. "He was beautiful."

"Sorry," I said. "I'm tired. I shouldn't try to mastermind
other people's lives. It never works out." I sat down in the
bowlegged chair and let the thoughts in my head string off in
whirling darkness.

Her touch on my shoulder straightened me up. She looked
down at me with a smile of wise innocence.

"Don't be sorry, and don't be angry with me. I wasn't
exactly nice."

Nice was her middle name, but I kept that to myself. I
looked at my wristwatch:

"It's nearly seven now. What are you going to say to her?"

"Whatever you think. Won't you take the call?"

"She knows my voice. You talk to her. Tell her you have
the money. You'll buy her information, provided it's backed
up by proof. If she's in Los Angeles or within driving
distance, make an appointment for ten to-night, later if she
insists. She's to go to West Hollywood and park in front of
8411½ Sunset Boulevard. You'll contact her there."

"I?"

"We both will." I printed the address in my notebook,
and tore the leaf out for her. "No matter how she gripes,
don't let her choose the meeting-place."

"Why not?"

"You're going to be with me. Bess may or may not be
dangerous herself, but she has dangerous friends."

She read the address I had printed. "What place is this?"

"My office. It's a good safe place to talk to her, and I
have built-in mikes. I don't suppose you take shorthand?"

"*Pas trop.* I can take some sort of notes."

"How's your memory? Repeat the instructions I gave
you."

She did, without an error, and said with the air of a child
remembering her manners:

"Come into the library, Mr. Archer. Let me make you
some tea while we're waiting. Or a drink?"

I said that tea would be fine. The telephone rang before I
got a taste of it. It was Bess calling from Los Angeles.

CHAPTER 29

At half past nine we were in my West Hollywood office. I called my answering service and was informed that a Mr. Elias McBratney of Beverly Hills had phoned twice on Saturday and would phone again on Monday. James Spinoza, Jr., of Spinoza Beach Garb, wished me to call him back as soon as possible about those shortages. A lady who declined to give her name had tried to reach me four times between eight ten and nine twenty. I thanked the operator and said I would take my own calls until further notice.

I turned out the desk lamp. The inner office was dimly lit by the rectangular white beam that fell from the outer room through the one way panel in the glass door. A changing light thrown up from the Boulevard silhouetted the girl against the window.

"Look at the lights all up the sides of the hills," she said. "I've never seen this city at night. It's so new and aspiring."

"New anyway."

I stood behind her watching the cars run by in the road. I felt very close to Sylvia in the half-dark, and very conscious of time. The headlights flashed and disappeared like a bright succession of instants plunging out of darkness into darkness.

"Some day we'll have to jack it up and put a foundation under it."

"I like it the way it is," she said. "New England is all foundation and nothing else. Who cares about foundations?"

"You do, for one."

She turned, and her shoulder brushed me like a friendly movement of the darkness itself. "Yes, I do. You have foundations, Archer, don't you?"

"Not exactly. I have a gyroscopic arrangement. I'm afraid to let it stop spinning."

"That's better than foundations. And I don't believe you're afraid of anything at all."

"Am I not." I emitted a cynical-uncle chuckle which turned into a real laugh. Sylvia didn't join in.

The telephone on the desk rang sharply. I reached for it and spoke into the mouthpiece:

"Hello."

No answer. Only a faint electric murmur, the sound of thin wire in thin space. A click at the other end. Dead line.

I dropped the telephone into its cradle. "Nobody there."

"Perhaps it was the woman. Bess." Sylvia's face in the upward light from the window was white and enormous-eyed.

"I doubt it. She has no way of knowing this is my address."

"Will she come, do you think?"

"Yes. She needs the money for a getaway." I patted my fat breast-pocketful of bills.

"Getaway," Syplvia said, like a tourist picking up a foreign word. "What a wretched life she must have led, and still be leading. Oh, I hope she comes."

"Is it so important?"

"I have to know about Charles, one way or the other." She added under her breath: "And I want to see her."

"You'll be able to." I showed her the one-way panel in the door, and the earphones wired to the mike in the outer room. "You stay in here and take your notes. I'll keep her in the other room. I don't expect any trouble."

"I'm not afraid. I was afraid of everything for so very long. I've suddenly got over it."

At eight minutes to ten, a blue Chevrolet sedan passed slowly on the far side of the road, in the direction of Los Angeles. The face of the woman behind the wheel was caught in a photoflash of approaching headlights.

"That was Bess. You stay in here now and be still. Away from the window."

"Yes."

Closing doors behind me, I ran downstairs to the street. At two minutes to ten the Chevrolet came back and pulled up to the curb directly opposite the doorway where I was waiting. I crossed the sidewalk in three steps, opened the car door, pushed my gun into the woman's side. She released the emergency brake and raced the engine. I plucked the key out of the ignition switch. She tried to scratch my face. I locked her fingers.

"Calm down, Bess. You're caught."

"When haven't I been." She drew in a long sighing breath.

"I could stand it better before I started bumping into you
Well, little man, what now?"

"The same as before, except that you're going to do your
talking to me."

"Who says I am?"

"Five grand says it."

"You mean you've got the money for me?"

"When you earn it."

"And I can go free?"

"If you're reasonably clean, and I don't mean vice-squad
stuff."

She leaned close to study my eyes as if her future lay
behind them. I leaned away.

"Let me see the money."

"Upstairs in my office."

"What are we waiting for then?"

She came out of the car, her body full and startling in a
yellow jersey dress with a row of gold buttons down the
front. I frisked her on the stairs and found no gun and
burned my hands a little. But in the lighted room I saw that
she was losing what she had had. Her past was coming out
on her face like latent handwriting. Her powder and lipstick,
alkali and orange in the fluorescent light, were cracking and
peeling off. Grime showed in the pores of her nose and at
the sides of her neck. Dissolution was working in her rapidly
like a fatal disease she had caught from her husband that day.

She felt my look cold against her, and reached up automatically to straighten her hair. It was streaked greenish
yellow and black. I guessed she had been working on it with
peroxide half the afternoon, trying to reconstruct her image
in a cheap hotel mirror. And I wondered what the girl behind
the one-way panel was thinking.

"Don't look at me," Bess said. "I've had a bad day."

She sat in a chair by the outer door, as far from the light
as possible, and crossed her legs. Nothing could happen to
legs.

"You've had a bad day coming," I said. "Now talk."

"Don't I get a peek at the money?"

I sat down facing her and placed the five brown-paper-
wrapped packages on the table between us. There was a

microphone built into the table lamp, and I switched it on.

" Five grand, you said?"

" You're dealing with honest people. You can take my word for it."

" How much do I have to give you?"

" The whole thing. All you know."

" That would take years."

" I wonder. We'll start with something simple. Who killed Singleton?"

" Leo Durano blasted him." Her clouded blue gaze had returned to the packages of money. " Now I guess you want to know who Leo Durano is."

" We've met. I know his record."

She was beyond surprise. " You don't know Leo like I know Leo. I wish I never set eyes on him."

" He was picked up for contributing about ten years ago. Were you the minor?"

" Uh-huh. He was the connection I told you about, the one with the hat-check concessions in the clubs. We both got sneezed the same night, and they found out we lived in the same hotel room. He got off easy. The court doctor said he was batty, I could of told them that. They stuck him away in the booby-hatch for a spell, until Una talked him out of there. She's been talking him out of jams since he was a kid."

" Not this one," I said. " Now what about Singleton?"

" Me and Charlie?"

" You and Charlie."

" He was the one big love of my life," her cracked lips said. Her bleached hands moved down her smooth jersey body from breasts to thighs, wiping out a memory, or reviving it. " I met him too late, after I married Sam. Sam and I were living together in Arroyo Beach, and Sam was all work and no play, and that was never for me. Charlie picked me up in a bar. He had everything, looks and class and an Air Force officer's uniform. Real class. Class was the one thing I really wanted. I went with him the first night and it worked like magic. I didn't know what it was before Charlie showed me. Leo and Sam and the others never even scratched my surface.

" Charlie had to go back to Hamilton Field but he'd fly

down weekends. I waited for those weekends. Then Sam
went to sea and I couldn't even remember what he looked
like. I can't remember now. It was different when Charlie
went. He went all the way to Guam. He couldn't fly back
from there. The waiting stretched out, and he didn't write

"Sam wrote though, and Sam was the first to come back
I made the best of a bad job. After all I was married to the
guy. We settled down in Bella City and I cooked his chops
for him and said hello how are you to the cheesy patients he
had. I never mentioned Charlie to him but I guess he figured
it out from the things I didn't say. It wasn't any good at all
after Sam came back. I stuck it for one year, keeping track
of Charlie in the Arroyo newspaper and marking off the days
on the calendar. I crossed off every day for a year. I got up
early in the morning to cross them off and then I went back
to bed.

"One Saturday morning I didn't go back to bed. I got on
a bus and rode to Arroyo Beach and phoned Charlie and we
started over again, nearly every weekend. That was the summer of forty-six, I guess. It didn't last. He said goodbye in
September and went back to Boston to take a course at
Harvard Law School. I stayed with Sam that winter. It was
a long winter. Summer was good when it came but it didn't
last. It never lasted. Next year when the rains came in the
valley and I saw that green stuff on the hills I couldn't stick
it. I couldn't even hear what Sam was saying any more; it
went through my head like wind.

"I got on a train for New York and from there to Boston
Massachusetts. Charlie was living in his own apartment in
Belmont, but he wasn't glad to see me. He said I was part of
his California vacations, I didn't fit into his Boston life. Scat.
I told him what he was, and I walked out of there with
nothing on but a dress. It was March, and it was snowing.
I was going to walk into the river because the name of it was
the Charles River and that would drive him crazy. I hoped.

"I looked at the river for a while with the snowflakes falling into it. Then I walked to the end of the subway and rode
downtown. I didn't even rate a cold out of it. For a long
time then I lived on Scollay Square, getting back at Charlie.
I phoned him once to tell him what I was doing. He hung up
on me. That night it was the third rail in the subway I looked

at. I stood and looked at it for over an hour, and I couldn't move forward or back.

" A character in a boiled shirt saw me watching the third rail and picked me up. He turned out to be an unemployed ballroom-dancer from Montreal. Paul Theuriet. I supported him the rest of that year while we tried to work up an act together. Ever hear of Lagauchetière Street in Montreal?"

" I never did."

" It's rugged, and so was the act. Paul said I could make a dancer out of myself. God knows I tried. I was too clumsy or something. *He* was old and gouty in the joints. We did get ourselves booked into a few third-string clubs in Niagara Falls, Buffalo, Toledo. Then we were stranded in Detroit. I was waiting table in a beer joint, trying to raise enough money for limber-legs to open a dance studio, getting nowhere. We tried the old badger a couple of times. Paul fumbled it and ran out to Canada, left me holding the bag. That was where Leo came into my life again."

" It's about time."

" You asked for all of it," she said with a wry stubborn smile. This was her saga, all she had to show for her life, and she was going to tell it her own way:

" Leo heard that I was in the Detroit clink for extortion. He was going good again, a medium big gun in Michigan numbers. He had pull with the cops, and he hadn't forgotten me. He sprung me out of that rap. After all those years, I moved back in with Leo and his sister. No class, but the chips. I was in the chips."

" So you lived happily ever after, and that's why you're not here."

" It isn't funny," she said. " Leo started to have the fantods, worse than ever. It got so bad I sent some money to Sam, for an insurance policy. I thought if it got too bad I could come out here and retire on Sam. They didn't know about Sam."

" They?"

" Leo and his sister. She handled the money for Leo after his memory faded. Leo blew his top the end of last year. He tried to gun an orchestra leader for no good reason at all. We took him to a doctor and the doctor said he'd been sick for twenty years and was in the final stage of paresis. We

couldn't keep him in Michigan after that. He had enemie
in the organisation. The money boys and the underdogs with
the irons were both turning against him. Leo never laid any
thing on the line for his share of those banks. All he ever
put up was his hard-nose reputation and his connections. If
they knew he'd lost his mind they'd cut him out, or cut him
down. So it was California here we came. I sold Una on
Arroyo Beach.

"Ever since Boston, when Charlie Singleton kicked me out
of his life, I had this certain idea busting my brain. He
thought I was from hunger, and I thought if I went back to
Arroyo Beach with money on my back I'd make him squirm.
Pass him on the street and pretend I didn't know him. Anyway, that was my idea. When I did see him again, I did a
quick reverse and there I was back at the old stand, Saturday
nights in his studio. I didn't care about anything he did to
me in the past. He was the only man I liked to be with. It
went along like old times until a couple of weeks ago the
lid blew off. When Leo found out about Charlie and me."
She paused, her eyes fogged blue steel.

"Did he find out from Lucy?"

"Not a chance. Lucy was my one real friend in that
house. Besides, she was a nurse. She had psychic—psychiat-
ric training. She wouldn't pull a raw deal like that on one of
her patients. She was the one who warned us Leo was on
the warpath. She came up the mountain in a cab one jump
ahead of him."

"Who sent Leo on the warpath?"

"Una did, at least that's what we figured afterwards. Lucy
drove me over to the hotel to keep my date with Charlie.
When Lucy got back to the house, Una cross-questioned her
about where I was and who I was with. Lucy wouldn't talk,
and Una fired her. I guess Una knew all about it already.
She turned Leo loose and sicked him on us.

"Maybe the fantods ran in the family. Anyway, she must
have been far gone with whatever it was she had, to give
Leo a loaded gun and a green light. I didn't understand it
at the time. I was in the studio with Lucy when it happened.
I looked out the window and saw Leo in the station-wagon
with Una, and Charlie walking out to him, not realising the
danger. Charlie went right up to the station-wagon, and Leo

shot him. Charlie fell down and got up again. Una took Leo's gun away from him. We all stepped in and got him under control. Then Una put on an act about how Leo forced her to bring him there. I believed her, then. I was scared not to believe her. I've always been scared of Una.

"She said the shooting had to be hushed up, or else. It had to be as if nothing happened. No hospital for Charlie, and him doubled up in his car. I was afraid to argue with Una. I took what clothes I had in the studio and drove Charlie and Lucy over the pass to Bella City.

"I'd been to see Sam Benning a couple of times in the spring and summer, in case I ever needed him. He thought I was working in L.A., modelling clothes. We were on pretty good terms, but I couldn't tell Sam the truth: that one boyfriend shot the other and Sam was to make it all come right in the end. I played it as strong as I could with Sam. I told him Charlie had made a rough pass and I shot him myself. Lucy backed me up. Charlie was past talking by then.

"Sam believed me. He made me promise if he fixed Charlie up I had to stick with him in Bella City from then on and be a wife to him. I promised. He had me over a barrel.

"Maybe the wound was worse than it looked at first, or Sam isn't much of a surgeon. He blamed Lucy for what happened, said she fouled up the operation trying to assist him. Sam was always a man to shift blame onto other people's shoulders. Anyway Charlie died that night, right on the table in the examination room, before he came out of the ether."

"Who gave him the anæsthetic?"

"I don't know. I wasn't there. I couldn't stand to see him bleeding."

"You're a strange woman, Bess."

"I don't think so. How could I watch Sam cutting into him? Charlie was my boy. I loved him."

"I'll tell you what's really strange," she added after an interval: "The people you love are never the ones that love you. The people that love you, the way Sam loved me, they're the ones you can't love. Sam was a good man when I first knew him. But he was too crazy about me. I couldn't love him, ever, and he was too smart to fool. It ruined him.

"He did a wild thing that Sunday morning. There was

Charlie dead in his house, and Sam thinking I had shot him.
I couldn't change my story at that late date. Sam was afraid
he was going to lose me again, and it pushed him over the
edge. He butchered Charlie, cut him into pieces like a butcher.
He locked the cellar door on me, wouldn't let me down there.
I could tell from the noises what he was doing. There was a
laundry tub and an old gas stove down there that his mother
left behind her when she died. When he was through, there
was nothing but bones left. He spent the next three nights
working on them, putting them together with wire. Sam
always was good with his hands. When it was all wired
together and varnished and dried, he riveted on a tag from a
medical-supply house and hung the thing in a closet. He said
that was the skeleton in my closet and if I ever left him——"
She drew a fingernail across her throat.

There was a muffled cry from the inner room.

"And that's your proof?" I said loudly.

"You'll find it in the closet off his examination room.
Unless you already did?"

"What did he do with Charlie's car?"

"Hid it in the barn, under some old boards and tarpaulins.
I helped him."

"Did you help him burn Max Heiss, when Max found the
car?"

Bess didn't hear me. An intermittent sobbing and gasping
rose and fell in the inner room. Bess was listening to it, the
flesh haggard on the bones of her face like wet clay drooping
on an armature.

"You crossed me, you," she said.

Something fell softly and heavily against the inside of the
glass-panelled door. I went to it. The door was hard to open
because Sylvia had fainted against it. I reached around its
edge and turned her onto her back. The metal earphones
pincered her closed white face. Her eyes came open:

"I'm sorry. I'm such a fool.

I started for the water cooler. Bess was at the outer door,
fumbling with the Yale lock. The packages of bills were
gone from the table.

"Sit down," I said to her straining yellow back. "I
haven't finished with you."

She didn't answer. All her remaining energy was focused

on escape. The lock snapped back. The door opened inwards with Una pushing it from the hallway.

Una's mouth was wet. Her eyes were blind with the same darkness I had seen on her brother's face. The gun in her hand was real.

"I thought you'd be here with him. This is the pay-off, Wionowski, to squealers and false friends."

"Don't do it." Bess was leaning off balance against the opening door, still bent on escape.

I moved sideways to the wall, bringing my gun out fast, not fast enough. Bess staggered backwards under the blow of the first shot from Una's gun and went down under the second. The twin explosions smashed like bones in my head.

I shot to kill. Una died on her feet, of a smudged hole in the temple, and thumped the floor. I held Sylvia's hand until the police arrived. Her hand was ice cold at first. After a while it was a little warmer, and I could feel her blood beating.

CHAPTER 30

The starred sky arched like a crystal roof over the town. The valley floor was like the floor of a cave, the mountains blunt stalagmites against its glimmering walls. Once I got off the highway, the streets of Bella City were deserted. Its midnight buildings, bleached of colour by the alkali moonlight, stood like grey shadows on their own black shadows.

Parking at Benning's curb, I rang the bell and heard its complaint inside the house. A door creaked open at the rear of the hallway. Benning passed through its widening shaft of light and shut the door behind him. His face appeared above the cardboard patch in the corner of the window. It was crumpled and streaked like a discarded charcoal-sketch of itself.

He opened the front door. "What is it? Why have you come here?"

"Let me see your hands, doctor." I showed him the gun in mine.

He stepped out onto the porch, bulky in a zippered blue coverall, and held out his empty hands.

"They're dirty," he said. "I've been doing some cleaning in the house."

"You're wife is dead."

"Yes. I know. They phoned me from Los Angeles. I'm getting ready to go." He glanced down at my gun as if it were an obscenity that shouldn't be mentioned. "Perhaps they sent you to fetch me?"

"I came on my own."

"To spy on my grief, Mr. Archer?" he asked with broken irony. "You'll be disappointed. I can't feel grief, not for her. I've suffered too much for her." He turned up his dirty palms and looked down into them. "I have nothing." His fists closed slowly on moonlight. "Who is this woman who murdered her?"

"Una Durano. She's dead, too. I shot her."

"I'm grateful to you for that." His words were as insubstantial as his double fistful of moonlight. "Why did she do it to Bess?"

"She had various reasons. Your wife was a witness to the Singleton shooting, for one."

"Bess? A witness?"

"She was there when Singleton was shot."

"Who on earth was Singleton?"

"You know as well as I do, doctor. He was your wife's lover almost as long as you were married to her."

Benning looked up and down the empty street. "Come inside," he said nervously. "I only have a few minutes, but we can talk there."

He stood aside to let me enter first, maintaining a formal politeness like a wire-walker afraid to look down. I waved him in with my gun and followed him through the waiting-room into the consultation room. The inside of the house was suffocating after the chilly night air.

I pulled his swivel chair into the middle of the room. "Sit down, away from the desk."

"You're very hospitable," he said with his down-dragging smile. "Bess was, too, in her way. I won't deny that I knew of her affair with Singleton. Or that I was glad she shot him. It seemed fitting that she should be the one to destroy that arrogant young man."

"Bess didn't destroy him."

" I'm afraid you're mistaken. Now that Bess is dead, I'm ree to tell you the truth. She confessed to me that she shot im."

" She was lying to you."

He stood wide-legged and stubborn under the light, shaking is long head from side to side. " She couldn't have been ying. No one would lie about such a thing."

" Bess did. It was the only way she could persuade you to ake care of him. The crime was actually committed by Una Durano. Bess was a witness, as I said."

He slumped into the chair. " Do you know that, for a act?"

" I couldn't prove it in court. I don't have to. Una is lead, along with the competent witnesses, Singleton and Lucy and Bess."

" Did this woman murder them all? What kind of a woman was she?"

" As hard and nasty as they come. But she didn't kill them all. Bess was the only one she killed. She thought Bess had turned informer against her."

" You said she murdered Singleton."

" Not exactly."

" You said she committed the crime," he insisted.

" The crime was attempted murder, done by proxy, but you finished Singleton off. I think he'd still be alive if you hadn't got your knife into him."

Benning's body jerked backwards. His large grimy hands moved towards each other across his denim-covered abdomen. The thumb and forefinger of one hand plucked at the coverall zipper as if it were a sutured incision in his flesh.

He found his voice: " This is utter nonsense. You can't prove either the fact or the intent. Singleton's death was pure accident. I couldn't stop the internal hæmorrhage."

" You destroyed the body. That carries a lot of weight."

" If you could prove it. But there is no body. You have nothing." It was an echo of what he had said about himself.

" Singleton's bones will do."

" Bones?"

" The skeleton you rigged to hold Bess in line. It's turned into a booby trap."

" You've left me far behind."

I moved the gun in my hand, drawing his attention to it. "Open the closet in the examination room."

He rose, still holding his middle where my accusation had hit him. I thought he was too willing. The closet was empty. He shut the door and leaned against it. His long-toothed melancholy grin mimicked the grin of the absent skull.

"Where is it, doctor?"

"I suppose Bess took it with her. That would be fitting, too."

There was an iron grate set in the baseboard beside the closet door. Benning's glance rested on it involuntarily, a second too long. The grate was the closed outlet of an old-fashioned hot-air system. Holding my gun on Benning, I stooped to touch it. It was warm, and under it I could sense the minute vibrations of fire.

"Show me the furnace."

Benning stood flat against the door, his eyes gleaming palely, as though they belonged to a tormented animal crouched inside of him. He drooped suddenly, but I distrusted his docility. It was taut and dangerous. I held my gun close to his back as we went through the house and down the basement stairs.

The light was still on in the basement. A naked bulb suspended on a wire cast a dingy yellow glare on shelves of empty jars, broken furniture, newspapers and magazines, generations of cobwebs. A rusty three-burner gas plate squatted on a bench beside the stairs, and a copper boiler dented and green with age, hung on the wall above it. Benning avoided that corner of the basement.

In the far corner, behind a rough board partition, an old cast-iron furnace was breathing like a bull. I used my toe to open the fire door, and saw what lay in the heart of the fire: a skull licked by flames in a phœnix nest of bones.

Beside me, Benning was lost in contemplation. The orange light of the fire played feebly on the lower part of his face. He seemed for an instant to be young and smiling.

"Put it out."

He came to himself with a start. "I can't. I don't know how."

"Find a way, and be quick about it. Those bones are worth money to me."

He attached a garden hose to a tap in the hot water tank, and turned its stream on the fire. Steam sizzled and gushed from the furnace door. He emerged from it coughing, and sat down on a pile of kindling against the board partition. I looked into the blackened firebox at five thousand dollars' worth of charred bones, all that remained of the golden boy. It was a hell of a way to make money, selling dead men's bones. I kicked the iron door shut.

With his eyes closed, his head lolling back against the boards, Benning looked like another dead man.

" Are you ready to give me a full confession?"

" Never," he said. " They can't convict me."

" They have three tries, remember."

" Three?"

" If it was only Singleton, there'd be some room for doubt, even for sympathy. He took Bess away from you. You had some justification for letting the scalpel slip in his bowels."

He said in a deeper voice: " My enemy was delivered into my hands." Then openend his eyes in bewilderment, as if he had talked in his sleep and waked himself from nightmare.

" That doesn't apply to Lucy. She tried to help you."

Benning laughed. With a great effort, he throttled the laugh and imposed silence on himself.

" Before Bess was killed to-night, she told me Lucy assisted at the operation. Lucy was in a position to know who and what killed Singleton. When things closed in on her—landlady trouble, no job, detectives tailing her—she thought of selling her knowledge to Singleton's family. But she made the mistake of coming to you yesterday and giving you a chance before she did anything final.

" If she could get money from you, she wouldn't have to sell you out or involve herself in a murder case. You gave her the money you had on hand, enough to buy a train ticket and get out of town. You also hedged against the chance that she wouldn't take that train, by filching her motel-key out of her purse. Lucy missed the train, in every sense. When she went back to the motel, you were waiting in her rom. She tried to defend herself with a knife. You were too strong for her."

" You can't prove it," Benning said. Bowed far forward, he was staring down at the wet concrete floor.

"A witness will turn up. Somebody must have seen you go out, even if Florie didn't. You must have passed somebody who knows you between here and the Mountview Motel, going or coming. If I have to, I'm going to canvass the whole population of the town."

His head came up as if I had tightened a knot under his jaw. He knew he had been seen. "Why do you want to do this? Why do you hate me?" He wasn't asking me alone. He was asking all the people who had known him and not loved him in his life.

"Lucy was young," I said. "She had a boy friend who wanted to marry her. They honeymooned in the morgue, and Alex is still in jail, sweating out your rap for you. Do you think you're worth the trouble you've caused?"

He didn't answer me.

"It's not just the people you've killed. It's the human idea you've been butchering and boiling down and trying to burn away. You can't stand the human idea. You and Una Durano don't stack up against it, and you know it. You know it makes you look lousy. Even a dollar-chaser like Max Heiss makes you look lousy. So you have to burn his face off with a blow torch. Isn't that what you did?"

"It's not true. He demanded money. I had no money to give him."

"You could have taken your medicine," I said. "That never occurred to you. It hasn't yet. When Max found the Buick in your barn, that made him your enemy. Naturally he had to die. And when he came back for his money, you were ready for him, with Singleton's clothes and a blowtorch and a can of gasoline. It must have seemed like a wonderful plan, to get rid of Heiss and in the same moment establish Singleton's death by accident. But all it accomplished was to tip Bess off on what you'd done. As soon as I told her about the car he was found in, she realised you killed Max. And she left you."

"She left me, yes. After all I'd done for her."

"Not for her. For you. You've killed two men and a woman because they threatened your security. You'd have killed Bess if she hadn't got out fast. She didn't tell me that, but I think she knew it. She was the one you wanted to kill from the start, if you hadn't been afraid."

He shuddered, covering his eyes with his spread fingers. "Why are you torturing me?"

"I want a confession."

It took him several minutes to bring himself under control. When he lowered his hands, his face had smoothed and thinned. His eyes seemed smaller and darker. No animal was using them.

He got up awkwardly from the pile of wood and took a halting step towards me:

"I'll give you a confession, Mr. Archer. If you'll let me have access to my drug cabinet, for just a moment?"

"No."

"It will save time and trouble, for all of us."

"It's too easy. I've promised myself one satisfaction out of this case. To see you go in and Alex Norris come out."

"You're a hard man."

"I hope so. It's the soft ones, the self-pity boys like you, that give me bad dreams." I had had enough of that basement, cluttered with broken objects, wet and hot and squalid with broken desires. "Let's go, Benning."

Outside, the flawed white moon was higher among the stars. Benning looked up at them as if the night had really become a cave of shadows.

"I do feel grief for her. I loved her. There was nothing I wouldn't do."

He started down the veranda steps, his short black shadow dragging and jerking at his heels.

Fontana Books

Fontana is best known as one of the leading paperback publishers of popular fiction and non-fiction. It also includes an outstanding, and expanding section of books on history, natural history, religion and social sciences.

Most of the fiction authors need no introduction. They include Agatha Christie, Hammond Innes, Alistair MacLean, Catherine Gaskin, Victoria Holt and Lucy Walker. Desmond Bagley and Maureen Peters are among the relative newcomers.

The non-fiction list features a superb collection of animal books by such favourites as Gerald Durrell and Joy Adamson.

All Fontana books are available at your bookshop or news-agent; or can be ordered direct. Just fill in the form below and list the titles you want.

FONTANA BOOKS, Cash Sales Department, P.O. Box 4, Godalming, Surrey, GU7, 1JY. Please send purchase price plus 7p postage per book by cheque, postal or money order. No currency.

NAME (Block letters)

ADDRESS